**W9-CFQ-678**

"TREVANIAN SERVES UP ANOTHER SUPERIOR THRILLER!
This is certainly one of the toughest suspense novels . . . overlaid with a sleek, sardonic wit."

Publishers Weekly

"TREVANIAN CAN WRITE HOKED-UP HOOPS AROUND IAN FLEMING."

The Boston Globe

Also by Trevanian
Published by Ballantine Books:

SHIBUMI

SUMMER OF KATYA

THE EIGER SANCTION

THE LOO SANCTION

Trevanian

BALLANTINE BOOKS ● NEW YORK

Library of Congress Catalog Card Number: 73-82951

ISBN 0-345-31738-6

This edition published by arrangement with
Crown Publishers, Inc.

Manufactured in the United States of America

First Ballantine Books Edition: November 1984
Eighth Printing: April 1990

THE LOO SANCTION

St. Martin's-In-The-Fields

His pain was vast. But at least it was finite. Sharp-edged waves of agony climaxed in intensity until his body convulsed and his mind was awash. Then, just before madness, the crests broke and swirled over his limen of consciousness, and he escaped into oblivion.

But always he emerged again from the delirium, cold and perspiring, weaker than before, and more frightened.

A crisp wind fluted through the arches of the belfry in which he was prisoner and drove his tears horizontally back to his temples. During troughs of awareness between crises of pain, his mind cleared, and he was bewildered by his reactions to impending death. Matthew Parnell-Greene ("Uranus" in the planet-code of the counterespionage agency that employed him) had always known that violent death was a very real alternative to retirement in his line of work. He was not physically brave—his imagination was too active for that—so he had sought to mute his fear by callusing that imagination. He had forced himself to rehearse being shot, being knifed, taking a faceful of cyanide gas from a tube concealed in a folded newspaper, being poisoned—his urbane flair always insisting upon the poison being in exotic foods consumed at really good restaurants. And he had attempted to toughen his tender imagination by abrading it with anticipations of the more disgusting alternatives. He had been drowned in a bathtub; he had been suffocated, his face blue and his eyes bulging within a polyethylene bag; air had been injected into his heart. Always he had died well, with a certain dignity, not struggling dumbly against impossible odds. He had imagined pain, but the end had always come quickly. He had long ago realized that he could not withstand torture and had decided he would cooperate fully with his questioners, should it come to that.

Fear, pain, anger, even self-pity had been anticipated so often that they held no more dread than he could stand. But his anxious fantasies had not prepared him for the emotion that now overwhelmed his mind: disgust. Disgust was bitter in the back of his throat. Disgust curled the corners of his mouth and dilated his nostrils. When they found him, he would be unsightly, revolting. The thought of it embarrassed him intensely.

In the two hours since a watery dawn had made London visible below him, Parnell-Greene's eyes had dimmed many times, with each fresh crisis of pain that carried him over the brink of unconsciousness as some membrane inside him ripped through, sending waves of shock through his body.

How long had he been there? Six hours? Half his

life? His existence seemed divided into two parts, one containing forty-seven active, colorful years; the other, six hours of pain. And it was the second half that really mattered.

He remembered them bringing him to St. Martin's. Although he had been heavily drugged, it was all perfectly lucid. The drugs had been pleasant, euphoric; they had sapped his will, but he remembered everything. Two of them had brought him. They had stood on either side of him because he was unsteady on his feet. He had sat for a time with one of them—The Mute—in a back pew, while the other went up to the belfry to see that the apparatus was in place. He remembered the oaken contribution box with its notice:

Contributions to keep
this church always open
and to maintain its services

They had led him up the winding metal staircase and out onto the dark windy platform of the belfry. And then they had . . . and then they . . . Parnell-Greene wept at the sadness of it.

He sobbed, and that was a mistake. The convulsion ruptured something inside, pain clawed through his body and throbbed in his head. He fainted.

The streets below the church streamed with people. Hundreds gushed up Villiers Street and poured from Charing Cross Station, all hurrying toward work or standing with turgid obedience in queues, waiting to crowd into red double-decker buses, bodies touching, eyes assiduously averted. Escalators spewed anonymities from the undergrounds: young office men, bareheaded and red-eyed; cloth-capped laborers, sullen and stunned with lives of monotony; shopgirls and secretaries, miniskirted despite the season, their hands, faces, and legs ruddy and chapped; older women on the prowl for bargains, waddling through the press, heavy objects in their dangling string bags a threat to passing shins.

Any one of them might have seen Parnell-Greene's huddled silhouette in the arch of the belfry, but no one looked up. In the automaton way of British workers, their chins were sunk in their collars, their minds involute.

Perspiration was cold on his forehead when he returned to consciousness. He breathed carefully, his mouth wide open so as not to make a movement. At last, his tightly bound arms were numb, and that was a blessing. For the first hour or so, the loss of circulation had caused a regular dull ache that was somehow more wearing than the irregular ecstasies of agony when something tore within him.

He did not shout for help. He had tried that at first, but no one could hear his feeble voice from the height of the belfry, and each attempt had been rewarded with a bursting sac of liquid pain.

Slowly, the numbing of his overloaded nerves came into balance with this new level of agony, and neutralized it. He knew that more exquisite levels of pain would come, but it was no longer an animate enemy he might get by the throat and crush, and crush! His pain and his life had welded into one. They would always be together now. When there was no longer pain, there would no longer be life.

He felt very cold, and very sad.

He looked out, across the river, over the bulk of

the Charing Cross Hotel. There were the elements of new London. The inarticulate, utilitarian bulk of the Royal Festival Hall. The addled architecture of Queen Elizabeth's Hall, a compromise between a penal institution and a space station. New London. Economical and unmerciful architecture. And beyond, cubes of aluminum and glass persuaded the skyline of London to imitate Chicago. Some of the bloodless hulks stood unfinished, victims of continual strikes. Above these ugly heaps, giant construction cranes lurked, dinosaur skeletons poised to feed on huge blocks of salt.

Distressed, he turned his eyes away. So much of it was going! Even the façades temporarily spared from Progress were masked by scaffolding and canvas as they were being steamed and scrubbed to rid them of the character of patina.

It was all going.

He felt liquid dripping down his legs. And not only blood, he realized with despair. Revolting. Disgusting.

A bit of sun broke through the low layers of zinc cloud. He began to feel warm. Light. As though he were floating. It would be good to be weightless. Merciful numbness began to spread upward. His throat thickened. He was so tired.

The whir and clatter of machinery tugged him back to consciousness. The clapper of the great bell was grinding back against its spring, and it hovered for a second before it shot forward. The belfry roared and vibrated! The apparatus shook violently. The pain was pyrotechnic as everything within him burst!

Now Parnell-Greene screamed.
Unheard.

That evening the facts were carried by the London newspapers, each reflecting the taste of its readership:

MAN IMPALED IN ST. MARTIN'S-IN-THE-FIELDS

OPPOSITION QUESTIONS SECURITY OF NATIONAL BELFRIES

BELL RINGER INVESTIGATES THUD!

EARLY CHURCHGOER GETS THE POINT!

BBC 2 interrupted its year-long series on the development of the viola da gamba for a special broadcast in which three university dons outlined the uses of torture in general and impalement in particular in the Western world. Then a panel of experts discussed the implications of this latest impalement on the eve of Britain's entry into the Common Market. Finally, a woman Labour MP made the point that this literal impalement had shocked and sickened the nation, while it remained perfectly indifferent to the figurative impalement of womanhood on the phallus of male chauvinism over the years, which, after all, was . . .

Bloomsbury

"You!" the singer accused, pointing over the heads of the crowd with an arched forefinger, the other fist on his hip, his eyes wild and round in their pits of green mascara, his gold-tinsel wig glittering under the spotlight. "You! . . .   *

> . . . you're driving me crazy.
> What can I do? What can I do?
> My love for you makes everything hazy . . ."

His thin metallic alto blended with the muted instruments as his stiff torso dipped in tempo to the song, his knees flexing mechanically. He stood on a raised platform, and his eyebrowless clown-white face bobbed rhythmically over the heads of the chit-chatting crowd. The showrooms of Tomlinson's Galleries buzzed with conversation: intimate talk, meaningful and intense; significant talk about art and life; witty talk designed to be overheard and repeated.

* from the song "You're Driving Me Crazy" by Walter Donaldson copyright 1930, 1957 by Donaldson Publishing Co. Used by permission of Mrs. Walter Donaldson.

13

". . . so I simply put myself into his hands. He designs all my clothes and even selects the shirts and ties. In effect, he does me as he sees me . . ."

". . . for God's sake, Midge, he's not only your husband, he's my friend. Do you think *I* want to hurt him? . . ."

". . . it would be a challenge to paint you. I would like to try and capture your—ah—depth and to express it in—well, frankly—in sexual terms . . ."

". . . well, if you ask me, it was a blatant act of defiance—a challenge to the police. To impale a man on a wooden stake right in the belfry of St. Martin's-In-The-Fields! Have you had your martini, love?"

The minute Jonathan Hemlock stepped into the crowded reception room, he was sorry he had come. He looked over heads, but he didn't find the woman he was supposed to meet, so he began slowly to ease toward the door, juggling his glass adroitly and nodding to the empty-eyed models who hung impatiently on the arms of older men, and who smiled at him as he passed. But just as he made the door, David Tomlinson caught him by the arm, directed him to the center of the room, and jumped up on a pouf.

"Listen, everybody! Everybody?" (Silence rippled reluctantly from the center outward.) "I have the very great honor to introduce you to Dr. Jonathan Hemlock who's come all the way from America to set us all straight on art and all that." (Titters and one "hear-hear.") "All sorts of people have consorted to get him over here: the Guggenheim, the Arts Council—all that benevolent lot. And we must make good use of him. No comments from you, Andrew!" (Titters.) "Now you'll all have to watch yourselves because Dr. Hemlock actually *knows* something about art." (Groans and one giggle.) "I'm sure you've all read his books, and now he's here in the flesh, as it were. And remember this! You saw him first at Tomlinson's." (Laughter and light applause.)

Tomlinson stepped down from the pouf and spoke with such sincerity that he appeared to be in pain. "I am truly delighted that Van was able to persuade you to come. You've *made* the evening. May I call you Jonathan?"

"No. Look, you haven't seen Van, have you?"

"In point of fact, I haven't."

Jonathan grunted and slipped away to the bar where he ordered a double Laphroaig. He didn't notice fforbes-Ffitch's approach in time to avoid it.

"Heard you were going to be here, Jon. Thought I'd drop around for the event." fforbes-Ffitch spoke with the crisp, busier-than-thou accents of the academic hustler. He had taken his doctorate in the United States, where apparently he had majored in grantsmanship, which training he applied with such industry that he became the youngest head of department at the Royal College of Art and had recently been made a trustee of the National Gallery.

"Say, Jon. Tell me, did you receive my memo?"

Jonathan never used fforbes-Ffitch's first name. He didn't even know what it was. "What memo?"

fforbes-Ffitch preened his drooping moustache by pressing it down with his thumb and cleared his throat to speak importantly. "That one about your doing a lecture series for us in Scandinavia."

Jonathan had received it weeks before and had dismissed it as an attempt by f-F to brighten his reputation as a man who knows important people and gets things done. "No, I never received it."

"How does the idea sound to you?"

"Terrible."

"Oh? Oh? I see. Well, that is too bad. Ah—quite a gathering here this evening, don't you think?"

"No."

"Well, yes. I agree with you. Not real scholars, of course. But . . . important people. Well! I have to be going. Desk piled with work crying out to be done."

"You'd better get to it."

"Right. Cheers."

Jonathan felt great social fatigue as he watched f-F depart through the crowd, shaking hands with all the "names," studiously ignoring the others. No doubting it, f-F was a man on his way to a knighthood.

Jonathan had just finished his whiskey and was ready to get out when Vanessa Dyke appeared at his side.

"Having fun, love?" she asked evilly.

He smiled blandly out onto the throng and spoke to her out of the side of his mouth. "Where have you been? You told me it wouldn't be another of these."

She waved at someone across the room. "The truth is, I lied. Simple as that."

"One of these days, Van . . ."

"I look forward to it." She tapped out a Gauloise on her thumbnail and lit it, cupping the match like a sailor on a windy deck, then she squinted through the curling acrid smoke to find a handy ashtray, failing which, she tossed the match onto the thick carpeting. One fist on her hip, she looked disdainfully over the party, the pungent French cigarette dangling from the side of her mouth, the hard, intelligent eyes examining and dismissing the guests. An expatriate American, Vanessa wrote the leanest, most penetrating art criticism current in England under the name of Van Dyke, which the uninitiated took to be an alias. Jonathan had known her for years and had always admired and liked her, even during the flamboyant stage of her life when she had turned up at parties with a young whore on either arm, flaunting her homosexuality with defensive vigor. They disagreed totally about art, and had great battles in private, but should someone less informed join in, they united to destroy him.

Jonathan looked at her profile and noticed with surprise that age was making rapid inroads on her. Still thin as a reed under the black slacks and turtle-necked sweater that were her trademark, she had short tousled hair shot with gray, and the alert, nervous movements of her expressive hands revealed nails bitten to the quick.

"Have you met the Struggling Young Person?" she asked, leaning against the bar with her elbows and surveying the gathering without sympathy.

"No. Why did you ask me to come here?"

Vanessa avoided the question. "Have you seen his shit?"

"I glanced around when I came in."

"That's him over there." She gestured with her pointed chin.

Jonathan looked through the milling bodies to a dour young man with a shaggy beard and a corduroy hunting jacket, flaunting his nonclass by drinking beer. He was surrounded by people so eager to be seen in his company that they were willing to pay the price of listening to him. Hovering in the background was a sere, uncertain girl in a long dress of madras, her nose sharp between falls of long oily hair. She had the intense look of a graduate student's wife concerned with social injustice, and Jonathan took her to be the painter's mistress.

Christ, they all look alike!

Knowing that the tenor of his thoughts would be identical to her own, Vanessa shrugged, saying, "Well, at least he's fairly unassuming."

Jonathan looked again over the modern daubs on the carpeted walls. "What are his options?"

A couple were pushing their way through the crowd toward Jonathan. "Oh, Christ," he said from between teeth clenched in a smile.

"Come on," Vanessa said, drawing her arm through his and guiding him away, leaning against him in a masque of romantic conversation. But as they turned the first corner they ran smack into a conversational group of three that blocked their passage.

"Van, you harlot!" greeted a young man in a pale blue suede jacket with metal-tipped fringe. "You've just taken our much-touted art expert here all for yourself and you're gobbling him all up!" He looked at Jonathan, his eyebrows arched in anticipation of an introduction.

Vanessa ignored him, turning to a middle-aged man wearing heavy clothes and an open, eager expression that had a canine flavor. "Sir Wilfred Pyles, Jonathan Hemlock. I believe your commission had something to do with getting him here."

"Good to see you here, Jon."

"You mean at this party, Fred?"

"Well, no. I meant in the country actually."

"Ah-ha!" Vanessa said. "I had no idea you two knew one another."

"Yes indeed," Sir Wilfred explained. "I've been an admirer of Jon's for years. But not as an art critic. I'm afraid I'm only one of those chaps who know what they like. No, my acquaintance with Jonathan Hemlock was under rather a different heading. I used to be an enthusiastic amateur mountaineer, don't you know. Just puffing about and hill bashing, really. But I read all the journals and became familiar with this fellow's exploits. And, when I had a chance to meet him, I grabbed it. That was—how long ago was it, Jon?"

Jonathan smiled, uncomfortable as he always was when talking about climbing. "I haven't climbed for years."

"Well, I shouldn't wonder. I mean—that must have been a nasty business on the Eiger. Three men, wasn't it?"

Jonathan cleared his throat. "I don't climb seriously anymore."

"Not only that," Vanessa said, squeezing his arm, realizing that he wanted to change the subject, "he's given up serious criticism as well. Or haven't you read his latest bag of garbage?" She turned to the crisp, beautiful woman of uncertain years who stood beside Sir Wilfred. "And you are . . . ?"

"Oh, yes. Sorry," Sir Wilfred said. "Mrs. Amelia Farquahar. A friend of mine, actually."

"No one's introduced me yet," the suede jacket said.

Vanessa patted his cheek. "That's because no one's noticed you yet, darling boy."

"Oh, I doubt that. I doubt that." But his peeve lasted only a second. "Actually, we were having a lively conversation when you broke in. Lively and a little naughty."

"Oh?" Vanessa asked Mrs. Farquahar.

"Yes. We were, in fact, discussing the myth of vaginal climax." Mrs. Farquahar turned to Jonathan. "What are your opinions on that, Dr. Hemlock?"

"As an art critic?"

"As a mountain climber, if you'd rather."

Sir Wilfred grunted. "All part of women's liberation, I shouldn't wonder. I hear you've been having quite a lot of that in your country."

"Mostly among the losers," Jonathan said, smiling.

Vanessa smiled back. "You turd."

"And you, Miss Dyke?" Mrs. Farquahar asked. "Do you have an opinion on that?"

Vanessa dropped her cigarette butt in suede jacket's wineglass. "I don't think it's a myth at all. The misconception is that it takes a penis to achieve it."

"How interesting," said Mrs. Farquahar.

"I say!" injected suede jacket, feeling somehow he had been left out of the conversation. "Did you read about that man found impaled in St. Martin's-In-The-Fields?"

"Oh, ghastly business," Sir Wilfred said.

"Oh, I don't know. If you have to go ..." He wriggled a shoulder and took a sip of wine.

While he was coping with the mouthful of tobacco, Vanessa said to Mrs. Farquahar, "Come, let

20

me introduce you to the young man who has drawn this sparkling company together."

"Yes. I'd like that."

They pushed off through the crowd, Vanessa leading the way and prowling through the congested sea of people. Suede jacket stood on tiptoe and waved extravagantly to someone who had just entered, then struggled off after a word of apology.

Jonathan and Sir Wilfred stood side by side against the wall. "What's all this about climbing, Fred?" Jonathan asked without looking at him. "You get a nosebleed from standing on a thick carpet."

"Just the first thing that came to my mind, Jon." The flappy tones of the bungling British civil servant dropped away from his speech.

"I see. Are you still in the service?"

"No, no. I've been on the shelf for several years now. The extent of my counterespionage activities now is trying to find out how much my chauffeur tells my wife."

"When I saw your name on my appointment to come over here, I assumed MI–5 had found you an elastic cover."

"I'm afraid not. I am well and truly out to pasture. The electronic age has caught up with me. One has to be a damned engineer these days to stay in the game. No, I serve my country by chairing committees devoted to the task of bringing cultural enrichment to our shores. You constitute a cultural enrichment." He laughed. "Who would have thought in the old days when we were flogging about Europe, now on the same team, now in opposition, that we would be brought so low."

"You *do* know that I'm out of it totally now?" Jonathan wanted to be sure.

"Oh, certainly. First thing I checked upon when your name came up. The chaps at the old office said you were—to use their uncomplimentary compliment—politically subpotent. By which I take it that you and CII have parted company."

"That we have. By the way, congratulations on your knighthood."

"Not so much of an achievement as you might imagine. These days few people escape that distinction. When you leave the Service they automatically lumber you with a K.B.E. They've found it's cheaper than a gold watch, I suspect. Ah, the ladies return."

As she approached, Vanessa said to Jonathan, "I didn't lure you here just to punish you with my acquaintances. There's something I want to show you." She turned to Mrs. Farquahar. "Jon and I have to run off for a moment."

Mrs. Farquahar smiled and inclined her head.

In the hall where it was relatively quiet Jonathan asked, "What's this all about, Van?"

"You'll see. A chance for you to pick up some pocket money. But look, don't get uptight, and for God's sake, don't cause any trouble. That could be very bad for me." She led the way down a corridor, past the table at which the maids and caterer's assistants were flirting, to the door of a small private display room. "Come on."

Jonathan entered, then stopped short. A bronze Horse and Rider by Marino Marini stood in the center of a darkened room, its ragged modeling accented by the acute angle of a shaft of dramatically placed light. About forty inches high, a sand-colored forced patina, the modeling seemed to combine those primitive, lumpy Etrurian characteristics typical of Marini with an almost oriental twist of the heads of both horse and rider that was most uncharacteristic. But the fat rider's stubbed cigar of a penis was a Marini signature. Jonathan walked slowly around the casting, pausing occasionally to take in some detail, his concentration totally committed. So absorbed was he that it was a while before he noticed a man leaning against the far wall, posed under a dim light that had been arranged with almost as much care as that given to the Horse. He wore an extremely trendy suit of dusty gold velvet, and a ruffle of starched lace stood at his throat. His arms were folded across his chest, his stance poised and practiced, but an inner tension prevented his posture from appearing relaxed. He watched Jonathan steadily, following him with gray eyes so pale they seemed colorless.

Jonathan examined the man with frank curiosity. It was the most beautiful male bust he had ever seen—an unearthly, bloodless beauty such as masters of the Early Renaissance sometimes touched upon. Intuitively, he knew the man was aware of the effect of his cold beauty, and he had stationed himself in that particular light to heighten it.

"Well, Jonathan?" Vanessa had been standing back out of the light. Her voice was hushed most uncharacteristically.

Jonathan glanced again at the Renaissance man. Something in his demeanor made it clear that he did not intend to speak and did not wish to be spoken to. Jonathan decided to let him play out his silly game.

"Well what?" he asked Van.

"Is it genuine?"

Jonathan was surprised at the question, forgetting as often he did that his gift was quite unique. As some people have perfect pitch, Jonathan had a perfect eye. Once he had seen a man's work, he never mistook it. It was, in fact, upon that gift that his reputation had been founded and not, as he preferred others to believe, on his scholarship. "Of course it's genuine. Marini cast three of these and later broke one. No one knows why. Some defect probably. But only two now exist. This is the Dallas Horse. I didn't know it was in England."

"Ah—" Vanessa fumbled for a Gauloise to cover her tension, then she asked offhandedly, "What price do you think it would bring?"

Jonathan looked at her, startled. "It's for sale?"

She took a deep drag and blew smoke up at the ceiling. "Yes."

Jonathan looked across at the Renaissance man who had not moved a muscle and who still watched him, the colorless eyes picked out by a shaft of light just under the dark eyebrows.

"Stolen?" Jonathan asked.

"No," Vanessa answered.

"Doesn't he talk?"

"Please, Jonathan." She touched his arm.

"What the hell's going on? Is he selling this?"

"Yes. But he wanted you to have a look at it first."

"Why? You don't need me to authenticate it. Its provenances are impeccable. Even a British expert

24

could have certified it." He addressed this to the man standing on the opposite side of the bar of light illuminating the Horse. When the man spoke, his tessitura was just as one would have predicted: precise, carefully modulated, colorless.

"How did you know it was the Dallas Horse, Dr. Hemlock?"

"Ah, you speak. I thought you just posed."

"How did you know it was the Dallas Horse?"

As curtly as possible, Jonathan explained that everyone who knew anything at all about the Marini Horses knew the story of the one purchased by the young Dallas millionaire who subsequently picked it up at the plane himself, loaded it into the back of his pickup, then brought it to his ranch. In unloading, it was dropped and broken. Subsequently it was brazed together by an auto mechanic and, because it was imperfect, it was relegated to adorning the barbecue pit. "Any novice would recognize it," he said, pointing to the rough brazing.

The Renaissance man nodded. "I knew the story, of course."

"Then why did you ask?"

"Testing. Tell me. What do you suppose it will bring in an open sale?"

"I'm a professional. I get paid for making evaluations."

Vanessa cleared her throat. "Ah, Jon, he gave me an envelope for you. I'm sure it will be all right."

Neither the voice nor the words were in character for the gruff, hard-drinking Vanessa Dyke, and Jonathan's distaste for this whole theatrical setup grew. He answered crisply. "Impossible to say. Whatever the buyer can afford. It depends on how

25

much he wants it, or how much he wants others to know he owns it. If my memory serves me, the Texan you got if from gave something in the neighborhood of a quarter of a million for it."

"What would it bring now?" Vanessa asked.

Jonathan shrugged. "I told you. I can't say."

The Renaissance man spoke without moving even a fold in the fabric of his suit. "Let me ask you an easier question. Something you *can* answer."

Jonathan's slum boyhood toned his response. "Listen, art lover. Keep your fee. Or better yet, shove it up your ass." He turned to leave, but Vanessa stood in his way.

"Please, Jon? A favor to me?"

"What's this yahoo to you?"

She frowned and shook her head, not wanting to go into it now. He didn't understand, and he was angry, but Vanessa was a friend. He turned back. "What do you want to know?"

The Renaissance man nodded, accepting Jonathan's capitulation. "The Horse will be offered for sale soon. It will bring a very high price. At what point would people in the art world find the price unbelievable? At what point would the newspapers make something of it?"

Jonathan assumed there was a tax dodge on. "There would be talk, but no one would be unduly astonished at, say, half a million. If it came from the right sources."

"Half a million? Dollars?"

"Yes, dollars."

"I paid more than that for it myself. What if the price were well beyond that?"

"How much beyond?"

"Say ... five million ... *pounds.*"

Jonathan laughed. "Never. The other privately held one could be loosened for a tenth of that. And that one's never been broken."

"Perhaps the buyer wouldn't want the other one. Perhaps he has a fondness for flawed statues."

"Five million pounds is a lot to pay for a perverted taste for things flawed."

"Such a price, then, would cause talk."

"It would cause talk, yes."

"I see." The Renaissance man looked down to the floor. "Thank you for your opinion, Dr. Hemlock."

"I think we'd better get back now, Jon," Vanessa said, touching his arm.

Jonathan stopped in the hall and collected his coat from the porter. "Well? Are you going to tell me what that was all about?"

"What's to tell? A mutual friend asked me to arrange a contract between you two. I was paid for it. Oh, here." She gave him a broad envelope, which contained a thick padding of bills.

"But who is that guy?"

She shrugged. "Never saw him before in my life, lover. Come on. I'll buy you a drink."

"I'm not going back in there. Anyway, I have an appointment tonight."

Vanessa looked over his shoulder in the direction of Mrs. Farquahar. "I think I have too."

As he slipped into his overcoat, he looked back toward the door to the private showroom. "You have some weird friends, lady."

"Do you really think so?" She laughed and butted her cigarette in the salver meant to receive tips, then she walked into the crowded reception room where

27

the singer with the gold-tinsel wig and the green mascara was bobbing over the heads of the company, chanting in thin falsetto something about a cup of coffee, a sandwich, and you.

The Renaissance man settled into the passenger seat of his Jensen Interceptor and adjusted his suit coat to prevent its wrinkling. "Has he left?"

The Mute nodded.

"And he's being followed?"

The Mute nodded again.

The Renaissance man clicked on the tape deck and settled to listen to a little Bach as the car crunched along the driveway, its lights out.

A young man with a checked sports coat and a camera depended from his neck stood in a red telephone kiosk beneath a corner streetlamp. While the phone on the other end of the line double-buzzed, he clamped the receiver under his chin awkwardly as he scrawled in a notebook. He had been holding the license number on the rim of his memory by chanting it over and over to himself. Hearing an answering click and hum, he pressed in his twopence piece and said in a hard "r" American accent, "Hi, there."

A cultured voice responded, "Yes? What is it, Yank?"

"How did you know it was me?"

"That hermaphroditic accent of yours."

"Oh. I see." Crestfallen, the young man abandoned his phony American sound and continued with the nasal drawl of public school. "He has left the party, sir. Took a cab."

"Yes?"

"Well, I thought you would like to know. He was followed."

"Good. Good."

"Shall I tag along?"

"No, that wouldn't be wise." The cultured voice was silent for a moment. "Very well. I suppose you have the Baker Street ploy set up?"

"Right, sir. By the way, just in case you want to know, I took note of the time of his departure. He left at exactly . . . Good Lord."

"What is it?"

"My watch has stopped."

The man on the other end of the line sighed heavily. "Good night, Yank."

"Good night, sir."

Covent Garden

Jonathan sat deep in the back of the taxi, attending only vaguely to the hissing pass of traffic over wet streets. He experienced his usual social nausea after public gatherings of reviewers, teachers, gallery owners, patrons—the paracreative slugs who burden art with their attention—the parasites who pretend to be symbions and who support, with their groveling leadership, the teratogenetic license of democratic art.

"Fucking grex venalium," he muttered to himself, displaying both aspects of his background—the slums and the university halls.

Forget it, he told himself. Don't let them get to you. He looked forward this evening to a pleasant hour or two with MacTaint, his favorite person in London. A thief, a rogue, and a con with a fine sense of scatology and a haughty disdain for such social imperatives as cleanliness, MacTaint seemed to be visiting modern London from the pages of Dickens or the chorus of *Threepenny Opera*. But he knew painting as did few people in Europe, and he was England's most active dealer in the gray market of stolen art. Although Jonathan had never before

31

been to MacTaint's home, they had often met in little pubs around Covent Garden to drink and joke
and talk about painting.

He smiled to himself as he recalled their first
meeting three months earlier. He had returned to his
flat after a day marred by lectures to serious, ungifted students; meetings with committees whose
keen senses of parliamentary procedure obscured
their purposes; and gatherings of academic people
and art critics, all fencing for position in their minia-
ture arena. He was fed up, and he needed to pass
some resuscitating time with his paintings, the eleven
Impressionists that were all that remained from the
four years he had worked for the Search and Sanction Division of CII. These paintings were the most
important things in his life. After all, he had killed
for them. Under the protection and blessing of the
government, he had performed a half-dozen coun-
ter-assassinations ("sanctions," in the crepuscular
bureaucratese of CII).

Tired and depressed, he had pushed open the
door to his flat, and walked in on a party in progress. Every light was on, his whiskey had been broken out, Haydn played on the phonograph, and the
furniture had been moved about to facilitate exami-
nation of the eleven Impressionists lining the walls.

But it was a party for only one person. An old
man sat alone in a deep wing chair, glass in hand,
his tattered overcoat still on, its collar up to his ears
revealing only tousled gray hair and a bulbous,
new-potato nose.

"Come in. Come in," the old man invited.

"Thank you," Jonathan said, hoping the irony
had not been too heavy.

"Have some whiskey?"

"Yes, I think I will." Jonathan poured out a good tot of Laphroaig. "Could I freshen up yours?"

"Oh, that's good of you, son. But I've had sufficient."

Jonathan tugged off his raincoat. "In that case, get the hell out of here."

"In a while. In a while. Relax, lad. I'm feasting my tired eyes on that bit of crusted pigment there. Manet. Good for the soul."

Jonathan smiled, intrigued by this old leprechaun who looked like a cross between a provincial professor emeritus and a dirty dustman. "Yes, it's a first-quality copy."

"Pig shit."

"Sir?"

The visitor leaned forward, dandruff falling from his matted hair, and enunciated carefully. "Pig shit. If that's a copy, I'm a glob of whore's spit."

"Have it your own way. Now get out." As he approached the gnomish housebreaker, Jonathan was deterred by a barrier of odor: ancient sweat, body dirt, mildewed clothing.

The old man raised his hand. "Before you set to bashing me about, I'd best introduce myself. I'm MacTaint."

After a stunned moment, Jonathan laughed and shook MacTaint's hand. Then, for several hours, they drank and talked about painting. At no time did MacTaint take off the tattered, heel-length overcoat, and Jonathan was to learn that he never did.

MacTaint downed the last of the whiskey, set the bottle on the floor beside his chair, and regarded Jonathan with an evaluative squint from beneath shaggy white eyebrows, the salient characteristic of which was maverick hairs that hooked out like antennae over the glittering eyes. "So! You are Jonathan Hemlock." He chuckled. "I can tell you, lad, that your appearance on the scene scared the piss out of a lot of us. You could have been a vast nuisance, you know, with that phenomenal eye of yours. My colleagues in the business of reproducing masters might have found it difficult to pursue their vocations with you about. There was even talk of relieving you of the burden of your bleeding life. But then! Then came the happy news that you, like all worthy men, were at heart a larcenous and acquisitive son of a bitch."

"I'm not very acquisitive anymore."

"That's true, come to think of it. You haven't made a purchase for—how long is it?"

"Four years."

"And why is that?"

"I parted company with my source of money."

"Oh, yes. There was rumor of some kind of government association. As I recall, it was the kind of thing no one wanted to know about. Still. You haven't done half badly. You own these grand paintings, two of which, if I may remind you, came through my own good offices."

"I've never been sure, Mac. What are you? A thief or a handler."

"A thief, by preference. But I'll flog another man's work when times are hard. And you? What are you—other than a frigging enigma?"

"Frigging enigma?"

MacTaint scratched the scruff on his scalp. "You know perfectly well what I mean. My comrades on the continent shared my curiosity about you at first, and we pooled our fragments of information. Bits and pieces that never seemed to form a whole picture. You had this gift, this eye that made it possible for you to spot a fake at a glance. But the rest didn't make much sense. University professor. Critic and writer. Collector of black market paintings. Mountain climber. Employed in some kind of nasty government business. Frigging enigma, that's what you are . . ."

The taxi driver swore under his breath and jerked back the hand brake. They were frozen in a tangle of traffic around Trafalgar Square. Jonathan decided to walk the rest of the way. His eagerness to be away from the people at Tomlinson's had made him an hour early for his appointment with MacTaint anyway, and he could use the exercise.

To get away from the crowds and the noise for a second, he turned down Craven Street, past the Monk's Tavern, to Craven Passage and The Arches where destitute old women were settling in to pass the night on the paving stones, scraps of cardboard beneath them to absorb the damp, their backs against the brick walls, bits of fabric tugged about them for warmth. They drowsed with the help of gin, but never so deep into sleep that they missed the odd passerby whom they begged for coins or fags with droning, liturgical voices.

Swinging London.

He held to the back streets as long as possible. His mind kept returning to the Renaissance man he had met at Tomlinson's. Five million pounds for a Marini Horse? Impossible. And yet the man had seemed so confident. The event had made Jonathan uncomfortable. It had those qualities of the deadly absurd, of melodramatic hokum and very real threat that he associated with the lethal game players of international espionage, that group of social mutants he had despised when he worked for CII, and whom he had driven from his memory.

He turned back up into the lights and noise of center city. The rain had developed into a dirty, hanging mist that blurred and blended the stew of neon and noise through which crowds of fun-seekers jostled their way.

Modern young girls took long steps with bony legs under ankle-length skirts, their thin shoulders stooped with poor posture, some with frizzly hair, others with lank. They were the kind who abjured cosmetic artifice and insisted upon being accepted for what they were—antiwar, socially committed, sexually liberated, dull, dull, dull.

Working-class girls clopped along in the thick-soled plastic shoes Picasso's kid had inflicted on mass fashion, their stride already displaying hints of the characteristic gait of adult British women: feet splayed, knees bent, backs rigid—seeming to suffer from some chronic rectal ailment. Substantial legs revealed to the crotch by miniskirts, vast liquid breasts sloshing about within stiff brassieres, chattering voices ravaged by the North London glottal gasp, complexions the victims of the Anglo-Saxon penchant for vitamin-free diets. Doughy bodies, doughy minds. Gastronomic anomalies. Dumpling tarts.

Swinging London.

Jonathan walked close to the buildings where passage was clearest.

"Penny for the Guy, mister?"

The voice had come from behind. He turned to find three leering hooligans in their early twenties, jeans and thick steel-toed boots. One of them pushed a wheelchair in which reclined a Guy Fawkes effigy composed of stuffed old clothes and a comic mask beneath a bowler.

"What do you say, mister?" The biggest hooligan held his sleeve. "A penny for the Guy?"

"Sorry." Jonathan pulled away. He walked on with the sense of their presence etching his spine, but they didn't follow.

He turned into New Row with its gaslights, shuttered greengrocers, and bakeries. His pace carried him slowly away from the Mazurka Clubs, Nosh Bars, and Continuous Continental Revues of Piccadilly, and deeper into Covent Garden with its odd mélange of market and theatrical activities. Italian wholesale fruit companies, seedy talent agencies, imported olive oil, and a school of modern dance and ballet—tap a specialty.

Near a streetlamp, a solitary hustler carnivorously watched him approach. She was plump and fortyish, her legs chubby above thick white knee socks. She wore a short dress and a school blazer with emblem, and her stiff platinum hair was done in two long braids that fell on either side of her full cheeks. Obedient to recent police regulations, she did not solicit verbally, but she put one thumb into her mouth and rocked her thick body from side to side, making her eyes round and little girllike. As he passed, Jonathan noticed the scaly cake of her makeup, patched over, but not redone each time she sweated some off in the course of her work.

As he got deeper into the market, the acrid smell of traffic gave way to the high sweet smell of spoiled fruit, and the litter of paper was replaced by a litter of lettuce leaves, slimy and dangerous underfoot.

Down a dark side street, an out-of-tune piano thumped ragged chords as the silhouettes of tired dancers leapt over drawn window shades. Young girls sweating and panting in their damp exercise costumes. Stars in the making.

"Penny for the Guy, mister?"

He spun around, his back against the brick wall, both hands open before his chest.

The two children yelped and ran down the street, abandoning the old pram and its pitiful, floppy effigy wearing a Sneezy the Dwarf mask.

Jonathan called after them, but his shout served only to speed them on. When the street was quiet again, he laughed at himself and tucked a pound note into the Guy's pocket, hoping the children might sneak back later to retrieve it.

He walked on through the gaggle of lanes, then turned off into a cul-de-sac where there were no streetlamps. The end of a dilapidated court was blocked off by heavy double doors of weathered, splintery wood that swung silently on oiled hinges. The black within was absolute, but he knew he had found his way because of the rancid, cumin smell of ancient sweat.

"Ah, there you are, lad. I'd just decided to come looking for you. It's easy enough to get lost if you've never been here before. Here, follow me."

Jonathan stood still until MacTaint had opened

the inner door, flooding the inky court with pale yellow light. They entered a large open space that had once been a fruit merchant's warehouse. Odd litter was piled in the corners, and two potbellied coal stoves radiated cheerful heat, their long chimney pipes stretching up into the shadows of the corrugated steel roof some twenty-five feet overhead. Well spaced from one another, three painters stood in pools of light created by bulbs with flat steel shades suspended on long wires from above. Two of them continued working at their easels, oblivious to the intrusion; the third, a tall cadaverous man with an unkempt beard and wild eyes, turned and stared with fury at the source of the draft.

Jonathan followed MacTaint through the warehouse to a door at the far end, and they passed into a totally different cosmos. The inner room was done in lush Victoriana: crystal chandeliers hung from an ornate ceiling; blue-flocked wallpaper stood above eggshell wainscoting; a good wood fire flickered in a wide marble fireplace; mirrors and sconces on all the walls made an even distribution of low intensity light; and comfortable deep divans and wing chairs in soft blue damask were in cozy constellations around carved and inlaid tables. A full-blown woman in her mid-fifties sat on one of the divans, her flabby arm dangling over the back. The bright orange of her hair contested with the blood red of her pasty lipstick, and festoons of bold jewelry clattered as she screwed a cigarette into a rhinestone holder.

"Here we are," MacTaint said as he shuffled in his ragged greatcoat over to the crystal bar. "He wasn't lost after all. This, good my love, is Jonathan

39

Hemlock, about whom you have heard me say nothing. And this vast cow, Jon, is Lilla—my personal purgatory. Laphroaig, I suppose?"

Lilla twirled her cigarette holder into the air in greeting. "How good of you to pay us a visit. Mr. MacTaint has never mentioned you. While you're at it, my dear, you might bring me a little drop of gin."

"Friggin' lush," MacTaint muttered under his breath.

"Come. Sit here, Dr. Hemlock." Lilla thumped dust out of the divan seat beside her. "I take it you're connected with the theatre?"

Jonathan smiled politely into the drooping, overly made-up eyes. "No. No, I'm not."

"Ah. A pity. I was for many years associated with the entertainment world. And I must admit that I sometimes miss it. The laughter. The happy times."

MacTaint shambled over with the drinks. "Her only dealings with theatre were that she used to stand outside and try to hustle blokes too drunk to care what they got into. Here you go, love. Bottoms up, as they used to say in your trade."

"Don't be crude, love." She tossed back the glass of gin and smacked her lips, a motion that jiggled her pendulous cheeks. Then she clapped a ham-sized hand onto Jonathan's forearm and said, "Of course, I suppose it's all changed now. The old artists have gone, it's all youngsters with long hair and loud songs." She relieved herself of a shuddering sigh.

"It's worse than you think," MacTaint said, drooping into a damask chair and hooking another over with his toe so he could put his feet up on it. "The law doesn't allow you to carry sandwich boards advertising the positions you specialize in.

And curb service on rubber mattresses is definitely not in."

"Fuck you, MacTaint!" Lilla said in a new accent that carried the snarl of the streets in it.

MacTaint instantly responded in kind. "Hop it, you ha'penny cunt! I'd kick your arse proper for you, if I wasn't afraid of losing me boot!"

Lilla rose with tottering dignity and offered her hand to Jonathan. "I must leave you gentlemen. I have letters to do before retiring."

Jonathan rose and bowed slightly. "Good night, Lilla."

She made her way to the door at the far end of the room, sweeping up a bottle of gin as she passed the bar. She had to tack twice to gain the center of the door, which then gave her some difficulty in opening. In the end she gave it a hinge-loosening kick that knocked it ajar. She turned and waved her cigarette holder at Jonathan before disappearing.

Jonathan looked questioningly at MacTaint, who bared his lower teeth in a grimace of pleasure as he dug his fingernails into the ingrown stubble under his chin. "She drinks, you know," he said.

"Does she?"

"Oh, yes. I found her out there in the yard fifteen years ago," he explained, shifting the scratching to under an arm. "Somebody'd beat her up pretty badly."

"So you took her in?"

"To my eternal regret. Still! An occasional spat is good for the glands. She's a good old hole, really."

"What was this number she was doing for me?"

MacTaint shrugged. "Bits of old roles she's done,

I suppose. She's more than a little mental, you know."

"She's not the only one. Cheers." Jonathan drank off half his whiskey and looked around the room with genuine appreciation. "You live well."

MacTaint nodded agreement. "I don't move many paintings anymore. Only one or two a year. But what with no income tax, I do well enough."

"Who are those painters outside?"

"Damned if I know. They come and they go. I keep the place warm and light, and there's always tea and bread and cheese about for them. Sometimes there's only one or two of them, sometimes half a dozen. That tall one who gave you the evil eye, he's been around for years and years. Still working on the same canvas. Feels he owns the place—by squatter's right, I shouldn't wonder. Complains sometimes if the cheese isn't to his liking. The others come and go. I suppose they hear about the place from one another."

"You're a good man, MacTaint."

"Ain't that the bleeding truth. Did I ever tell you that I was once a painter myself?"

"No, never."

"Oh, yes! More than forty years ago I came down to The Smoke to study art. Full of theories I was, about art and socialism. You didn't look at my paintings, you read them. Essays, they were. Hungry children, strikers being bashed up by police, that sort of business. Trash. Then finally I discovered that my calling lay in stealing and flogging paintings. It's fun to do what you're good at."

They fell silent for a time, watching the fire loop yellow and blue in the hearth. It settled with a hiss of sparks, and the sound pulled MacTaint from his musings. "Jon? I asked you to drop over this evening for a reason."

"Not just to drink up your whiskey?"

"No. I've got something I want you to see." He grunted out of his chair and crossed to a painting that had been standing in an ornate old frame, its face to the wall. He carried it back tenderly and set it up on a chair. "What do you think of that?"

Jonathan scanned it and nodded. Then he leaned forward to examine it in detail. After five minutes, he sat back and finished off his Laphroaig. "You're not thinking of selling it, are you?"

MacTaint's eyes twinkled beneath his shaggy eyebrows. "And why not?"

"I was thinking of your reputation. You've never peddled a fake before."

"Goddamn your eye!" MacTaint cackled and scratched his scruffy head. "That would pass muster anywhere in the world."

"I'm not saying it's not a good copy—in fact it's extraordinary. But it is a forgery, and you don't flog fakes."

"Don't bother your head about that. I've never sold a piece of shoddy goods before, and I never shall. But slake my curiosity, lad. How can you tell it's phony?"

Jonathan shrugged. It was difficult to explain the almost automatic processes of mind and eye that constituted his gift. "Oh, a thousand things," he said.

"For instance?"

He sat back and closed his eyes, dredging up the original of J.-B.-S. Chardin's *House of Cards* from the lagan of his memory and holding it in focus as he studied the mental image. Then he opened his eyes slowly and examined the painting before him. "All right. This was done in Holland. At least, the Van M. technique was used. A relatively valueless painting of the proper age and size was sanded down, and the surface crackle was brought up by successive bakings of layers of paint."

MacTaint nodded.

"But the crackle was not perfect here." He touched the white areas around the face of the young man in a three-cornered hat. "And when the crackle didn't bake through perfectly, your forger rolled the canvas to force it. Basically a good job, too. But in these areas it ought to be deeper and more widely spaced. Your man seems to have forgotten that white dries more slowly than other pigments."

"And that's the only flaw? Crackle?"

"No, no. Dozens of other errors. Most of them are excessive precision. Forgers tend to be more exact in their draftsmanship than the artist was. Look here, for instance, at the perspective on the boy's left eye."

"Looks all right to me."

"Precisely. On the original, Chardin made a slight error—probably caused by two sittings during the drawing. And look here at the coin. It's as carefully drawn as the marker there. In the genuine painting, the coin has blurred outlines, as though it were in a different field of focus from the marker."

MacTaint shook his head in admiration, and a fall of dandruff floated to his lap. "Goddamn those eyes of yours."

"Even forgetting my eyes, this thing would

bounce the minute it hit the market. The original hangs in the National Gallery."

"Oh, get along with you!"

They laughed, knowing that many forgeries hang bravely and unchallenged in the major galleries of the world, while the originals hang in clandestine splendor in private collections. This was, in fact, the case with all but one of Jonathan's own Impressionists.

"Would this pass inspection, Jon?"

They both knew that the real skills of major curators were limited to the documentation of ownership patterns, despite their tendencies to report in terms of genuine knowledge. "With what provenance?" Jonathan asked.

"Oh ... let's say it was hanging in the National Gallery in place of the real one."

Jonathan raised his eyebrows, his turn to feel admiration. "No question at all," he pronounced with confidence. "But how would you get at the real Chardin, Mac? Since the '57 thing, they've stiffened their security and there hasn't been a successful theft."

"What makes you think that?" MacTaint's eyes were round with feigned surprise, and he looked more than ever like a mischievous leprechaun.

"But there's a weight alarm system. You couldn't possibly get one off the wall without being detected."

"Of course it would be detected. It's always detected."

"Always? Tell me, Mac. How many paintings have you nicked from the National Gallery?"

"All told?" MacTaint squinted sideways in concentration. "Over the years? Ah—h, let's see ... seven."

"Seven!" Jonathan stared at the old man. "I'll take that drink now," he said quietly.

"Here you go."

"Ta."

"Cheers."

They drank in silence. Jonathan shook his head. "I'm trying to see this in my mind, Mac. First, you walk to the gallery."

"I do that. Yes. In I walk."

"Then you take the painting from the wall. The alarms go off."

"Dreadful noise."

"You hang up a reasonably good forgery in its place, and you stroll out. Is that it?"

"Well, I don't stroll, exactly. More like running arse over teakettle. But in broad terms, yes, that's it."

"Now the alarm system tells them which picture has been tampered with, right?"

"Correct."

"And yet it never occurs to them to give the painting a professional scrutiny."

"They give it a great deal of attention. But not scrutiny." MacTaint was enjoying Jonathan's confusion immensely. "You're dying to know how I do it, aren't you?"

"I am."

"Well, I'm not going to tell you. Give that mind of yours something to chew on. You'll figure it out easily enough when you read about it in the newspapers."

"When will that be?"

"Exactly one week from tonight."

"You're a crafty and secretive son of a bitch."

"Part of my charm."

"MacTaint . . ." Jonathan didn't pursue it. He had no doubt at all but that the old fox would get the painting.

"All right," MacTaint relented, "I'll give you a little hint." He fished up a penknife from the depths of his overcoat pocket and pulled open one of the blades with a broken crusty thumbnail. Then he leaned over the painting for a second before slashing it twice, making a broad ✕ through the face of the boy. "There. How's that?"

"You are a nut, MacTaint. I'm getting out of here."

MacTaint chuckled to himself as he showed Jonathan to the door. "Haven't you ever wanted to do something like that, lad? Slash a painting? Or break a raw egg in your hand? Or kiss a strange lady in an elevator?"

"You're a nut. Give my love to Lilla."

"I have enough trouble trying to give her my own."

"Good night."

"Yes."

The warehouse-cum-studio was in darkness, save for a single light hanging from the corrugated roof and the reddish glow of banked coal fires through the mica windows of the pot-bellied stoves. Only one painter was still at work, alone in absorbed concentration within the single circle of light. Jonathan walked silently across the cement floor and stood at the edge of the light, watching. His attention was so

taken by the alert, feline motions of the painter attacking the canvas, then drawing back to judge effect, that it was some moments before he realized
she was a woman. Seemingly oblivious to his
presence, she squeezed off the excess paint from her
brush between her thumb and forefinger and wiped
them on the seat of her jeans, then she put the brush
between her teeth sideways and took up a finer one
to correct some detail. Her cavalier method of cleaning brushes was evidently habitual, because her bottom was a chaos of pigment, and Jonathan found
this more interesting than the modernistic daub on
the easel.

"What do you think of it?" she asked between her
teeth, without turning around.

"It's certainly colorful. And attractively taut. But
I think its potential for motion is its most appealing
feature."

She stepped back and scrutinized the canvas criti-
cally. "Taut?"

"Well, I don't mean rigid. More lean and compact."

"And *interesting?*"

"Most interesting."

"That's the kiss of death. When people don't like
what you've done, but they don't want to hurt your
feelings, they always fall back on "interesting.""

Jonathan laughed. "Yes, I suppose that's true."
He was delighted by her voice. It had the curling
vowels of Irish, and the range was a dry contralto.

"No, now tell me true. What do you honestly
think of it?"

"You really want to know?"

"Probably not." With a quick movement she

brushed a wisp of amber hair away with the back of her hand. "But go ahead."

"Like most modern painting, I think it's undisciplined, self-indulgent crap."

She took the brush from her mouth and stood for a moment, her arms crossed over her chest. "Well now. No one could accuse you of trying to chat a girl up just to get into her knickers."

"But I am chatting you up," he protested, "and probably for that reason."

She looked at him for the first time, her eyes narrowed appraisingly. "Does that work very often—just saying it out boldly like that?"

"No, not very often. But it saves me a hell of a lot of wasted energy."

She laughed. "Do you really know anything about art?"

"I'm afraid so."

"I see." She thoughtfully replaced her brushes in a soup tin filled with turpentine. "Well. That's it, I guess." She turned to him and smiled. "Are you in a mood to celebrate?"

"Celebrate what?"

"The end of my career."

"Oh, come now!"

"No, no. Don't flatter yourself that it's just your opinion, informed though you assure me it is. As it happens, I agree with you totally. I suppose I'm a better critic than painter. Still, I've made one great contribution to Art. I've taken myself out of it."

He smiled. "All right. How would you like to celebrate?"

"I think dinner might be a good idea for starts. I haven't eaten since morning."

49

"You're broke?"

"Stoney."

"The only thing open this time of night would be one of the more fashionable restaurants." He glanced involuntarily at her clothes.

"Don't worry. I shan't embarrass you. I'll just clean up and change before we go."

"You have your clothes here?"

She nodded her head toward two suitcases standing against the wall. "My rent came due this morning, you see. And the landlady never cared for the stink of turps in the halls anyway." She began scrubbing the paint from her hands with a cloth dipped in turpentine.

"You intended to sleep here?"

"Just for the night. The old geezer won't mind. Other painters have done it from time to time. I used the last of my money to send an SOS telegram to relatives in Ireland. They'll be sending something down in the morning, I suspect. You can turn your back if the female nude disturbs you—not that I'll be all that nude."

"No, no. Go ahead. I've passed some of my happiest moments in the presence of the nude figure."

She wriggled out of her close-fitting jeans and kicked them up into her hands. "Of course, as a nude, I wouldn't have been much to Rubens's taste. I'm quite the opposite of ample, as you can see. In fact, I'm damned near two-dimensional."

"They're two of my favorite dimensions."

She was just pulling her jumper over her head, and she stopped in mid-motion, looking out through the head opening. "You've a glib and shallow way of talking. I suppose the girls find that dishy."

"But you do not."

"No, not especially. But I don't hold it against you, for I suppose it's just a habit. Will this do, do you think?" She drew up from the open suitcase a long green paisley gown that set off the cupric tones of her hair.

"That will do perfectly."

She tossed it on over her head, then patted down her short fine hair. "I'm ready."

He gave her her choice of restaurants, and she selected an expensive French one near Regent's Park on the basis that she had never had the money to go there and it was fun to be both beggar and chooser. Nothing about the meal was right. The butter in the scampi meunière tasted of char, the salade niçoise was more acid than bracing, and the only wine available at temperature was a Pouilly-Fuissé, that atonic white that occupies so large a sector of British taste. But Jonathan enjoyed the evening immensely. She was a charmer, this one, and the quality of the food did not matter, save as another subject for laughter. The lilt and color of her accent was contagious, and he had to prevent himself from slipping into an imitation of it.

She ate with healthy appetite, both her portions and his, while he watched her with pleasure. Her face intrigued him. The mouth was too wide. The jawline was too square. The nose undistinguished. The amber hair so fine that it seemed constantly stirred by unfelt breezes. It was a boyish face with the mischievous flexibility of a street gamine. Her most arresting feature was her eyes, bottle green and too large for the face, and thick lashes like sable brushes. Their special quality came from the rapid eddies of expression of which they were capable. Laughter could squeeze them from below; another moment they would flatten to a look of vulnerable surprise; then instantly they were narrow with incredulity; then intense and shining with intelligence; but at rest, they were nothing special. In fact, no single element of her face was remarkable, but the total he found fascinating.

"Do you find me pretty?" she asked, glancing up and finding his eyes on her.

"Not pretty."

"I know what you mean. But it's a good old face. I enjoy doing self-portraits. But I have to suppress this mad desire I have to add to my measuring thumb. Your face is not so bad, you know."

"I'm glad."

She turned to her salad. "Yes, it's an interesting face. Bony and craggy and all that. But the eyes are a bother."

"Oh?"

"Are you sure you're not hungry?"

"Positive."

"Actually, they're smashing. But they're not very comfortable eyes." She glanced up and looked at them professionally. "It's difficult to say if they're green or gray. And even though you smile and laugh and all that, they never change. You know what I mean?"

"No." Of course he knew, but he liked having her talk about him.

"Well, most people's eyes seem to be connected to their thoughts. Windows to the soul and all. But not yours. You can't read a thing by looking into them."

"And that's bad?"

"No. Just uncomfortable. If you're not going to eat that salad, I'll just keep it from going to waste."

Over coffee, over cognac, over more coffee, they talked without design.

"Do you know what I've always wished?"

"No. What?"

"I've always wished I was a tall, terribly handsome black woman. With long legs and a chilling, disdainful sideways glance."

He laughed. "Why have you wished that?"

"Oh, I don't know really. But think of the clothes I could get away with wearing!"

". . . oh, it was a typical middle-class Irish childhood, I suspect. Cooed over and spoiled as a baby; ignored as a child. Taught how to pass tests and how to stand with good posture. My father was a rabid Irish nationalist, but like most he had suspicions of inferiority. He sent me off to university in London—to get a *really good* education. And they were delighted when I came back with an English accent. I hated school as a girl. Sports and gymnastics particularly. I remember that we had a very, very modern physical culture teacher. A great bony woman, she was, with a prissy voice and a faint moustache. She tried to introduce the girls to the joys of eurythmics. You should have seen us! A gaggle of awkward girls—some with stick legs and knobby knees, others placid and fat—all trying to follow instructions 'to writhe with an inner passion and reach up expressively for the Sun God and let him penetrate your body.' We'd giggle about inner passions and penetrations, and the teacher would call us shallow, silly girls and dirty-minded. Then she'd writhe for us to show how it should be done. And we'd giggle some more. Cigarette?"

"I don't smoke."

She didn't seem to realize that she had stopped her story midway and had turned her thoughts inward.

He allowed the silence to run its course, and when she focused again on him with a slight start, he said, "So you won't be going back to Ireland?"

She butted her cigarette out deliberately. "No. Not ever." She lit another and stared at the gold lighter as though she were seeing it for the first time. "I should never have gone to the North. But I did and ... too much happened there. Too much hatred. And death." She sighed and shook her head briskly. "No. I'll never go back to Ireland."

"Say, do you like Sterne?" she said.

"Ah ... funny you should mention him."

"Why?"

"I haven't the slightest idea who you're talking about."

"Sterne," she said, "the writer."

"Oh. That Sterne."

"I've always had this deep intuition that I would get on well with any man who had a fondness for Sterne, Trollope, and Galsworthy."

"Has it worked out like that?"

"I don't know. I've never met anyone who liked Sterne."

"More coffee?"
"Please."

". . . and you took up painting?"

"Oh, little by little. Not with much courage at first. Then I took the plunge and decided I would do nothing but paint until my money ran out. The family was dead against it, especially as they had wasted so much money sending me over here to school. I suppose they would have been happier if I had gone into prostitution. At least they would have understood the profit motive. Well, I painted and painted, and nobody at all noticed. Then I ran out of money and sold everything I had of any value. But the first thing I knew, I was stoney broke and didn't even have rent money."

"And that was that."

"And that was that." She looked up and smiled. "And here I am."

"I have a confession to make," he said seriously.

"You're a typhoid carrier?"

"No."

"You're designed to self-destruct in seven minutes?"

"No."

"You're a boy."

"No. You'll never guess."

"In which case I give up."

"I have never liked the films of Eisenstein. They bore me to screaming."

"That is serious. What do you do for espresso talk?"

"Oh, I'm not excusing myself. I recognize it to be a great flaw in my character."

". . . oh, I love to drive! Fast, at night, in back lanes, with the lights off. Don't you?"

"No."

"Most men do, I think. British men especially. They use fast cars sexually, if you know what I mean."

"Like Italians."

"I suppose."

"Maybe that's why both countries produce so many competent grand prix drivers. They get practice on public roads."

"But you don't like to drive fast?"

"I don't need it."

She smiled. "Good." The vowel was drawn out and had an Irish curl.

". . . Philosophy of life?" he asked, smiling to himself at the idea. "No, I've never had one. When I was a kid, we were too poor to afford them, and later on they had gone out of fashion."

"No, now, don't send me up. I know the words sound pompous, but everyone has some kind of philosophy of life—some way of sorting out the good things from the bad . . . or the potentially dangerous."

"Perhaps. The closest I've come to that is my rigid adherence to the principle of leave-a-little."

"Leave a little what?"

"Leave-a-little everything. Leave a party before it becomes dull. Leave a meal before you're cloyed. Leave a city before you feel that you know it."

"And I suppose that includes human relationships?"

"Most especially human relationships. Get out while they're still on the upswing. Leave before they become predictable or, what is worse, *meaningful.* Be willing to lose a few events to protect the memory."

"I think that's a terrible philosophy."

"I'm sorry. It's the only one I've got."

"It's a coward's philosophy."

"It's a survivor's philosophy. Shall we have the cheese board?"

He half stood in greeting as she returned to the table. "A last brandy?" he asked.

"Yes, please." She was pensive for a second. "You know, it just now occurred to me that one might make a useful barometer of national traits by studying national toilet tissues."

"Toilet tissues?"

"Yes. Has that ever occurred to you?"

"Ah . . . no. Never."

"Well, for instance. I was just noticing that some English papers are medicated. You'd never find that in Ireland."

"The English are a careful race."

"I suppose. But I've heard that American papers are soft and scented and are advertised on telly by being caressed and squeezed—right along with adverts for suppository preparations and foods that are finger-licking good. That says something about decadence and soft living in a nation with affluence beyond its inner resources, doesn't it?"

"What do you make of the waxed paper the French are devoted to?"

"I don't know. More interest in speed and flourish than efficiency?"

"And the crisp Italian papers with the tensile strength of a communion wafer?"

She shrugged. It was obvious that one could make something of that too, but she was tired of the game.

She took his arm as they walked along the wet street to a corner more likely to produce taxis.

"I'll drop you off at Mac's. It's more or less on my way."

"Where *do* you live?"

"Right here." They were indeed passing the entrance to the hotel in which he had a penthouse apartment.

"But you said—"

"I thought I'd give you a way out."

She walked along in silence for a while, then she squeezed his arm. "That was a nice gesture. Truly gentle."

"I'm like that," he said, and laughed.

"But it *is* a bit odd that you just happen to live two doors from the restaurant."

"Now wait a minute, madam. *You* picked the restaurant."

She frowned. "That's true, isn't it. Still, it's a troubling coincidence."

He stopped and placed *his* hands on her shoulders, searching her face with mock sincerity. "Could it be . . . fate?"

"I think it's more likely a coincidence."

He agreed and they started off again, but back toward the hotel.

The phone double-buzzed several times before an angry voice answered. "Yes? Yes?"

"Good evening, sir."

"Good Lord! Do you know what time it is?"

"Yes, sir. Sorry. I just thought you'd like to know that they just went into his hotel on Baker Street."

"Is there any trouble? Is everything prepared?"

"No trouble, sir."

"Then why are you calling?"

"Well, I just thought you would want to be kept in the picture. They entered the hotel at exactly ... oh, my. I must get this watch seen to."

There was a silence on the other end of the line. Then, "Good night, Yank."

"Good night, sir."

Baker Street

"Lord love us!" she said. "This is ghastly!"

Jonathan laughed as he passed on ahead, turning on lights as he went. She followed him through two rooms.

"Is there no end to it?" she asked.

"There are eleven rooms. Including six bedrooms, but only one bath."

"That must cause some awkward traffic problems."

"No. I live here alone."

She dropped into the spongy pink velvet upholstery of an oversized chaise longue carved with conchs, serpentine sea dragons, and bosomy mermaids painted in antique white enamel and picked out in metallic gold. "I'm afraid to touch this rubbish. Afraid I'll catch something."

"Not an unfounded fear. Nothing is more communicable than bad taste, as Ortega y Gasset has warned us. Look at pop art or the novels of Robbe-Grillet."

She looked at him quizzically. "You really are an academic, aren't you?" She scanned the pink marble fireplace, the harlequin wallpaper, the Danish modern furniture, the yellow shag rug, the burgundy-tinted glass sconces, the wrought-iron wall plaques. The saccharine profusion caused her nostrils to dilate and her throat to constrict. "How can you stand to live here?"

He shrugged. "It's free. And I have a little flat in Mayfair. I only stay here when I'm in this end of town."

"Goodness me. Impressive, sir. *Two* flats in the midst of a housing shortage. And he reads Ortega y ... whoever. What more could a beggar girl ask?"

"She could ask for a drink." He poured from a hammered aluminum decanter in the form of a wading bird. "The single advantage of this place is that it makes going out into the street a pleasure. And you need something like that in London. Cheers."

"Cheers. You don't find London attractive?"

"Well, it's made me reevaluate my aesthetic ranking of Gary, Indiana."

She took her drink and wandered into the next room, which was less tastefully appointed. "How did you come by this place? Do you have enemies in real estate?"

"No. It belongs to a film producer who took a twenty-year lease on it years ago to soak up some of the 'funny money' he had made in England, but couldn't take out of the country. He uses it as a *pied-à-terre* when in London, and he gives keys to friends who might be passing through. When I told him I'd be spending a year in England, he offered to lend it to me."

"Did he decorate it himself?"

"He used furniture and props from his films. The Doris Day/Rock Hudson sort of things."

"I see. Where do you stay to get away from the noise?"

"Come along." He led her through two rooms to one that had been left unfurnished. He had dragged in some of the quieter pieces and had hung his collection of Impressionists around the slate gray walls. It was in this room that he had first found MacTaint drinking his whiskey and admiring his paintings.

The canvases arrested her. She set down her glass and stood before a pointillist Pissarro in silence.

"I have a hobby of collecting the best copies I can find," he told her.

"Beautiful."

"Oh, yes. Even copies, they're capable of putting modern painting in its place."

"All right, sir," she said in a heavy brogue, "that will be enough of that altogether." She crossed to the tall windows and looked out on the pattern of lamplights in the park below. "Six bedrooms, is it? Choice of room must be an interesting cachet for the women you bring up here."

"Don't fish."

"Sorry. You're quite right."

"In point of fact, it occurs to me that I have never invited a woman up here."

She looked at him over the top of her glass, her green eyes round with a masque of ingenuousness. "And I am the very, very first one?"

"You're the first one I've *invited.*" He told her about waking one morning to find a woman staggering about in his bathroom. Despite her sunken eyes and greenish look of recent dissipation, he had recognized her as a film actress whom cosmetic surgery and breast injections kept employed past her time.

She had evidently gotten a key from the producer years before, and had come there drunk after a night on the town with a brace of Greek boys. They had dropped her off after taking what money she had in her purse. She hadn't remembered anything of the night and after Jonathan had given her a breakfast bland enough to keep down, she had tucked a straying breast back into her gown, bestowed a snickering leer upon him through bloodshot eyes, and asked him how they had done.

"And what did you tell her?"

Jonathan shrugged. "What could I tell her? I said she had been fantastic and it had been a night I would never forget. Then I got her a cab."

"And she left?"

"After giving me her autograph. It's over there."

She went to the mantel and unfolded a sheet of paper. "But it's blank."

"Yes. The pen was out of ink, but she didn't notice."

She folded the paper carefully and replaced it. "Poor old dear."

"She doesn't know that. She thinks she's having a ball."

"Still, it makes me want to cry."

"If she ever found that out, she'd leave blank autographs behind her everywhere."

She returned to the window and looked out in silence, her cheek against the drapery. After a time she said, "It was nice of you."

"Just the easiest way out."

"I suppose so." She turned and looked at him thoughtfully. "What's your name?"

"Jonathan Hemlock. And yours?"

"Maggie. Maggie Coyne."

"Shall we go to bed, Maggie?"

She nodded and hummed. "Yes, I'd like that. But . . ." Her eyes crinkled impishly. "But I'm afraid I have some rather bad news for you."

He was silent for several seconds.

"You're kidding. This doesn't happen to good guys."

"I wish I were kidding. I really didn't mean to cheat you. But I didn't have a place to stay, don't you see?"

"I'll be goddamned."

"Pity we didn't meet a day or two later."

"Only a day or two?"

"Yes."

Jonathan rose. "Madam! It has always been my contention that the more subtle pleasures of love-making are reserved for those with daring and abandon. How do you feel about that?"

She grinned. "I have always felt the same way, sir."

"Then we're of a mind."

"We are that."

"En route."

At the first light of morning he woke hazily and turned to her, fitting her bottom into his lap. She snuggled against him slightly in response, and he wrapped her up in his arms.

"Good morning." His voice was husky as a result of little sleep and much exercise.

"Good morning," she whispered.

He rested his forehead against the back of her head and buried his face in her hair. "Maggie."

"What?"

"Nothing. Saying your name."

"Oh. That's nice. It isn't much of a name, though. Not romantic. No vowels to sing. Like Diane, or Alexandra, or Thomasyn. Maggie is a substantial name. Beefy. You may not waste away dreaming of a Maggie, but you can always trust a good old Maggie."

He smiled at the curling sound of her vowels. Proximity and body heat began to work their effect, apparent almost at once to her because of their postures. "I think I'll just make a little trip to your WC first, if you can stand the wait."

He released her. "Don't come back cold."

She slipped out of bed, and he slipped back toward sleep.

"Jonathan?"

He was fully awake immediately. She had spoken softly, but there was a brittle tension in her voice that set off alarms in him. He sat up.

"What is it?"

She stood in the doorway, an unlit cigarette dangling between her fingers. With only her brief panties on, she looked frail and vulnerable.

"What is it, Maggie?"

"The bathroom." Her voice was thin.

"Yes?"

"Jonathan?" Tight terror in her voice.

As he swung out of bed, he took up his robe and handed it to her, then he went quickly down the hall to the open door of the bathroom.

A man sat on the toilet seat, huddled over with his arms wrapped around his stomach. He was dressed in a black suit, and his graying hair was perfectly combed. The scene was denied dark humor by the terrible stench that filled the room and by the thick amoeba of blood that spread over the tile floor, fed by drips from his saturated trousers.

Jonathan's experience with CII told him exactly what had happened. The man had been gut shot, and as always in such cases, a convulsion of the sphincter had caused him to defecate. The mixed smells of blood and excrement were potent.

Jonathan stepped to him, carefully avoiding the thickening blood on the floor. He placed his fingertips against the throat. The man was not dead, but the pulse was faint and fluttery. The man lifted his head and looked blearily at Jonathan. There was no chance for him. The eyes had that wall-eyed spread that attends death. The pupils were contracted. There was dope in him.

Jonathan's attention was attracted to a slight pulsing motion in the man's lap. He was holding his guts in with his hands. He tried to speak, but only a glottal whisper came out. Jonathan put his ear close to the mouth, resisting the revulsion caused by the stink of human feces.

"I . . . I'm awfully . . . sorry. Disgraceful thing . . . I . . ."

"Who are you?"

"Shameful . . ."

"Who are you?"

Out of the tail of his eye, Jonathan saw Maggie standing at the bathroom door. Her face was a plane of disgust and horror. She was trying to calm herself by lighting her cigarette, but in her nervousness she couldn't operate the lighter.

"Get out."

"What?" She was confused.

"Get out. He's ashamed."

She disappeared.

"Oh, God . . . Oh, good God . . ." The man's body tensed. He stared up at Jonathan with anguish and disbelief, his teeth clenched, his head shuddering with his vein-bursting effort to cling to life. "Oh! God!"

Then he let it go. He slumped and let life go.

He made one last sound. A name.

Then he slipped off the toilet seat almost gracefully, and his cheek came to rest in his own blood. His hands fell away, and the gray green guts protruded. The seat of his trousers was wet and stained with excrement.

Jonathan stood up and stepped back. For the first time he noticed something crammed in behind the toilet bowl. It was a Halloween mask—Casper the ghost. He stepped out of the bathroom and closed the door quietly behind him.

Maggie was standing down the hall, her back pressed against the wall defensively, her face pale with terror. He put his arm around her for support and conducted her to the bedroom.

"Here. Lie down. Put your feet up."

"I think I'm going to be sick," she said faintly.

"It's shock. Go ahead, be sick. Put your finger down your throat."

She tried, and gagged. "I can't!"

"Listen to me, Maggie! I don't mean to be cruel or unfeeling, but you've got to pull yourself together. We've got to get out of here. That man in there . . . This is a setup. I've seen them before. For your own good, do exactly what I tell you. If you're going to be sick, do it. If not, get dressed. Then lie down and rest until I've done a couple of things. OK?"

She stared at him, confused and frightened by his cool efficiency. "What is this? What's happening?"

"Just do what I told you. Here. Give me that. I'll light it for you."

"Thank you."

"There. Now, move over."

"What are you going to do?"

"Nothing." Jonathan lay full length on his back beside her and closed his eyes. He put his palms together in a prayerlike gesture and brought them to his face, the thumbs under his chin and the forefingers touching his lips. Then he regulated his breathing, taking very shallow breaths deep in the stomach. He focused his mind on the image of an unrippled pond, calm in a chill dawn light. Tension drained from him; the adrenaline seeped away; his mind grew peaceful and clear.

In three minutes he opened his eyes slowly and brought the room back into focus. He was all right.

He rose and moved around the room quickly, getting dressed and emptying pockets and drawers in search of money.

Maggie finished her cigarette, her eyes never leaving him; something in his adroit, professional movements fascinated her. And frightened her.

He looked over the room to see that everything was done, then he knelt on the bed and brushed the hair away from her forehead. "Come on, now. Get dressed, dear." He nuzzled into the closure of her dressing gown and kissed each of her breasts lightly.

69

Then he left to collect money from the other bedrooms.

Typical of poor boys who have finally become financially comfortable, he was ostentatiously careless with money and kept a fair amount around in cash. By the time he had come back to their bedroom, combed and shaved, he had gathered almost three hundred pounds, largely in crumpled forgotten notes.

She was sitting on the edge of the bed, dressed, but still dazed.

He sipped his third café crème. Maggie had desultorily stirred hers when it arrived, but had not drunk it; a tan scum had formed on its surface. She stared into the glass unseeing, her thoughts focused within her. From their table deep within a coffee shop across the street, Jonathan watched the entrance of his Baker Street residence carefully. They had not spoken since ordering.

She broke the silence without looking up from her glass. "Are we safe here? Right across the street?"

He nodded, his eyes not leaving the hotel's revolving door. "Fairly safe, yes. They'll expect us to try to make distance."

"They? Who are they?"

"I don't know."

"But you have some idea?"

"It could be CII. An American intelligence organization I used to work for. Years ago."

"Doing what?"

He glanced at her. How could he tell her he had been an assassin? Or even, to split moral hairs, a

70

counterassassin? He returned to watching the doorway across the street.

"But why would they want to implicate you in ... in that terrible business back there?"

"They have devious, perverted minds. Impossible to know what they're up to. Chances are they want me to work for them again."

"I don't understand."

"Drink your coffee."

"I don't want it."

They returned to silence and to their own thoughts. And after a time the impulse to speak came to both at once.

"Do you know what was the worst ... Pardon? You were saying?"

"Look, Maggie, I'm very sorry ... Excuse me ... The worst what?"

"Sorry ... No, you go ahead."

"Sorry ... I was just going to say the obvious, love. I'm terribly sorry you're implicated in this."

"Am I? Really implicated, Jonathan?"

He shook his head. "No, no. Not really. I'll get you clear of it. Don't worry."

"And what about you?"

"I can take care of myself."

"True." She searched his eyes. "Too well, really."

"What is that supposed to mean?"

"Well, that's what I was going to say before. When I think about it, the worst part of the whole thing was your reaction. So brisk. Professional. As though you were used to this sort of business. You were terribly calm."

"Not really. I was scared and confused. That's why I had to take that unit of light meditation."

"On the bed?"

"Yes."

"And you can sort yourself out just like that? In a few minutes?"

"I can now. After years of practice."

She considered that for a moment. "There must have been some terrible things in your life, for you to have to develop—"

"There! There they are!"

She followed his eyes to the hotel entrance. Through gaps in the traffic, she saw two men emerge and stand on the pavement, looking up and down the street. One of them was dressed oddly in flared trendy trousers, cowboy boots, and a longish, tight plaid sports jacket. The collar of his aloha shirt was folded over the jacket collar in the style of twenty-five years ago, and a bulky camera dangled from around his neck. The other man was tall and powerfully built. His bullet-shaped head was shaved, and there were deep folds of skin halfway up the back of his neck. He wore a thick turtleneck sweater under a tweed jacket, and gave the impression of a prize-fighter, save for his large, mirror-faced sunglasses.

Aloha Shirt said something to Bullet Head. From his expression, he was angry. Bullet Head barked back, clearly not willing to take the blame. They looked again up and down the street, then Aloha made a signal with his hand, and a dark Bentley pulled up to the curb. They got in, Bullet in front, Aloha alone in back. The Bentley pulled into the traffic, bullying its way into the flow on the strength of its prestige.

Maggie looked at Jonathan, who was studying the

faces of the other passersby in front of the hotel. "That's all," he said to himself. "Just the two."

"How do you know—"

He held up his hand. "Just a moment." He watched the street narrowly until, in about three minutes, the Bentley passed again, slowing down as it went by the hotel entrance, the men within leaning forward to examine it carefully. Then the car sought the center lane and drove off.

"OK. They won't be back. Not for a few hours, anyway. But they've undoubtedly left someone inside."

"How do you know they were the ones?"

"Instinct. They have the look of the weird types you find in espionage. And their subsequent behavior nailed it."

"Espionage? What on earth is going on, Jonathan?"

He shook his head slowly. "I honestly don't know."

"Have you done something?"

"No." He felt anger and bitterness rise inside him. "I think it's something they want me to do."

"What sort of thing?"

He changed the subject curtly. "Tell me, how would you describe the boss one? The one with the camera and the gaudy shirt?"

She shrugged. "I don't know. An American, I suppose. A tourist?"

"Not a tourist. Even in his excitement, he checked the traffic from right to left. As though he were used to driving on the left. Americans check it from left to right."

"But the cowboy boots?"

"Yes. But the trousers were of British cut."

"He did look odd, come to think of it. Like an American. But like an American in old movies."

"Exactly my impression."

"What does that tell you?" She leaned forward conspiratorially.

Jonathan smiled at her, suddenly amused by the tone of their conversation. "Nothing, really. Drink your coffee."

She shook her head.

He withdrew into himself for several minutes, his brow furrowed, his eyes focused through the patterned wall he was staring at. Unit by unit he put together the flow of his necessary actions for the rest of the day. Then he took a deep breath and resettled his attention on Maggie. "OK, listen." He drew his wallet from his jacket pocket. Folded in it were his checkbook, several sheets of writing paper, stamps, and envelopes, all of which he had collected in his tour of the penthouse flat. "I'll be damned!" He had also drawn out the envelope containing money the Renaissance man had given him for his ad hoc appraisal of the Marini Horse. He had completely forgotten about it. So he wasn't working all that lucidly after all. His reactions had rusted in the years since he had quit this kind of business forever. He opened the envelope and counted the money: ten fifty-pound notes. Good. He wouldn't have to use a check after all. "Here," he said, passing two hundred pounds over the table, "take this."

She moved her hand away from the notes, as though to avoid contaminating contact. "I don't need it."

"Of course you need it. You don't have a room.

You don't have any money. And you can't go back to MacTaint's."

"Why not?"

"They'll have someone watching it. This thing is pretty carefully put together. They must have been on me most of the night. I don't too often sleep up there. I usually stay in my Mayfair flat."

"If you hadn't met me . . ."

"Nonsense. If they really wanted to get to me, they'd have done it sooner or later."

"Something occurs to me, Jonathan. How did they get in?"

"Oh, any number of ways. Picked the lock. Used a key. And there are a lot of keys around. I told you about that drunk actress."

"Still, it must have been difficult. Carrying that poor man."

"He was alive when they brought him in. They shot him there in the bathroom. No blood in the hall. He was heavily doped up."

"But still, how did they get him up to your flat?"

He shook his head. While they had waited for the elevator to bring them down from his apartment, he had noticed a folding wheelchair against the wall. That, together with the Casper mask stuffed behind his toilet, told him that they'd brought the poor son of a bitch there as a Guy Fawkes dummy. Jonathan saw no reason to share this grisly detail with Maggie.

"Here, take the money."

"No, really . . ."

"Take it."

Her hand shook as she accepted the folded notes. "I know, dear. And I'm sorry. It's really a piece of bad luck that you got mixed up in this. But you'll be all right. They're not after you."

Tears appeared in her eyes, as much in reaction to the stress and fear as anything else. She didn't apologize for them, nor did she try to blink them away. "But they are after *you*. And I'm afraid for you." She pulled herself together by the technique of assuming a broad Irish accent. "I've grown rather fond of you, don't you know?"

"I've grown fond of you too, madam. Maybe after I've sorted this thing out . . ."

"Yes. Let's do try."

"Will you have some coffee now?"

She nodded and sniffed back the last of the tears.

He ordered more coffee and some croissants, and they didn't speak until after the waiter had brought them and departed. She drank her coffee and broke up a croissant, but she didn't eat it. She pushed her plate aside and asked, "Will you be able to let me know how you're getting on?"

"That wouldn't be wise. For you, Maggie. Anyway, I won't know where you're staying. And I don't want to."

"Oh, but I'd feel dreadful not knowing if you were all right."

"All right. Look, tomorrow afternoon I will be giving a lecture at the Royal Institute of Art. You can attend. That way you'll be able to see me and you'll know I'm all right. If it looks as though we can meet afterward, I'll end the discussion by saying that I hope to have the opportunity to pursue some of these matters with interested individuals in private. And about an hour later, I'll meet you right here. OK?"

She frowned, confused. "You intend to go ahead with this lecture?"

"Oh yes. With all my social engagements. In this sort of game, they win if they can completely disrupt my life. That would force me either to come to terms with them, or to go on hiding forever. I'm reasonably safe in the open, in public places. You notice that they didn't bring the police with them just now. The big trick will be getting to and from the lecture, and keeping out of sight in the meanwhile. But I've been trained in this sort of game. So don't worry."

"What kind of advice is that?"

He smiled. "Well, don't worry too much anyway."

"Do you really think you can avoid them forever?"

"No. Not forever. But I'll get a chance to think. And I'll try to pick my own ground for meeting them."

"What are you going to do now? After I leave you?"

"I have to arrange some mechanical things. I don't have clothes. I don't have a place to stay. Once I've settled that, I suppose I'll go to the movies."

"Go to the movies?"

"Best place to lose yourself for a few hours. One of those porno houses where you can rent a raincoat."

"Rent a raincoat?"

"Never mind."

"What are you going to do about that man . . . we found? You can't just leave him there."

"I can't do anything else. Anyway, unless I miss my guess, he won't be there in an hour. They don't

77

want the police in on this if they can help it. I wouldn't be much use to them in prison. No, they were supposed to walk in on me and get hard evidence. A photograph or something. Then they'd have the leverage to force me to work for them. But something went wrong—what, I don't know. Maybe we woke up too early and got out too fast. They'll have to drop back and think up something else. And I'm hoping that will take them a little while."

She shuddered. "I'm sorry. I try not to think of him . . . the man in your loo . . . but every once in a while the image of him—"

Jonathan looked up at her suddenly. "In my loo?"

"Yes. In your bathroom. What is it?"

"The man said a word just before he died. A name, I thought. I thought he said Lew, as in Lewis. Or Lou as in Louise. But he could have meant loo as in bathroom."

"What would that mean?"

Jonathan shook his head. "I haven't the slightest idea."

Just before they parted, after they had gone back over the arrangements for meeting after the Royal Institute lecture, Maggie made an observation that had occurred to Jonathan as well. "It's an odd feeling. The change of tone between this morning and the bantering in the restaurant last night. I can't help this curious sensation that we have known one another for years and years. In just a few hours we've been through laughter, and love, and all this trouble. It's an odd feeling."

"I admire the way you've braced up under this."

"Ah, well, you see, I've had practice. The troubles

in Belfast got very close to me. The soul develops calluses very quickly. That's the real terror of violence: a body gets used to it."

"True." Indeed, he had surprised himself with the speed with which he had swung into the patterns and routines of a kind of existence he had thought was far behind him. "I'll see you soon, Maggie."

"Yes. Soon."

He stood in the red public telephone box and memorized the numbers of two railroad hotels.

"Great Eastern Hotel?" The operator's voice had the singsong of rote.

He pushed the twopence in. "Reservations, please."

At the Great Eastern, he reserved a room under the name Greg Eastman. Then he called the Charing Cross Hotel and reserved a room under the name Charles Crosley. Railroad hotels were the kind he needed. Quiet, middle class, very large, and used to transients. He would actually stay at the Great Eastern where a lift could bring him directly from the Underground station into the lobby, making it unnecessary to go onto the open street. His reservation at the Charing Cross was only for a pickup of clothes.

Next he called his tailor on Conduit Street.

"Ah, yes. Dr. Hemlock. May we be of service?"

"I need two suits, Matthew."

"Of course, sir. Shall we make an appointment for a fitting?"

"I haven't time for that. You have my paper there."

"Quite so, sir."

"I need the suits this evening."

"*This* evening? Impossible, Dr. Hemlock."

"No, it isn't. You carry Bruno Piattellis, don't you? Pull a couple off the racks, and have one of your tailors alter them to my paper. Conservative in color, not too trendy in cut. You could do it in three or four hours, if you put two men on it."

"We *do* have other commitments, sir."

"Double the price of the suit. And twenty quid for you."

The clerk sighed histrionically. "Very well, sir. I'll see what can be done."

"Good man. Have them delivered to the Charing Cross Hotel, to Mr. (he had to think for a second of the mnemonic device he had used for names) Mr. Charles Crosley."

The next call was to his shirtmaker in Jermyn Street. A little more pot-sweetening was necessary there because he despised ready-made shirts, and they would have to be cut from his patterns on file. But eventually he received their commitment to have six shirts delivered by five o'clock, together with stockings and linen.

Jonathan's last call was to MacTaint.

"Ah, is that you, lad? Just a minute." (The hiss of a phone being cupped over with a hand.) "Lilla! I'm on the phone. Shut your bleeding cob!" (An angry babble from off phone.) "Put a sock in it! ... now, what can I do for you, Jonathan?"

"I'm going to mail off three hundred quid to you this afternoon."

"That's nice. Why?"

"I'm in a little trouble. I want a source of money that's not on my person."

"Police?"

"No."

"Ah. I see. *Real* trouble. What do I do with the money?"

"Keep two fifty handy to send to me if I contact you. I'll probably be at the Great Eastern. My name will be Greg Eastman."

"The remaining fifty's for my trouble?"

"Right."

"Done. Keep well, lad."

Jonathan rang off. He appreciated MacTaint's professionalism. It was right that he accept the fee without whimpering protestations of friendship, and it was right that he ask no questions.

The telephone box was near an Underground entrance, and Jonathan took the long escalator into the tube. Until this trouble was sorted out, he would travel primarily through the anonymous means of the Underground.

He reemerged into the sunlight near Soho, and he made his way to a double-feature skin flick: *Working Her Way through the Turkish Army* and *Au Pair Girls in the Vatican.* For four hours he was invisible in the company of the lost, the lonely, the ill, and the warped, who pass their afternoons in torn seats that smell of mildew, candy-wrapper litter under their feet, staring with frozen pupils at Swedish "starlets" moaning in bored mock ecstasy as they make coy orificial use of members and gadgets.

London

Jonathan stayed in the cover of the crowds around Charing Cross Monument, keeping the façade of the Charing Cross Hotel under observation. It was nearly five, and the go-home traffic had thickened. Queues for buses coiled and re-coiled: in a few minutes vehicular and human traffic would nearly coagulate. He was relying on that, in case the people who were after him had had the experience or intelligence to think of checking with his tailor.

He looked up to the belfry clock of St. Martin's-In-The-Fields for the time, and he recalled the newspaper reports of the unfortunate fellow who had been found impaled there. A delivery van bearing the name of his shirtmaker had already arrived at the front entrance of the hotel, but he had seen nothing of the bullet-headed boxer in sunglasses or of the 1950 vintage American tourist. Still the suits hadn't arrived from his tailor; that was disconcerting because everything depended on his being able to pick up his clothes during the rush hours.

At five o'clock straight up, a taxi pulled into the bustle of the rank outside the hotel, and a young man alighted. He breasted his way through the press of people, a large white box carried high. That would be the suits. Jonathan strolled across the street and stood against the façade of the hotel. No sunglasses, no Aloha Shirt, no Bentley. He waited until a taxi stopped to discharge passengers, then approached the driver.

"Wait for me here, will you? Five minutes."

"Can't do that, mate. Rush hour, you know."

Jonathan took a ten-pound note from his pocket and ripped it in half. "Here. The other half when I get back in five minutes."

The driver was undecided for a second. "Right." He glanced through the rearview mirror at the growing queue of taxis behind. "Make it quick."

Jonathan entered the lobby through the restaurant and glanced around before picking up a house phone.

"This is Charles Crosley in 536. There will be some parcels for me. Would you ask the porter to have them sent up?"

Through the glass of the telephone cabinet he watched the receptionist, hoping she would not check to see if his key had been picked up. In the rush of guests and inquiries at this hour, she did not. A bellboy responded to a summons and went to the parcels room where he collected a small and a large box. As he carried them toward the lifts, Jonathan stepped out from the telephone booth and fell in behind him. Just as the lift doors closed, Jonathan caught the bustle of two men entering the main lobby hurriedly. Aloha Shirt and Bullet Head.

So they had thought to check with his tailor after all. But just a little too late, if everything worked out well.

"You must be bringing those to me."

"Sir?"

"Crosley? Room 536?"

"Oh, yes, sir."

Jonathan pushed the fourth-floor button. "Here, I'll take them." He passed the bellboy a pound note.

"But you're on five, sir."

"That's true. But my secretary is on four.'" He winked, and the lad winked back.

Waiting for the elevator car to bring him back to the lobby, he watched the indicator for the next car count its way to five, then stop. He had a minute on them. Time enough, provided his taxi driver had been able to resist the anger and impatience of men behind him in the rank.

The Bentley was parked at the entrance, and the driver, a beefy lad with longish hair, recognized Jonathan as he passed. He clambered out of the car and took a step or two toward Jonathan, changed his mind and turned toward the hotel entrance to alert his comrades, then thought better of it and decided that he must not lose sight of Jonathan. He ran back to the Bentley and, not knowing what to do, leaned in the driver's window and pressed his horn. Startled taxi drivers in the rank sounded their horns in retribution. Confused by the blare of horns, a car stopped at the intersection, and a lorry behind him slammed on its brakes and barked irritation with its two-toned air horn. Passing cars swerved aside and blasted their horns angrily. Bus drivers slammed their fists onto their horn buttoms. Traffic around the Circus joined in.

Jonathan shouted to his taxi driver over the din, "Charing Cross Underground!"

"But that's only a block away, mate!"

Jonathan passed forward the other half of the torn note. "Then you've made out, haven't you?"

The driver added his horn to the cacophony and pulled away from the curb. "Bleeding Americans," he muttered. "Bloody well mental they are."

Just as the taxi turned the corner, Aloha Shirt and Bullet Head burst through the revolving doors, flinging out before them a bewildered old woman who spun around twice before sitting on the steps, dizzy. The Bentley was only half a block behind as Jonathan jumped out at the Underground entrance. Holding his bulky packages over his head, he ran down the long double escalator, passing those who obediently kept to the right. The passageways were crowded with commuters, and the parcels were both a burden and a weapon. Instantly he came out on the waiting platform, he walked along to the "Way Out" end, so he had an avenue of escape should the train not come in time.

And he waited. No train. Girls babbled to one another, and old men stared ahead sightlessly, in the coma of routine. The train did not come. An advertising placard requested readers to attend a benefit concert for Bangladesh, and a scrawled message beside it enjoined them to "Fuck the Irish" and another said "Super Spurs." No train.

There was a flutter in the crowd at the far end of the tunnel, and Bullet Head and Aloha Shirt rushed out to the platform. The former's head was glistening with sweat as he looked up and down, scanning the faces of the throng. Jonathan pressed against the wall, but no good. They spotted him, and the two of them were breasting through protesting commuters in his direction.

Jonathan slipped out the exit and up a tiled passageway toward the double escalators. A train had pulled in at another dock, and just behind him came a flood of people, rushing to make connections. At the head of this mob, he was able to trot up the long escalator two steps at a time. At the top he looked back. Aloha Shirt and Bullet Head were crowded into the center of the human ice jam, slowly oozing up the escalator. Jonathan U-turned and stepped onto the nearby empty down escalator. His pursuers watched with helpless rage as he passed them, not five yards away. They struggled to push ahead, but sharp words and threats of physical retribution from men in cloth caps forced them to accept the inevitable, if not philosophically. As they drew abreast, Jonathan nodded in sassy greeting and slipped his middle finger along the side of the box in his arms. They did not react to the taunting gesture, and Jonathan realized he had used the one-finger American version, rather than the two-finger British orthography for the universal symbol.

No sooner had he stepped back out onto the platform than he felt the rush of stale air that signaled the arrival of a train. It stopped with a clatter of opening doors, there was a gush and countergush of people, the doors slammed shut, and it pulled out with a squeal. Bullet Head, outstripping his panting companion, ran along just outside the window, shouting his rage and frustration. Jonathan leaned over and communicated with him in sign language, this time in British. As they plunged into the black tunnel, Jonathan glanced up to see a look of frozen

87

indignation on the face of a prim old lady on the seat opposite. He had inadvertently made the gesture within inches of her nose.

"Well, tipped up this way, it *could* mean Victory, you know. Or Peace? I'll bet you don't want to talk about it, right?"

Jonathan took breakfast in the Victorian abundance of the grand dining room of the Great Eastern. The railroad hotel was a perfect cover. With his native panache, he would have been conspicuous in a bed and breakfast place, and they—whoever they were—would already have checked the ranking hotels.

The night before, he had taken a long, very hot bath in a bathroom so cool that it rapidly filled with thick swirling steam. He had lain soaking in the deep tub, the open hot tap keeping the temperature of the water high, until the stresses and fatigues of the day had seeped out of his body. His skin glowing from the bath, he had gotten into bed naked between stiffly starched sheets. He would need rest when the business began again tomorrow, so he emptied his mind and set his breathing pace low as he folded his hands together and brought on sleep through shallow meditation. Each stray thought that eddied into his mind he pushed aside, gently, so as not to disturb the unrippled surface of the pond in his imagination. The last conscious image—Maggie's imperfect but pleasing face—he allowed to linger before his eyes before easing it aside.

Whatever happened, he had to keep her to the lee of trouble.

Luncheon at the Embassy was, as always, both vigorously animated and abysmally dull. Jonathan considered his attendance at such functions the price he had to pay for their lavish support of his stay in England, but he made it a practice to be dull company, talking to as few people as possible. It was in this mood that he carried his glass of American champagne away toward the social paregoric of an untrafficked corner. But it was not sufficiently insulated.

"Ah! There you are, Jonathan!"

It was fforbes-Ffitch, whom Jonathan seemed fated to encounter at every function.

"Listen, Jonathan. I've just been in a corner with the Cultural Attaché, and he gives his support to this idea of mine to send you off for a few lectures in Sweden. The American image isn't particularly bright there just now, what with the Southeast Asia business and all. Could be an excellent thing, jointly sponsored by the USIS and the Royal College. Sound enticing?"

"No."

"Oh. Oh, I see."

"I told you the other evening I wasn't interested."

"Well, I thought you might just be playing hard to get."

Jonathan looked at him with fatigue in his eyes. "Don't rush at it, f-F. You'll make it. With your hustle and ambition, I have no doubt you'll be Minister of Education before you're through. But don't climb on my back."

fforbes-Ffitch smiled wanly. "Always straight from the shoulder, aren't you? Well, you can't blame a fellow for trying."

Jonathan looked at him with heavy-lidded silence.

"Quite," f-F said perkily. "But you will honor your commitment to lecture for us at the Royal College this afternoon, I hope."

"Certainly. But your people have been remiss in their communications."

"Oh? How so?"

"No one has told me the topic of my lecture. But don't rush. It's still an hour away."

fforbes-Ffitch frowned heavily and importantly. "I am sorry, Jonathan. My staff has been undergoing a shake-up. Heads rolling left and right. But I've not put together a trim ship yet. In any department I run, this kind of incompetence is simply not on." He touched Jonathan's shoulder with a finger. "I'll make a call and sort it out. Right now."

Jonathan nodded and winked. "Good show."

fforbes-Ffitch turned and left the reception room with an efficient bustle, and Jonathan was in the act of retreating into another low traffic corner when he was intercepted by the host, the Senior Man Present. He was typical of American Embassy leadership—a central casting type with wavy gray hair, a hearty handshake, and an ability to say the obvious with a tone of trembling sincerity. Like most of his ilk, his qualifications for statesmanship were based upon an ability to get the vote out of some Spokane or other, or to contribute lavishly to campaign funds.

"Well, how's it been going, Dr. Hemlock?" the Senior Man Present asked, pulling Jonathan's hand. "We don't see enough of you at these affairs."

"That's odd. I have quite the opposite impression."

"Yes," the Senior Man Present laughed, not quite

understanding, "yes, I imagine that's true. It's always like that though, really. Even when it doesn't appear to be. That's one of the things you learn in my line of work."

Jonathan agreed that it probably was.

"Say," the SMP asked with a show of offhandedness, "you're out in the wind of public opinion. What kind of ground swells do you get concerning the American elections?"

"None. People don't talk to me about it because they know I wouldn't be interested."

"Yes." The SMP nodded with profound understanding. "No—ah—no comments about the Watergate bugging business?"

"None."

"Good. Good. Nothing to it, really. Just an attempt to implicate the President in some kind of messy affair. Between you and me, I think the whole thing was cooked up either by the other party or by the Communists. I imagine it will blow over. This sort of thing always does. That's one thing you learn in my line of work."

"Good Lord, Jonathan, there's been a ballup." fforbes-Ffitch was back. "Ah!" He smiled profuse greetings to the SMP. "Did I catch you two chatting about my plans for a lecture series in Sweden?"

"Yes, you did," the SMP lied with practiced insouciance. "And I'm all for it. If there's anything my office can do to move things ahead . . ."

"That's awfully good of you, sir."

After shaking hands with warm cordiality, both his hands cupped around Jonathan's, the SMP returned to his hostly duty of pressing a drink on a visiting Moslem.

"You say there's been a ballup?" Jonathan asked.

"Yes. I am sorry. Our fault entirely. I'll cancel, if you want."

Jonathan had been looking forward to seeing Maggie in the audience during this lecture, perhaps even meeting her in the cafe afterward.

"What's the trouble?" he asked.

"They've advertised that you're going to lecture on *cinema*. I've got the title here: 'Criticism in Cinema: Use and Abuse.'"

Jonathan laughed. "No problem. Not to worry. I'll vamp it."

"But ... cinema? You're in painting, aren't you?"

"I'm in just about everything. And, despite Godard, cinema is still essentially a visual art. Do you have a car here?"

"Why, yes." fforbes-Ffitch was surprised and pleased. "Could I run you over to the college?"

"If you would." f-F's lickspittle conversation would be fair pay for the cover of traveling with him, in case Aloha Shirt and Bullet Head should be hanging about outside the post office bulk of the Embassy.

"... which rhythms are established by cutting rate and cutting tone. While the intensity of the visual beat is a function of what Whitaker, in his lean description of film linguistics, has called 'cutting volume.' Does that answer your question?"

Jonathan scanned the packed audience for a glimpse of Maggie while he responded automatically to the questions. The hall was filled, and a few people were standing at the back of the house. Because of the overcrowding, a policeman was present. In his tall hat and stiff uniform, he was in sharp contrast to the earthy-arty appearance of the audience.

Someone with a thin nasal voice in the back of the hall was proposing a question when Jonathan caught sight of Maggie against the back wall. She stood under one of the conical light fixtures set in the ceiling of the overhanging balcony, and the soft narrow beam isolated her from the mass and mixed with the amber of her soft hair. He was pleased she was there.

". . . and therefore ineluctably interrelated with it?"

He had not caught the whole of the question, but he recognized the style of inquiry: another involute question asked by a bright young person, not to learn, but to demonstrate the level of his recent reading.

Jonathan faked his way out. "That's a sinewy and complicated question with ramifications that would take more time than we have to explore adequately. Suppose you break off the fragment that most puzzles you and phrase that concisely."

The thin voice hemmed and hawed, then restated his question in full, adding additional fragments of erudition that occurred to him.

But Jonathan's attention was even slighter than it had been before. At the back of the hall, leaning against the wall, was Bullet Head. Jonathan scanned around. Aloha Shirt was making his way down the right aisle. Jonathan looked for Maggie. She still stood in her beam of light, evidently unaware of them.

A pause and a cough. The question had been posed, and they awaited an answer. A couple of remembered key words in the question gave Jonathan adequate cue to form an answer: "That shifts us from the discussion of film qua film to a look at the state of film study and criticism in the world. But I'm willing to make the shift if you are. In broad, it is safe to say that current film study and criticism are both a chaos and a desert. First, we must acknowledge that, with the exception of Mitry and perhaps Bazin, there are no film critics of substance."

Where the hell was that bobby?

"All we really have are reviewers on varying altitudes of diction. The French school—if one can call that colloidal suspension of spatting personalities a school—works from the principle that cinema is a Gallic invention, the subtleties of which can never properly be mastered by peoples of less fortunate nativity."

Bullet Head was making his way down the left aisle. Maggie still stood alone in the cone of light.

"Their most insidious export since the French pox has been their capricious insistence that American cinema is greatest at its most common denominator. They have seduced spineless American and British scholars into giving the benediction of serious study to such thin beer as the films of Capra, Hawks, and Jerry Lewis."

The young driver of the Bentley was moving across the back of the hall toward Maggie! Where in hell was that policeman?

"The situation is no healthier in the United States, where the ranking reviewers operate as petulant social starlets. Snide infighting, phrasemaking, and pantheon building are the symptoms of their critical affliction. Then, of course, you have the Village Blat types pandering to their young readers' assumption that befuddlement is Obscurantism and that technical incompetence denotes social concern. But the greatest burden to American film criticism is that it is resident in the universities and therefore blighted by the do-nots."

Aloha Shirt stood at the foot of the stage steps on one side, Bullet Head on the other. The young driver had slipped to Maggie's side.

"The East Coast universities devote their attention to obscure films, sequences, and film makers that require the beacon of critical analysis to rescue them from the limbo of deserved obscurity. This symbiotic affair between film maker and critic has entangled them in studies of Vertov and Antonioni that delight small coteries of wide-eyed apostles, but contribute nothing to the mainstream of cinema. The West Coast schools are little better. All hardware and hustle, they produce students in whom the technical proficiency of Greenwich Village is blended with the sensitivity of 'I Love Lucy.' "

The driver leaned over and said something to Maggie. She looked at Jonathan, her eyes wide. He shook his head in answer. The driver took her arm and guided her out the back door. Where the fuck was that bobby?

"And in the center of the continent, insulated by landmass and disposition from contradictory thought, is what might be called the Chicago School of Criticism. Here we find bitter, envious young men who, lacking the spark of creativity, attempt to deny its existence in others by focusing their attention on filmic *genres*. As though films made themselves, and the men who direct them are no more artists than are they, the leveling critics."

A question came from the hall. Jonathan glanced into the wings and was relieved to see the dependable bulk of the policeman, his hands behind his back, his eyes on the lights in the grid, stoic and bored. A rock in the storm.

"As a guest in your country, I should say nothing about the state of British film study other than it's well financed and the government seems particularly patient with the several institutions who have been sorting themselves out for years now. I feel sure they will get around to making a contribution to film study by the end of the century."

Ignoring the applause, Jonathan made quickly for the wings, where he addressed the police officer, who appeared to be surprised at being approached by him. "There are three men out there, officer."

"Is that a fact, sir?"

"They've got a girl with them."

"Have they, sir?"

"I haven't time to explain. Come with me."

"Right you go, sir."

A quick glance over his shoulder told Jonathan that Aloha Shirt and Bullet Head had not come onto the stage. The bobby following along, he pushed through the exit doors from the wings and ran down a deserted outer corridor. Echoing footfalls advanced toward them from around the far corner. Jonathan stopped, the policeman beside him. The footsteps continued to near. Then the four of them came around the corner, Bullet Head and Aloha Shirt in front, the driver with Maggie behind. They stopped at their end of the hall.

Jonathan and the bobby walked slowly toward them. "Let her go," Jonathan said, his voice unexpectedly loud in the empty corridor.

The policeman spoke. "Is this the man, sir?"

"Yes."

"Yes."

Jonathan and Aloha Shirt had spoken at the same time.

"Right you are then!" The big bobby took Jonathan by the arm with a grip like metal.

"What the hell is going on?" Jonathan protested.

"Our car is just outside, officer," Aloha Shirt said. "Bring him along, won't you?"

"Come on now, sir." The officer spoke with condescending paternalism. "Let's not have any trouble."

Bullet Head closed the distance between them with a menacing swagger. "Maybe *I* should take him. He wouldn't give me no trouble." He brought his porcine face close to Jonathan's. "*Would* you, mate?"

Jonathan looked past the ape to Aloha Shirt, who seemed to be in charge. "The girl isn't in this thing."

"Isn't she?"

"Let her go."

"Can it, buddy," Aloha Shirt said. The sound was odd: American words with a British accent.

"If you let her go, I'll come with you without trouble."

Bullet Head sucked his teeth and thrust out his head. "You're coming along with us no matter what, mate."

Jonathan smiled at him. "You'd love me to make a run for it, wouldn't you?"

97

TREVANIAN

"You got it right there, chum. I'm sick of chasing your arse around London."

"But you're not carrying a gun. Fat though you are, I can see you're not carrying a gun."

"Here, none of that," the policeman warned.

"I got *these*, mate." Bullet Head held out his hands, blunt and vast.

Jonathan turned to the bobby. "Officer?"

The policeman's politeness was automatic. "Sir?"

That was it! At that instant Jonathan had it!

For a fraction of a second everything was right—the position of Jonathan's body relative to Bullet Head's, the slight relaxing of the policeman's grip as he answered—at that instant Jonathan could have made it. The heel of his hand into the tip of Bullet Head's nose would have disabled him, possibly killed him if a bone splinter were driven into the brain. He could have been away from the officer with one jerk, and he'd have had Aloha Shirt by the larynx before the driver could react. That would have given him the life of one man between his thumb and forefinger as hostage. Once on the street, he knew he would be an odds-on favorite in any game of hide-and-seek.

But he let it go. Maggie was three strides too far away. The driver would have had her before Jonathan had Aloha Shirt.

Damn it!

"Sir?" the bobby asked again.

Jonathan's shoulders slumped. "Ah . . . did you enjoy my lecture?"

"Oh yes, sir. Not that I followed all of it. It's your accent, you know."

"Come on!" Bullet Head growled, "let's get it moving!"

The Bentley was parked outside, and behind it was another dark sedan with a driver. As they descended the long sweep of shallow granite steps, Jonathan felt the Kafkaesque anomaly of the situation. They were being abducted with the help of a policeman, in the middle of the afternoon, with people all around.

Maggie was deposited in the back seat of the sedan with a young man who had seemed to be loitering against a postbox, while Jonathan was conducted into the back of the Bentley. Aloha Shirt got in back with him; Bullet Head and the driver in front; and they pulled away from the curb, the two cars staying close together until they got onto a motorway. They picked up speed and started off toward Wessex.

"Care for a coffin nail?" Aloha Shirt asked, producing a pack of American cigarettes.

"No, thanks."

Aloha Shirt smiled affably. "No need to get uptight, Dr. Hemlock. You struck out, but everything's going to be A-okay."

"What about the girl?"

"She's fine and dandy. No sweat." Aloha Shirt smiled again. "I should make introductions. The driver there is Henry."

The driver stretched to seek Jonathan's reflection in the rearview mirror and grinned in greeting. "Good to meet you, sir."

"Hello, Henry."

"And my burly sidekick there is The Sergeant."

"Not 'Bullet Head'?"

The Sergeant scowled and turned to stare out the windscreen, his jaw set tight.

"And I'm called Yank." He grinned. "It's kind of a weird moniker, but they call me that because I dig American things. Clothes. Slang. Everything. For my money, you guys are where it's at."

In the space of a few minutes, Yank had used slang sampling a thirty-year span of American argot, and Jonathan assumed he got it from late night movies. "Where are we going, Yank?"

"You'll see when we get there. But don't worry. Everything's cool. We're from Loo." He said this last with some pride.

"From where?"

"Loo."

The Olde Worlde Inn

As they rushed along the motorway, Yank sketched in the history and function of the Loo organization. Though his instructions allowed him to impart no information beyond this, he said they would meet a man at their destination who would clarify everything.

Following the typical pattern of development for espionage organizations in democratic countries, England's earliest felt need was for a domestic agency to ferret out and control enemy espionage and sabotage within its borders. Building up its information files on real and imagined enemies, and occasionally stumbling onto a genuine spy cell while groping about for a fictive one, this bureaucratic organism grew steadily in size and power, justifying each new expansion on the basis of the last. From a single cluttered desk in the Military Intelligence building, it swelled to occupy an entire office: Room #5. And by the simplistic codes of the service, it became known as MI–5.

It eventually occurred to the intelligence specialists that they might do well to assume an active as well as passive role in the game of spy-spy, so they set up a sister organization to control British agents operating abroad. The traditional British penchant for independence dictated that these two agencies be fully autonomous, and the rivalry between them extended to refusal to admit of the existence of the other. But this resulted in a certain erosion of manpower, inasmuch as the agents of each organization spent much of their time spying on, thwarting, and occasionally killing the agents of the other. In a master stroke of organizational insight, it was decided to open communications between the two agencies, and the international branch was installed in the next office down the corridor, becoming known in official circles as MI–6.

In harness, they muddled their way through the Second World War, relying largely on the French organizational concept, "système D." Their agents earned reputations for bravery and enterprise, which qualities were vital to survival, considering the blunderers who insisted on parachuting French-speaking agents into Yugoslavia. No energy was spared in the rounding up of Irish nationalists on the basis of the rumor that Ireland was a secret signatory of the Axis Pact.

At home, their operatives uncovered spy rings that were passing information by means of cryptic keys in the knitting patterns of balaclavas that women's institutes were supplying to troops in Africa. And they captured no fewer than seven hundred German parachute spies, nearly all of whom had been trained with such insidious thoroughness that they spoke no German at all and pretended to be innocently pushing their bicycles to work in munitions plants. It was obvious that these were agents of the highest importance, because their controls had gone to the trouble of giving them covers that included homes hit by the blitz and county clerk records supplying them with generations of British ancestors.

In Europe, MI–6 agents blew up bridges in the path of the advancing Allied armies, thus preventing hasty and ill-considered thrusts. It was they who uncovered Switzerland's intention to declare war on Sweden as a last resort. And on three separate occasions only bad luck prevented them from capturing General Patton and his entire staff.

When the war was over, each agent was required to write a book on his adventures, then he was permitted to enter trade. But the romance surrounding MI–5 and MI–6 was tarnished somewhat by a pattern of defections and information leaks that embarrassed British Intelligence almost as much as the existence of that agency was an embarrassment to British intelligence. Clearly, something had to be done to prevent these defections and leakages and to maintain the honor and reputation of the organization. Following the fashion of the day, the government turned to the United States for its model.

At about the same time in America, the 102 splinter spy groups that had sprung up in the Army, Navy, State Department, Treasury, and Bureau of Indian Affairs were merged into a vast bureaucratic malignancy, the CII. This organization, like its British opposite number, was having its share of defections and its share of witch-hunting self-examination spawned by the McCarthy panic. In reaction, it organized an internal cell designed to police and control its own personnel and to protect them from assassination abroad. This last was achieved by the sanction threat of counterassassination, and the cell that performed these internal and external sanctions was known as the Search and Sanction Division—popularly known as the SS Squad. It was for SS that Jonathan had worked, before he managed to release himself from their coils.

Emulating the American structure, the British developed an elite inner cell which they installed in the next room up the corridor, which room happened to be a toilet. Despite the fact that they refurbished the space to accommodate its new function, wags immediately gave the assassination group the nickname: The Loo.

". . . and that ought pretty much put you into the big picture," Yank concluded. "At least you know who we are. Any questions?"

Jonathan had been listening with only half an ear as he watched the countryside flow past his window, a grimy twilight beginning to soften the line of the background hills. They had left the motorway and were threading through country lanes. When they passed through a village, Jonathan noticed the arms over a public house: vert, three blades of grass proper, a bend of the first. Obviously they were still in Wessex and had been weaving through back roads without making much linear progress. He glanced out the back window to make sure the car carrying Maggie was still following close behind.

"No sweat," said Yank, "they know where they're going. Everything's real George."

"That's wonderful. Now, why don't you tell me what this is all about?"

"No can do. The Guv will lay it on you when we get there. You'll like the Guv. He's old school and all that, but he's no square from Delaware. He's hip to the scene."

The Bentley turned in at a roadside inn called the Olde Worlde and crunched over a gravel drive to the back where it stopped against a retaining log. The car carrying Maggie followed and parked twenty yards away. Two young men conducted her to the back door of the inn.

"Well, what do you think of it?" Yank asked as Jonathan stepped out and was flanked by The Sergeant and Henry. "Nice pad, eh?"

Jonathan scanned the sprawling warren. It was phony Tudor, built at the end of the last century by the look of it, and certainly not originally designed to be an inn. Dozens of details had that inorganic appliqué quality of a style imitated. But where taste and constraint had been lacking, funds had not, for the glass, the wood, the brick were of the best quality available in the 1880s—that last moment before craftsmanship fell victim to the machine and the union.

"This way, sir." Henry's accent had the chewed diphthongs of the working class. They conducted Jonathan around to the front of the inn where, at the reception desk, they were greeted by a healthy, overly made-up young lady wearing a tight sweater and a mini so short that the double stitching of her panty hose showed. Her accent, clothes, and makeup clubbed her with Henry's class, and by the looks they exchanged, it was evident that Henry and she had something going.

"Is this the 'special' you've got with you?" she asked, giving Jonathan a head-to-toe look meant to be sultry.

"That's right," Yank said. "He's to see the Guv straight off."

"The Guv's down to the church. Evening service. Will he be staying long?"

Jonathan resented being spoken of in the third person. "No, I won't be staying long, duck."

"A few days," Yank said.

"Then I'll put him in 14," the bird said. "You and The Sergeant can have the rooms on either side. How's that?"

Yank took the key and led the way as they climbed a narrow, ornately carved staircase to the second floor where, after passing through a maze of dark broken corridors with irregular floors that squeaked under carpeting, they stopped before a door. The Sergeant opened it and gestured Jonathan in with a flick of the thumb.

The room was large, uncomfortable, and cold, as befitted its period. The first thing that caught Jonathan's eye was the open wardrobe in which the clothes he had had brought to the hotel were hung.

"We were expecting you," Yank said, openly proud of his organization's efficiency.

Jonathan crossed the room and looked out over the vista. Beneath his window was a neat garden, scruffy now with autumn brownness, in the center of which was a formal quatrefoil pond, the water green with algae and rippling in the brisk wind. Beyond the garden rolled the gentle hills of Wessex, sucked empty of color by the metallic overcast. The prospect was marred by the thick bars on the window.

"The bars help to keep out the draft," The Sergeant said with a heavy chuckle.

Jonathan glanced at him wearily, then spoke to Yank. "They're all your people, I suppose. Hotel personnel and all?"

"That's right. Loo owns the whole shooting match. By the way," he said with a knowing ogle, "what did you think of the girl at the desk? Slick chick, eh? Lucky bugger!"

Jonathan wasn't sure, but he assumed the bird did tricks for the special guests. "When do I meet the head crapper?"

"Who?"

"Mr. Loo. The *Guv*."

"Soon," Yank said, obviously annoyed at Jonathan's irreverence. "I think you'll be comfortable here. There'll be one inconvenience, though. You'll be locked in until the Guv says otherwise, and the WC's down the hall, so . . ." Yank shrugged, embarrassed that British inns lacked the convenience of American ones.

The Sergeant broke in. "So if you have to go potty, mate, just rap on the wall, and I'll take you down by the hand. Got it?"

Jonathan regarded The Sergeant languidly as he asked Yank, "Does he have to stay around? Don't you have a kennel?"

The Sergeant rankled. "I hope I'm not going to have any trouble from you, mate!"

"Hope's cheap, anus. Indulge yourself." He turned to Yank. "What about Miss Coyne, the young

107

lady you picked up with me? There's no reason to hold her. She's nothing to me."

"Don't worry about her. She'll be all right. Now why don't you wash up and grab a few Zs before your chat with the Guv."

Left alone in the room, Jonathan stood by the window, feeling off-balance and angry. His sense of déjà vu was total. These people with their ornately staged machinations, this feeling of the ring closing in on him, the vulgar Sergeant for whom murder and mayhem would be an exercise, the veneered Americanism of Yank—everything here was a British analogue of the CII. And if this "Guv" was true to form, he would be urbane, hale, friendly, and ruthless.

He lay back on the bed, his fingers pressed lightly together and his eyes set in infinity focus on the wall before him, and he began deliberately to empty his mind, image by image, until he had achieved a state of neutrality and balance. The muscles of his body softened and relaxed, last of all his stomach and forehead.

When they knocked at his door twenty minutes later, he was ready. The machinery of his mind and body was running calmly and smoothly. He had reviewed the events of the past two days and had come to one distasteful realization: it was possible, it was likely even, that Maggie had set him up for the Loo people.

With the threatening presence of The Sergeant close behind him, Yank and Jonathan walked some two hundred yards down the road from the Olde Worlde Inn before turning off into a yew-lined lane that led through an arched gateway to a curious church.

As they stepped into the vestibule, the teetering tonal imbalance of amateur singers making a joyful noise unto the Lord announced that evening service was in progress. The Sergeant remained outside, while Yank and Jonathan advanced into the church. It amused Jonathan to see Yank tiptoe across to a back pew and kneel briefly in rushed and mumbled prayer before sitting up and staring at the serving priest with an expression of bland and dour piety. Jonathan glanced around at the decor of the church and was surprised to find it was Art Nouveau: a style unique in his experience for religious architecture. He examined it with open curiosity as the vicar began his sermon to the handful of faithful scattered sparsely among the pews.

"No doubt you will recall," the voice was a rumbling bass with the nasal and lazy vowels of the well-educated Englishman, "we have begun to examine the meaning of the sacraments. And this evening I should like to take a look at baptism—the one sacrament that, for most of us, is an involuntary act."

The decor of the church fascinated Jonathan without pleasing him. Mother-of-pearl and pewter were inlaid into the ornate floral carving; tubercular angels, their long-waisted bodies curved in limp S-forms, their fragile-fingered hands pressed lightly together in prayer, looked down on the congregation with large, heavy-lidded eyes; exotic, short-lived flowers drooped from slender stems up the stained glass windows; and above the altar a glistening effeminate Christ in polished pewter trampled the head of a snake with ruby eyes.

The service continued through communion, and everyone but Jonathan went up to receive the Host. Jonathan watched Yank return from the rail, his palms pressed together, his eyes lowered, Christ melting in his mouth.

At a signal from Yank, Jonathan remained seated as the rest of the faithful filed out after a last vigorous attack on Song. Then Yank conducted him to the vestry where the Vicar was finishing off the last of the communion bread.

"Sir?" Yank's voice was diffident. "May I introduce Dr. Hemlock?"

The Vicar turned and with an open gracious smile of greeting took Jonathan's hand between his large hirsute paws. "This *is* a pleasure," he said, winking. "So good of you to come." His mellow basso warmed with practiced civility. "Just allow me to finish and we'll have a good natter." He drank off the last of the communion wine and wiped out the chalice carefully, while Jonathan studied his full puffy face with its tracery of red capillaries over the cheekbones and in ruddy abundance on the substantial amorphic nose. His hair had retreated beyond the horizon line of his broad forehead, but was long on the sides and blended with his full muttonchop sideburns.

"Odd ritual, this," the Vicar said, replacing the utensils. "The last morsels of consecrated bread and wine must be consumed by the priest. I suppose it arose out of some fear of contamination and sacrilege, should the body and blood of Christ find its way into the alimentary canal of an unbeliever." He winked.

"What is missionary work but the effort to introduce Christ to the uninitiated?" Jonathan commented.

The Vicar laughed robustly. "Precisely! Precisely! You, I dare to assume, do not avail yourself of the sacrament often."

"No form of cannibalism appeals to me."

"Oh. I see. Yes." The Vicar folded the last of his vestments carefully and set them aside. From behind, his formidable bulk seemed to fill the black flowing garment. "Shall we take a turn around the churchyard, Dr. Hemlock. It's quite lovely in the last light. We shall not be needing you, Yank. I'm sure you can find something to amuse yourself with for a few minutes."

Yank made a gesture akin to a salute and left the vestry. The Vicar looked after him with paternal warmth. "There's a very bright young man for you, Dr. Hemlock. Energetic. Zealous. We pulled him away from another project and made him your liaison with our organization because we thought you might be more comfortable working with someone who was au courant with things American." He put his heavy arm around Jonathan's shoulders and conducted him on a leisurely stroll down the nave of the Art Nouveau church. "Beautiful, isn't it? Quite unique."

"Is it yours?"

"God's, actually. But if you are asking if I am the regular vicar, the answer is no. I am standing in for him for a fortnight while he is on honeymoon in Spain. But the less said of that the better." He made a wide gesture with his arm. "When would you guess this church was built?"

Jonathan stepped away from the encircling arm and glanced around. "About 1905."

The Vicar stopped short, his bushy salt-and-pepper eyebrows arched high. "Amazing! Within a year!" Then he laughed. "Ah, but of course! Art is your province, isn't it." He glanced quickly at Jonathan. "That is, it is *one* of your occupations."

"It is my only occupation," Jonathan said with mild stress.

The Vicar clasped his hands behind his back and studied the parquet floor. "Yes, yes. Your Mr. Dragon informed me that you had left CII in some disgust after that nasty business in the Alps." He winked.

Jonathan leaned against the side of a pew and folded his arms. This vicar evidently knew a great deal about him. He even knew the name of Yurasis Dragon, head of Search and Sanction Division of CII: a name known to fewer than a dozen people in the States. Obviously, the Vicar would prefer to approach whatever dirty business he had in mind through the gentle back alleys of trivial polite conversation, but Jonathan decided not to cooperate.

"Yes," the Vicar continued after an uncomfortable pause, "that must have been a nasty affair for you. As I recall the details, you had to kill all three of the men you were climbing with, because your SS Division had been unable to specify which one was your target."

Jonathan watched him steadily, but did not respond.

"I suppose it takes a rather special kind of man to

do that sort of thing," the Vicar said, winking. "After all, a certain camaraderie must grow up amongst men making so dangerous a climb as the Eiger. Isn't that so?"

No answer.

The Vicar broke the ensuing silence with artificial heartiness. "Well, well! At all events, the little project we have in mind for you will not be so grisly as that. At least, it need not be. You have that much to be grateful for, eh?"

Nothing.

"Yes. Well. Mr. Dragon warned me that you could be recalcitrant." The tone of robust friendliness dropped from his voice, and he continued speaking with the mechanical crispness of a man accustomed to giving orders. "All right then, let's get to it. How much did Yank tell you about us?"

"Only as much as you instructed him to. I take it that your Loo organization is a rough analogue of our Search and Sanction, and is occupied with matters of counterassassination."

"That is correct. However, what we have on for you is a little out of that line. What else do you know?"

Jonathan began walking down the nave toward the vestibule. "Nothing, really. But I have made certain assumptions."

The Vicar followed. "May I hear them?"

"Well, you, of course, are Mister Loo. But I haven't decided whether this church business is simply a front."

"No, no. Not at all. I am first and always a man of the Church. I served as chaplain during the Hitlerian War and afterward found myself still involved

113

in government affairs. We are, after all, a state church." He winked.

"I see." Jonathan passed out through the vestibule and turned up a path that led through the church-yard, cool and iridescent in the gloaming. Yank and The Sergeant were standing at some distance, watching them as the Vicar fell into step alongside.

"It is not uncommon, Dr. Hemlock, for C. of E. churchmen to have some hobby to occupy their minds. Particularly if their livings are of the more modest sort. Nature study claims a great number; and some of the younger men toy about with social reform and that sort of thing. Circumstance and personal inclination directed me along other paths."

"Killing, to be specific."

The Vicar's response was measured and cool. "I have certain organizational talents that I have placed at the service of my country, if that's what you mean."

"Yes, that's what I meant."

"And, tell me, what else have you assumed?"

"That this young lady—Maggie Coyne, if that is her real name—"

"As it happens, it is."

". . . that this Miss Coyne is one of your operatives. That she set me up in that little affair of the man in my bathroom."

"My, my. You *are* perceptive. What brought you to this conclusion?"

Jonathan sat on a headstone. "In retrospect, the thing was too neat, too circumstantial. I seldom use the Baker Street penthouse. But your men knew I would be there that particular night. And it was

Miss Coyne who proposed the restaurant a half block away."

"Ah, yes."

"And along with a rack of trumped-up circumstantial evidence linking me with the poor bastard, there must be some hard evidence—probably photographic. Right?"

"I blush at our being so transparent."

Jonathan rose and they continued their stroll.

"How did you get the photographs?"

"The young woman took them."

"When? With what?"

"The cigarette—"

". . . The cigarette lighter!" Jonathan shook his head at his stupidity. A gold cigarette lighter in the possession of a girl who didn't know where her next meal was coming from. A camera, of course. And she had fumbled with it, unable to light her cigarette, as she stood there at the bathroom door.

He snatched a twig from a shrub, stripped the leaves with an angry gesture, and crushed them in his hand. "And the gun, of course, would be found in my apartment."

"Very well hidden. It would be found only after an extensive search. But it *would* be found." The Vicar winked.

Jonathan walked on slowly, rolling the leaf pulp between his palms. "I'm curious, padre . . ."

"The sign of a healthy intellect."

"After hitting that man in my john, your men left. They didn't try to put the hand on me then, presumably because they didn't yet have the photographs."

"Just so."

"Why did they come back later?"

"To pick up the cigarette lighter and develop the film. Miss Coyne was supposed to leave it behind."

"But she didn't."

"No, she did not. And that threw my chaps into some confusion."

"Why do you suppose she broke the plan?"

"Ah." The Vicar lifted his hands and let them fall in a gesture of helplessness. "Who can probe the human heart with only the brutish tools of logic, eh, Dr. Hemlock? She was shocked perhaps by the sight of that poor fellow in your bathroom? It is even possible that some affection for you misdirected her loyalties."

"In that case, why didn't she destroy the films?"

"Ah, there you go. Asking for sequential logic in the workings of emotion. Man is nothing if not labyrinthine. And when I say 'man' I include, of course, woman. For in this context, as in the romantic one, man embraces woman. I shall never understand why Americans doubt the Briton's sense of humor."

Jonathan could. "So your men were running around London looking for both Miss Coyne and me."

"You gave us a few difficult hours. But all that is behind us now. But come now! Let's not look on the gloomy side. Provided you lend your skills to our little project, the police will be allowed to remain in that state of blissful ignorance so characteristic of them." The Vicar stopped beside a fresh grave that did not yet have a headstone. "That's poor Parnell-Greene," he said, sighing deeply, "unfortunate fellow."

"Who's Parnell-Greene?"

"Our most recent casualty. You'll learn more about him later." He made a sweeping gesture with his arm. "All of them here," he said, his voice resonant and wavering, "they're all ours. All Loo people."

Jonathan glanced at the inscriptions on nearby stones, just legible in the fading light. *Passed into the greater life. Went to sleep. Returned home. Found everlasting glory.*

"Didn't any of them die?" he asked.

"Pardon me?"

"Nothing."

"The names and dates on the stones are false, of course. But they're all our brave lads." He sighed stentoriously. "Good youngsters, every one."

"No shit?"

The Vicar stared at him with reproof, then he laughed. "Ah, yes! Mr. Dragon warned me of your tendency to revert to the social atavism of your boyhood. It used to pain him, or so he said."

"You seem to be on good terms with Dragon."

"We correspond regularly, share information and personnel, that sort of thing. Does that surprise you? We also have arrangements with our Russian and French counterparts. After all, every game must be played by certain rules. But I must admit that Mr. Dragon was not of much help in the matter now before us, occupied as he is with the dire events on his own doorstep. No doubt you have heard about this Watergate business?"

"Oddly enough, it was mentioned just today at the Embassy. It seems to me to be a lot of fuss over a trivial and incompetent bit of spy-spy."

"One would think so, but it can't be all that trivial

if CII has been brought in on it. The affair evidently requires fairly heavy hushing up, and Mr. Dragon is involved in that side of it. I shouldn't be surprised if the statistics on death by accident showed an unaccountable rise over the next month or so. But I take it from your distant expression that you are not overly concerned with this election."

"It's difficult to get excited when the choice is between a fool and a villain."

"Personally, I prefer villains. They are more predictable." The Vicar winked vigorously.

"So it was Dragon who put you onto me?"

"Yes. We knew, of course, that you were in the country, but we had been informed that you had retired from our line of work, so we did not interfere with your visit. At that time we had no intention of using you. There is nothing more dangerous than an unwilling and uncooperative active. But. This business came along and ..." The Vicar blew out his broad cheeks and shrugged fatalistically. "... we had no other option, really."

"But why me? Why not one of your own people?"

"You will learn that in due course. Lovely evening, isn't it? That precious moment when day and night are in delicate balance."

Jonathan knew he was hooked. If he refused to cooperate, Loo would certainly hang him for the murder of that poor bastard on the toilet, even though it would make his services unavailable. Like CII, Loo realized that threats and blackmail were effective only if the mark was sure that the threat would be carried out at all cost.

"All right," Jonathan said, sitting on a grave marker, "let's talk about it."

"Not just now. I'm awaiting some last odd bits of information from London. Once I have them, I shall be able to put you totally into the picture. Shall I see you at the rectory tomorrow? Say, midmorning?"

The Vicar made a simple gesture with his fingertips and Yank, who had been keeping them under close surveillance, straining his eyes in the gloom, came trotting over. Literally trotting.

As he ascended the narrow stairs to the second floor of the inn, Jonathan stepped aside to allow Maggie to pass on her way down. She paused and looked at him with troubled eyes. "I suppose it would sound a little foolish to say I'm sorry?"

"Foolish certainly. And inadequate."

She brushed back a wisp of amber hair and forced herself to maintain eye contact with him. "I'll run the risk, then, of being foolish."

"Come on," The Sergeant growled from behind, "I don't have all night to stand about!"

Jonathan turned to him and smiled his gentle combat smile. He beckoned him closer and spoke softly into the bland moon face with its shaved head and crisp military moustache. "You know something? I am becoming very annoyed with everything that's happening here. And I have this conviction that my annoyance is eventually going to purge itself on you. And when it does ..." Jonathan grinned and nodded. "... and when it does ..." He patted The Sergeant's cheek. Then he turned away and went up to his room.

The Sergeant, not sure what had just happened, scratched the patted cheek angrily and mumbled after the retreating figure, "Anytime, yank. Anytime!"

Yank had come to fetch him down to supper in the low-ceilinged, pseudo-Tudor dining room, a recent addition featuring stucco with capricious finger-swirl patterns and pressed plastic wooden beams placed in positions that could not possibly bear weight. There were fewer than a dozen diners served by a Portuguese waiter in an ill-fitting tuxedo who went about his task with great style and flourish that interfered with his efficiency.

Jonathan and Yank occupied a corner table, while The Sergeant sat alone three tables away and occupied himself, when he was not pushing great forkloads of food into his mouth, by glowering at Jonathan with a menacing intensity that was almost comic. Henry, the driver, sat in close conversation with the bird from the reception desk, who often giggled and pressed her knee against his. The rest of the guests were young men stamped from Henry's mold: longish hair, beefy faces, dark suits with flared jackets, and belled trousers.

"I see that Miss Coyne hasn't come down to supper," Jonathan said.

"No," Yank said. "She's eating in her room. Not feeling too well."

"A girl of delicate sensitivities."

"I reckon so."

It was a classically English meal: meat boiled until it was stringy, waterlogged potatoes, and the ubiquitous peas and carrots, tasteless and mushy. Directly the edge of his hunger was dulled, Jonathan pushed his plate away.

Although he had been eating with great appetite,

Yank imitated Jonathan's gesture. "This English chow's a crime, isn't it?" he said. "Give me hamburgers and French fries any old time."

"Who are all these young men?" Jonathan asked.

"Guards, mostly," Yank said. "Shall I order some Java?"

"Please. All these guards for me? I'm flattered."

"No, they don't work here. They work . . ." He was visibly uncomfortable. ". . . up the road."

"At the church?"

Yank shook his head. "No-o. We have another establishment. Back in the fields."

"What kind of establishment?"

"Ah! I think I caught the waiter's eye." Yank held his coffee cup in the air and pointed to it. The Portuguese waiter was at first confused, then with a dawn of understanding, he help up a cup from an empty table and pointed to it, raising his eyebrows high in question. Yank nodded and mouthed the word: C-o-f-f-e-e, with exaggerated lip movement.

When the tea arrived, Jonathan's curiosity made him ask, "This other establishment you mentioned. What goes on there?"

Yank's discomfort returned. "Oh. It's nothing. Say!" He changed the subject without subtlety. "I really envy you, you know."

"Oh? Always had a secret desire to be kidnapped?"

"No, not that. I guess I envy every American. Can't understand why you came to live among us limeys. If I ever get to the old forty-eight, you can bet your bottom dollar I'll hang in there. And I'm going to do it some day. I'm going to the States and get a ranch in Nebraska or somewhere and settle down."

"That's just wonderful, Yank."

"It's not just a dream, either. I'm going to do it. As soon as I get the loot together."

Back in his room Jonathan lay in the dark and stared up toward the ceiling. His deep anger at being used, boxed in, manifested itself as pressure behind his eyes that built up and began to throb. He was rubbing his temples to relieve the pressure when he heard the sound of a key turning in his lock. He opened his eyes and, without moving his head, watched the bird from the reception desk enter and approach his bed.

"You asleep?"

"No."

She sat on the edge of his bed and put her hand on him. "Feel like having a go?"

He smiled to himself and examined her face in the gloom. She was pretty enough in the plastic way of English girls of her class and age. "I had the impression that you had something going with the young man who drove me here."

"Who, Henry? Well, I do, of course. We're thinking about getting married one of these days. But that's my private life, and this is my work. The blokes who come here are always tensed up, and I help them to relax. It's all part of the service, you might say."

"A civil service trollop."

"It's a job. Good pension. Henry and me have decided that I should go on working after we're married. Until we have kids, that is. We're saving our money, and we got fifteen books of green stamps. One of these days, we're going to get a little off license in Dagenham. He's got a level head on him, Henry has. Well, then. If you won't be wanting me, I'll get back to the telly. Wouldn't want to miss 'It's a Knockout' if I could help it."

"No, I won't be needing you. You're a cute little girl, but this is a bit clinical for me."

She shrugged and left. There was no understanding some men.

He was in a deep layer of sleep when the visceral throb of the discotheque snapped him into consciousness—sticky-minded and stiff-boned. He could not believe it! The volume was so high that the thump of the back-beat bass was a physical thing vibrating the floor and rattling the drinking glass on the washstand. The singsong, hyperthyroid patter of the disc jockey introduced the next selection in a rapid, garbled East End imitation of American fast patter deejays, and the room began to vibrate again. He swung out of bed and pounded on the wall to be let out. There was no response, so he rattled the door, and it opened in his hand. So. He was no longer locked in. The Vicar must have told them that he was firmly hooked and would not try to escape.

After splashing his face and changing shirts, he went down to the foyer to find it and the adjacent pub packed with young people, shouting at each other, pushing through, beer mugs held high, and brandishing cigarettes. He pressed through the crowd in the saloon bar, trying to find a way out of the din, and instead found himself in a discotheque, surrounded by youngsters who hopped and sweated to the deafening throb of amplifiers in a murky darkness broken occasionally by a flash of color from a jury-rigged strobe light. The noise was brutal, particularly the amplified bass, which vibrated in his sinuses.

A form approached him through the smoky dark. "Did the noise wake you up?" Yank asked.

"What?"

"Did the noise wake you up?"

Jonathan shouted into Yank's ear. "Let's not do that number. Show me how to get out of here."

"Follow me!"

They threaded through bodies gyrating in a miasma of smoke and stale beer, and out a back door to the parking area, now filled with cars and small knots of young men, talking together and erupting into jolts of forced laughter whenever one of them said something bawdy.

Well beyond the car park, in the garden Jonathan could look down on from his window, the noise was low enough to permit speaking. They stopped and Yank lit up a cigarette.

"What is going on here?" Jonathan asked.

"We have discotheque five nights a week. Kids come all the way from London. It's the Guv's idea. It provides cover for our operation here, and a little extra income."

Jonathan shook his head in disbelief. "When does it come to an end?"

"Closing time. About ten thirty."

"And what am I supposed to do in the meantime?"

"Don't you dig music?"

124

Jonathan glanced at him. "My door is no longer locked. I take it I'm free to wander about now?"

"Within limits. Perhaps it would be better if I came along."

They strolled through the garden and up a footpath that led away from the inn. Yank babbled on about the virtues of America, things American, places he was going to go and things he was going to do when he saved up enough money to emigrate. "I guess it sounds as though I had it in for old Blighty. Not true, really. There are a lot of British things— ways of life, traditions—that I admire and that I'll miss. But they're really gone anyway. Gone, or on their way out. England has become a sort of low-budget United States. And if you have to live in the United States, you might as well live in the real one. Right?"

Jonathan, who had not been listening, indicated a fork in the path. "What's up this way?"

"Oh . . . nothing really." Yank started to take the lower fork.

"No. Let's go on along here."

"Well . . . you can't go very far up that way anyway. Fenced off, you know."

"What's up there?"

"Another branch of our operation. The guards you saw come from there. I don't have anything to do with it."

"What is it?"

"It's . . . ah . . . it's called the Feeding Station."

"A farm?"

"Sort of. Let's be getting back."

"You go back. I can't take the noise."

"OK. But don't go too far up this path. The dogs are loose at night."

"Dogs? To keep people out of the Feeding Station?"

"No." Yank took a long drag on his cigarette. "To keep people in."

Jonathan sat in the darkness on a stone bench beside the quatrefoil pool. A light mist was settling in the windless air, and his skin tingled with cold. There was a crimson smear in the northern sky, the last burning off of the stubble fields; and the air carried the autumn smell of leaf smoke. The discotheque had closed down, and the crowds had poured out to their cars, laughing and hooting in the car park. Horns had sounded and gravel had been sprayed, and one last drunk, alone and stumbling in the dark, had called for "Alf" several times with growing desperation before staggering onto the road to hitchhike.

There was a period of deep silence before the night creatures felt safe; then began the chirp of insects, the rustle of field mice, the plop of frogs.

Jonathan sat alone and depressed. He had been so sure his break with CII was permanent. He had repressed all the nasty memories. And here he was. They had him again. But what bothered him most was not the irony of it, or the loss of freedom of choice. It was the discovery that he had not left this business as far behind as he had thought. Already, the high-honed, aggressive mental set necessary to survive in this class of action had returned to him, quite naturally, as though it had always been there buried under a thin cover of distaste.

He heard her approach from fifty yards away. He didn't bother to turn his head. There was no stealth in the footfalls, no urgent energy, no danger signals.

"Do you have a light?" she asked, after she had stood beside him for some time without attracting the least recognition of her existence.

"What happened? Your cigarette lighter run out of film?"

She made a pass at laughter. "It doesn't matter really. I don't have a cigarette anyway."

"Just this deep desire to communicate. I know the feeling."

"Jonathan, I hope you don't feel too badly toward me, because—"

"Yes, this lack of communication is the major problem in the world as we know and love it around us in everyday life. All people are essentially good and loving and peace-seeking, but they have trouble communicating that fact to one another. Right? Perhaps it's because they raise barriers of mistrust. People ought to learn to trust one another more. The only people you can really trust are women named Maggie. Someone once told me that the name Maggie, while not melodious, was at least substantial. You could always trust good old Maggie."

"All right. I give up."

"Good." He rose and started back toward the inn. She followed. "There is one thing, though."

"Let me guess. You'd give anything in the world if you hadn't had to set me up. You could almost weep when you think of me, lying there in the deep sleep of the sexually exercised and satisfied—probably a boyish smile on my face—while you slipped out of bed and opened the door to let the Loo men in and gutshoot that poor bastard on my crapper."

"Really, I didn't know——"

"Certainly! After all, I was just a cipher to you at first. But later, it was different. Right? After we'd exchanged trivial confidences and fucked a bit, you discovered deeper feelings. But by then it was too late to back out. Maggie! . . ." He reined his anger and lowered his voice. "Maggie, your actions lack even the charm of new experience for me. I was nailed once before by a lady. The only difference is that she was in the major leagues."

Her eyes had not left his, and she had not flinched through his tirade. "I know, Jonathan."

He realized that he had reached out and was grasping her upper arms tightly. He released her, snapping his hands open. "How do you know?"

"Your records. CII sent us your entire file, and I was required to study it carefully before . . ."

"Before setting me up."

"All right! Before setting you up!"

He believed the shame in her sudden rush of anger. Suddenly he felt very tired. And he regretted his loss of control. He looked away from her and forced his breathing to assume a lower rhythm.

She spoke without temper and without pleading. "I want to tell you this."

"I don't need it."

"*I* need it. I didn't know what they had in mind. I thought they were going to set you up with a drug plant or something. When they appeared at the door with that poor man, I . . . I . . ."

"He was alive at that time."

She swallowed and looked past him, down the

road gleaming faintly in the ghost light of moon above fog. Talking about it required that she pick at the painful scab of memory. "Yes. He was badly doped up. He couldn't even stand without help. And he was wearing that horrid grinning mask. They had to carry him in and put him onto the . . . But he was aware of what was happening. I could see it in his eyes—just the eyes behind the cutouts in the mask. He looked at me with such . . ." She blinked back the tears. "There was such sadness in his eyes! He was begging me to help him. I felt that. But I . . . Lord God above, it's a terrible business we're in, Jonathan."

He drew her head against his chest. It seemed the only reasonable thing to do.

"Why didn't they kill him cleanly?"

She couldn't speak for a while, and he heard the squeaking sound of tears being swallowed. "They were supposed to. The Vicar was very angry with them for bungling it. They went into the bathroom while I waited outside. Then you turned over in your sleep and made a sound. I was frightened you might wake up, so I tapped at the door, and at the same moment I heard a popping sound."

"A silencer."

"Yes, I suppose. They rushed out immediately, but one of them was swearing under his breath. My knock had startled him and spoiled his aim."

He rocked her gently.

"I crept back into bed, trying not to wake you. I didn't know what to do. I just lay there, staring into the dark, concentrating as hard as possible, trying to keep dawn from coming."

"But no luck."

129

"No luck at all. Morning came. You woke up. Then . . . I just couldn't make love when you wanted."

He nodded. That was to her credit. "Come on. Let's take a walk around the inn before turning in."

She sniffed and pulled herself together. "Yes, I'd like that."

They strolled slowly, arm about and arm about, each accommodating for their difference in stride. "Tell me," he said, "why didn't you throw the cigarette case away?"

"You know about that? Well, I suppose the real question is why didn't I leave it behind in your room, as I was supposed to do. I don't know. At the moment, I thought I might be protecting you by denying them the films. But directly I had time to think it out, I realized that they were determined to get you. There was no point in denying them the films. They'd only have set something else up, and you would have had to go through that."

"I see." He looked down, watching their shoes step out in rhythm. "Who were the men who came to my flat?"

"The two you rode here with in the Bentley. Not Yank, the other two.

"And who did the shooting?"

"The Sergeant."

"Figures." He added another line to the bill The Sergeant was running up with him. The payoff became inevitable.

They walked without speaking for a time, breathing in the moist freshness of the night air.

"It may be silly," she said at last, "but I'm glad you didn't take Sylvia up on it."

"Who is Silvia?"

"The girl who works here. You know, Henry's friend."

"Oh, her. Well, she isn't my type."

They were at the door again. She turned to him and asked, "Am I your type?"

He looked at her for several seconds. "I'm afraid so."

They went in.

"I'm sorry about that," she said out of a long silence. She was sitting up, braced against the carved oaken headboard, and she had just lit another cigarette.

He hugged her around the hips and put his cheek into the curve of her waist. They had made love, and slept, and made love again, and now his voice was ragged with sleepiness. "Sorry about what?"

"About that last bit—those internal contractions when I climax. I can't help them. They're beyond my control."

He growled and mumbled, "By all means, do let's talk about it."

She laughed at him. "Don't you like to talk about it afterward? It's supposed to be very healthy and modern and all."

"I suppose. But I'm old-fashioned enough to be sentimental about the operation. For the first few minutes anyway."

"Hm-m." She took a drag on her cigarette, her face briefly illuminated in the glow. "Your kind of people are like that."

He turned over. "My kind of people?"

"The violent ones. They tend to be sentimental. I

131

guess sentiment is their substitute for compassion. Kind of a surrogate for genuine feelings. I read somewhere that ranking Nazis used to weep over Wagner."

"Wagner makes me weep too. But not from sentiment. Go to sleep."

"All right." But after a moment of silence: "Still, I am sorry if my little spasms ruined any plans you had for epic control."

"Sorry for me? Or sorry for yourself?"

"Oh, you *are* feeling a bit bristly, aren't you? Do you always suffer from postcoitus aggression?"

He rose to one elbow. "Listen, madam. It doesn't seem to me that I started any of this. The only thing I'm feeling at this moment is postcoitus fatigue. Now good night." He dropped back on his pillow.

"Good night." But he could tell from the tension of her body that she was not prepared to sleep. "Do you know what I wish you suffered from?" she asked after a short silence.

He didn't answer.

"Intracoitus camaraderie, that's what," she said, and laughed.

"OK. You win." He pulled himself up and rested against the headboard. "Let's talk."

She scooted down under the covers. "Oh, I don't know. I'm kind of tired."

"You're going to get popped right in the eye."

"I'm sorry. But you are fun to tease. You rise to the bait so eagerly. What do you want to talk about, now that you've got me wide awake?"

"Let's talk about you, for lack of more interesting things. Tell me, how did a nice girl like you, et cetera . . ."

"Why am I working for Loo?"

"Yes. We both know why *I* am."

She knew that taunt was not completely in jest, but she decided he had a right to some bitterness. Perhaps the best thing to do would be to share the truth with him. After all, the truth did mitigate her complicity. "Well, most of what I told you about myself the other night was true. I was born in Ireland. Went to university over here, then returned. I was young and silly and politically committed—looking for a cause, I suppose. Or bored maybe. I used to meet my brother and some of his friends at a coffee shop, and we would talk about a united Ireland. Angry speeches. Plans and plots. You know the sort of thing. Then one day my brother was gone. I discovered that he had gotten into Ulster. He had always said he wanted to take an active part in the thing, but I had written that off as romantic game-playing. He was a poet, you see. Flashing eyes and floating hair and all that. I don't imagine you would have liked him."

"He died?"

He felt her nod. "Yes. He was found in his car." Her voice became very soft. "They shot him through the ear. And I . . . I . . ."

He hugged her head to his side. "Don't talk about it."

"No, I want to. It's good for me. For months the image of him being shot in that car haunted me. I used to have nightmares. And do you know what image used to shock me awake, all sweating and panting?"

He patted her.

"The noise of it! Can you imagine the terrible noise of it?"

Jonathan felt helpless and stupid. He was sorry for her, but he knew the emptiness of saying so. "Who did it?" he asked. "UDA? IRA?"

She shrugged. "It doesn't really matter, does it? They're all the same."

"I'm surprised you realize that. Good for you."

"Oh, I didn't know it then, of course. I wanted revenge. More for myself than for my brother, I suppose. I went to Belfast and joined a cell of activists. And ..."

"You got your revenge?"

"I don't know. We set bombs. People got hurt—probably the wrong people. After a while, I came to my senses and realized how stupid the whole business was, and I decided to return to Dublin. And that's when I was picked up and arrested. Things always happen that way."

"You were sentenced?"

"No. They were taking me from one prison to another in an army vehicle, when they were run off the road by armed hijackers. The soldiers were all shot. The hijackers took me with them. Only me. They left the other prisoners."

"I assume the hijackers were Loo people."

"Yes."

"How long ago was this?"

"Only a month. They brought me here for a week of briefing on your background file from CII. Then they placed me at Mr. MacTaint's where we met. And that's it."

Jonathan slid down beside her, and they lay for a time staring into the dark above them. "Why *you*, I

134

wonder," he said at length. "Not that I'm complaining."

She took a deep breath. "I don't know. I could paint—well, in a way. And there was no question about my being cooperative. All the Vicar has to do is lift a telephone, and I'm back in Belfast facing charges. And this time I'll have to answer for those dead soldiers as well."

Jonathan's fists clenched and unclenched. "He's quite a number, that vicar. No messing around with fluctuating loyalties for him. When he wants you, he ties you up properly."

"True. He's got both of us. And he does the whole thing with a hearty handshake and polite small talk."

"And a wink."

"Oh, yes. And a wink. I suppose that winking is just a nervous tic, but it's a nuisance. It's infectious when you're talking to him. You have this urge to wink back, and that wouldn't do at all."

Jonathan was relieved that the talk was taking this lighter tone. The last thing in the world he needed was the burden of this girl's problems or, worse yet, her affection. Lovemaking was no threat to his precious insulation. Two people meet on the neutral ground of lust, they scratch their itches, then they go back into themselves. Nothing shared, nothing lost. But this sort of thing—this sharing of ideas and problems, this quiet talk into the common dark— this could be dangerous. Sapping.

Maggie leaned across him and butted her cigarette out in the bedside ashtray. Then she resettled herself against him and ran her fingers over his stomach idly. "This is kind of old hat for you, isn't it? I read in your file about that Eiger affair—about that girl who roped you into it." She felt his stomach tighten, but she plunged ahead with that well-intentioned instinct for the emotional jugular that characterizes good women grimly determined to understand and help. "Her name was Jemima Brown, wasn't it?"

There was no inflection in Jonathan's voice when he said, "Yes."

"Was she at all like me?"

"No. Not at all."

"Oh." She removed her hand from him. "Did you love her?"

Jonathan got up and sat on the edge of the bed. Beyond the window, the night horizon was still smudged by a reddish glow of burning stubble out in the fields, but this false dawn was not so distant from the real one, for the birds were beginning to sound the odd chirp in expectation.

Maggie sat up and patted the bed beside her. "I'll make you a bargain," she said in comic broad brogue. "Bring your fine body back here, and I'll not plague you with me queries into your emotional life. Which is not to say that I won't be making any demands upon you at all, at all."

He rejoined her, stretching out flat on his back and feeling that he had been childishly touchy. She scooted down beside him and pressed her forehead against his. He looked into her impish green eye—one only and large at this distance. "You have a way of coming out one up, haven't you?" he said.

"Instinct for emotional survival. Do you realize that we've made sexual pigs of ourselves in the little time we've had together?"

"Shameful."

"Isn't it just. Physically prodigal, I'd call it."

"I think it's only fair to warn you that I'm an aging man. I may not be up to it."

"Lord, I hate double entendre."

Breakfast, the only meal English cooks feel comfortable with, was interrupted by The Sergeant bursting into the dining room, his face flushed and steaming with sweat. "Where the 'ell 'ave you been!" he shouted at Jonathan, who was finishing a last cup of tea with Yank and Maggie at a corner table somewhat out of the draft. "I've been runnin' me arse off around these bleedin' 'ills!"

Jonathan set down his napkin and looked out the window on the countryside, where the corn stubble was pastel under the lowering gray sky.

The Sergeant crossed to their table in three angry strides, and his bulk hovered over Jonathan.

"More tea?" Jonathan asked Maggie.

"No, thank you."

"I'm talking to you, mate!" The Sergeant put his heavy hand on Jonathan's shoulder. Jonathan glanced down at the thick fingers as though they had dropped from a passing bird, then he looked across at Yank with raised eyebrows.

Yank intervened nervously. "Come on, now. No need to get your dander up. He's just been sitting here having breakfast with us. Cool it, man."

"When I went into his room this morning, the bleedin' bed 'adn't been slept in. Looked like he'd scarpered. The lads and me's been all over the grounds lookin' for 'im!"

"You must have worked up quite an appetite,"

Jonathan commented softly. "And it's obvious that you needed the exercise."

"I'm fitter than you'll ever be, mate."

"In which case you don't need my support to stand up." Jonathan glanced again at the hand, which was removed from his shoulder with an angry snap.

"Let's drop it," Yank told The Sergeant. "After all, the Guv has given Dr. Hemlock the run of the place."

"You know he don't want 'im up ... there." The Sergeant jerked his head in the direction of the path leading to the Feeding Station. "And anyway, nobody told me nothin' about 'im having the run of the place."

"I am telling you now," Yank said distinctly, clarifying for Jonathan the chain of command from the Vicar. "Now be a good lad and sit down to your breakfast."

The Sergeant glowered at Jonathan, then left, grumbling.

Yank leaned forward and spoke confidentially to Jonathan. "I wouldn't put him on, if I were you. He's no quiz kid, but he's got a temper, and he's a master of hand-to-hand combat."

"I am forewarned."

"By the way. Just out of curiosity, where *did* you pass the night?"

Maggie smiled into her plate.

Jonathan answered offhandedly, timing his response to catch Yank with a forkful of eggs on the way to his mouth. "At the Feeding Station."

The fork hovered, then returned to the plate still laden. The color had drained from Yank's face.

"That's a good deal less funny than you fancy, Dr. Hemlock."

It amused Jonathan to note that all traces of American accent fled from Yank's voice under pressure, just as multilingual people always return to their native language when they swear, count, or pray.

Unable to eat, Yank excused himself and left.

"That was cruel," Maggie said.

"Uh-huh. What do you know about this Feeding Station?"

"Nothing really. It's up the path there. Guards and dogs and all. Sometimes the guards come down here to the bar or to take lunch, but they never talk about it."

"Can you find out about it for me?"

"I can try."

"Do that."

It had turned wet and blustery by the time Jonathan was allowed to walk to the vicarage with only the light guard of Yank, who kept up a running conversation of trivia, quite recovered from his crisis of distrust over the mention of the Feeding Station. When they reached the gate, Yank joined two other young men dressed in the flared dark suits and wide bright ties that were almost a Loo uniform. Jonathan could not help noticing how much like East End hoods they looked.

He found the Vicar in his garden, dressed in a stout hunting jacket and twill breeches tucked into thick stockings. His shoes were heavy, boat-toed brogans. The costume contrasted sharply with Jonathan's close-fitting city clothes and custom-made light shoes. The Vicar did not seem to be aware of Jonathan's presence as he muttered angrily to himself while scattering fish food to the carp in his pond. Then he looked up. "Ah, Dr. Hemlock! Good of you to come."

"You seem distressed."

"What? Oh. Well, I am a bit. Nothing to do with your affair. It's that damned Boggs! Will you take something? Coffee, perhaps, or tea?"

"Thank you, no."

"Just as good. I was hoping we might take a little walk through the fields as we chatted. No place like the open country for privacy. There are insects in the hedgerows, but no bugs—if you have my meaning there."

Jonathan looked up at the threatening, gusting sky.

"No worry about the weather," the Vicar assured him. "Forecast predicts only occasional rain." He winked.

Jonathan shrugged and followed him to the bottom of the garden where the path became a narrow foot trail through a tangled coppice. "How did this Boggs get damned?" he asked the back of the figure trudging out briskly before him.

"Pardon? Oh, I see. Well, Boggs owns the land next to the church. A farmer, you know. Been ripping out hedgerows again. Do you know that more than five thousand miles of hedgerows are ripped up annually in England?"

"Pity they didn't get this one," Jonathan mumbled after stumbling over a root.

"What?"

"Nothing."

"Five thousand miles of homes for small creatures and nestings for birds torn out every year! And some of our hedgerows were planted in Saxon times! But the farmers say they get in the way of modern machinery. They are sacrificing the inheritance of centuries for a few pounds profit. No sense of responsibility to nature. No sense of history. Oh, I *am* sorry! Did that branch catch you as I let it go? And do you know what Boggs has done now?"

Jonathan didn't care.

"He sold off the tract next to the church to construction speculators. Think of it! In a year's time there may be an estate of retirement homes abutting the churchyard. Thin-shelled boxes with names like 'End O' The Line,' and 'Dunroam Inn'!"

"Does all this really matter to you? Or is this a little show for my benefit?"

The Vicar stopped and turned. "Dr. Hemlock, the Church is my life. And I take a special interest in preserving the living monuments of its architecture. Every penny I make from my avocation with the government goes to that end." He winked.

"And is that how you justify the ugly things your organization does?"

"It might be. If patriotism required justification."

"I see. You picture yourself as a kind of whore for Christ. Presumably Magdalen was your college."

The Vicar's expression frosted over, his face seemed to flatten, and he spoke with crisper tones. "It occurs to me that we might do better to confine our communication to the problem before us." He turned and continued his walk, pushing through the brush to a field of stubble.

"Let's do that."

"It goes without saying," the Vicar spoke over his shoulder, "that everything you learn in the course of your work with us is absolutely confidential. My young assistant—the man you know as Yank—has told you in outline the function of the Loo organization. Rather like the Search and Sanction Division of your CII, Loo is assigned the thankless task of providing protection for MI–5 and MI–6 operatives by technique of counterassassination. For good or for ill, our position as most secret of the secret and most efficient of the efficient brings extraordinary tasks to my doorstep. The affair at hand is one such. It is not in essence what your people would call a sanction. There is no specific assignment to kill a given person. To state it better: The affair does not absolutely require assassination. But the chances are you will be pressed to that extreme in an effort to remain alive yourself. Oh, my goodness! I should have warned you about that boggy spot. Here, give me your hand. There! Ah, you seem to have left a shoe behind. Never mind, I'll fetch it out for you. There. Good as new!"

The Vicar pressed on, inhaling deeply the brisk breeze that carried needles of rain with it. "I think it would be clearer if I presented the situation to you in terms of morals, for modern trends in turpitude lie at the core of the issue. Sexual license, to be specific. The New Morality—which is neither true morality nor particularly new, as a casual reference to the social lives of the Claudian emperors will affirm—has infected every stratum of society, from the universities to the coal pits—not that that is such a great gulf fixed, what with the democratization of the schools. Perhaps it is only natural that a generation that has passed the greater part of its life under the covert threat of atomic annihilation, that has seen the traditional bulwarks of family and class crumble under the pressures of enforced egalitarianism and liberalism gone to seed, that has experienced the decline of formal literature and art and the rise of television, pop art, folk masses, thriller novels, happenings, and the rest of it—all of which appeal to the nerve ends rather than to the mind, and to immediate reaction rather than to tranquil contemplation—perhaps it is only natural that such a generation would seek the sexual narcotic. Although as a churchman I cannot condone such activities, as a humanitarian I can grant the existence of powerful stimuli prompting people toward burying their minds in the mire of flesh and orgasm. Wish we had a flask of tea with us. That would warm you up. Come, let's press on and get the blood circulating.

"It suffices to say that a general retreat into sexual excess has become a fact of life in all circles, save the working class, which has been protected from infection by virtue of its want of imagination. And it would seem that unnatural sexuality is a habit-forming vice. Once he embarks on its use, the thrill-seeker develops a tolerance for the more ... ah ... commonplace activities, and finds they no longer serve to relax him and to dim his mind. The nerves seem to develop calluses, as it were. And so the sybarite is pressed toward more ... ah ... unconventional ... ah ..."

"I see."

"I thought you might. For some years now this grass fire of the senses, if I may avail myself of metaphor, has been spreading amongst persons in the government and civil service. At first it was limited to the relatively safe and pallid practice of exchanging wives while on holiday. But in time, the fire demanded more occult fuels. And, as one might expect, certain organizations sprang up to supply these demands. Most of them are smutty little operations offering simple varieties of number, race, and posture, together with the dubious advantage of becoming famous through the efforts of spying newspaper photographers. A little higher on the scale were places that offered variants long popular on the Continent—particularly in France, of course. Girls dressed as nuns, girls in caskets—that sort of thing. Look there! Did you see them? Two hares bounded across that bit of meadow. The autumn hare! Memories of boyhood, eh?"

Jonathan turned up the collar of his jacket and stared ahead miserably.

"At the apex of this pyramid of vice—Oh, my, I *do* wax Victorian. At the apex is a small and terribly expensive operation that offers to elite clientele what might be described as sexual maxima. I shall not abuse you with the details of these events. Suffice it to say that the organization in question is also involved in the importation of Pakistanis—illegal immigrants who cannot find gainful employment and who are driven to extremes to stay alive. This organization finds particular use for Pakistani children of both sexes between the ages of nine and fifteen. And I must confess that it is not only men in government that frequent this establishment, but often their wives and daughters as well. And all this nastiness goes on to the accompaniment of excellent wines and lobster—in season."

"I assume the clientele is not limited to clerks and middle-management personnel."

"Sadly, it is not. I blush to admit that among the clients are certain Very Highly Placed Persons." He winked.

"Do the bed linens bear the stamp 'by appointment'?"

The Vicar flushed, angry. "Certainly not, sir!"

Jonathan held up one hand in a gesture of peace. "Just wanted to know what league I was playing in."

"I see." The Vicar was not mollified. He turned and continued trudging on, entering an overgrown wood, anger making him increase his stride and breast his way through the tangle. When his anger had burned out, he continued. "For a year or two, this activity went on. A deplorable business, but not one that endangered the security of the country, so far as we knew. But then something happened that required me to review my evaluation of The Cloisters—for that is the ironic name of the resort in which these excesses take place."

"It's in the country somewhere?"

"No. London. Hampstead, in fact. Look there! A rhododendron! Like you, a visitor to our shores."

"What happened with The Cloisters? Blackmail?"

"No. Not really. And that's the uncomfortable part of it. But I'll get to that in a moment.

"One afternoon—just after tea, as I recall—I received a confusing call from my opposite number in MI-5. He had a report, the content of which had galvanized that normally lethargic branch of the service into activity. As one might suspect, they had no idea what to do with the information, but they had the good sense to push it over onto my plate. A man had stopped by at their office, a civil servant in the middle ranks with the Defense Ministry, and had boldly revealed to them a number of astonishing facts. Getting a bit above himself, he had participated in the leisure activities offered at The Cloisters. I don't know whether his money ran out or his conscience prevailed, but after a time he discontinued his visits. Then one afternoon he was visited by a caller who, with all the trappings of civility, demanded that he come later that evening to The Cloisters. The poor wretch dared not refuse. When he arrived, he was taken to a private salon where he was treated to a private showing of motion pictures."

"And he was surprised to find himself the star of the film. Argh-ga!"

"You anticipate correctly. Good Lord! I knew it! I told Boggs a dozen times that stile was rotten and wanted mending. I *knew* it would give way just when someone was straddling the fence. You didn't by any chance—"

"No! I'm all right!"

"Could I give you a hand down?"

"I'll make it!"

"You're quite sure you're all right? You're walking a bit oddly."

Jonathan crashed angrily on through the pathless thicket.

"The strange thing," the Vicar continued, "was that there was no threat of blackmail. Indeed, no pressure was brought to bear on the official to continue frequenting The Cloisters. But it was made perfectly clear to him that any mention of their activities would be met by an immediate publication of the film. As you might suspect, he was distressed

146

beyond telling, but he was assured that he was not alone in this uncomfortable position. They evidently had a large number of films implicating a wide spectrum of government personalities."

"Why do you assume they are collecting this evidence, if not blackmail?"

"We don't know. But it doesn't really matter in any substantive way. The very existence of this information constitutes a time bomb planted in the seat of government—ah, there's the kind of maladroit metaphor that used to set us to laughing in school—and we have no idea when it will go off, or who will be harmed in the explosion. One thing is certain: a revelation of this caliber would damage Her Majesty's government beyond repair."

For a time the Vicar seemed to be lost in gloomy contemplation of so terrible a fate. They walked along a footpath that had been pulverized by horses into a ribbon of gummy slime.

To get on with the thing, Jonathan asked, "Why did this man come to MI–5 with information that would certainly end his career?"

"I couldn't know, of course. Shame, one might conjecture. Or a sense of patriotism. As I said, he was a *middle* rank in the civil service. Mere clerks are seldom affected by patriotism, and the leadership is immune to shame. The entire question is academic, however, inasmuch as our first move had to be to assure ourselves of this chap's silence. Inner pressures had driven him to divulge all of us. Who could know what his next action might be? The popular newspapers? At all costs, this scandal had to be kept from public view. And *that*, you had better know, remains our primary concern."

"So you had him sanctioned?"

The Vicar did not respond at once. "Not exactly," he said in a distant voice.

The truth dawned on Jonathan. "Oh, I see. That is lovely. The poor bastard showed up on my toilet, having failed to pull his trousers down."

"Just so. And I must tell you how much I regret the bungling of that matter. There was no call to burden you with the poor fellow's last words, to say nothing of the disgusting olfactory effect of the misplaced bullet. I can assure you the man responsible has been reprimanded." He winked.

"I have a feeling he will be punished further."

"Oh? Then you know who it was?" The Vicar's voice carried genuine admiration. "You certainly have a flair for getting information quickly. I feel vindicated in my choice of you for this somewhat delicate mission."

"Which is? . . ."

The Vicar refused to abandon his sequential progression through events. "Directly we received this information, we began our investigation. One of our best men was set to the task—a man who, because of his Grecian penchant in matters sexual, would have a subtle entrée into the goings-on at The Cloisters. That man's name was Parnell-Greene."

"The fresh grave I saw yesterday evening?"

"I'm afraid so. But before they got onto him, he was able to pass on some valuable fragments of information. We know, for instance, the identity of the man in charge of The Cloisters. He is best known to us as Maximilian Strange. German, by birth. Born as Max Werde in October of 1922 in Munich. The Werde family had been in the business of flesh-selling for three generations. Posh dens of vice catering to the upper classes—well, to the rich, at least. Young Max seems to have taken to the family line with rare energy, for we find him in 1943 at the tender age of twenty-one catering to the rather vigorous sexual appetites of ranking German officers. In Berlin and in at least two provincial cities, he managed sumptuous pleasure establishments stocked with girls and boys he had hand-picked from the concentration camps. The activity was ... ah ... irregular. Indeed, there was one small house on the outskirts of Berlin that was called the Vivisectory because . . ."

"I get the picture."

"Good. Recounting it is painful."

"You're a man of delicate sensibilities," Jonathan said.

"Irony, if it is to be effective, should lightly etch a phrase. Not drip from each word. But rhetoric is not our study here. When next our researchers catch sight of Werde—or Strange, as he calls himself now—the war is over and he is purveying rather Roman entertainments in such places as Morocco, the Antibes, Samos—all the haunts of what you call the jet set. These amusements involve young people painted with gilt, participants from the audience daubed with grease, and activities between animals and humans—the favored beast being, for some obscure reason, the camel." He winked.

"It is at this time that we get our first description of the man. There are no photographs in existence. He is described as a handsome man in his early twenties. This is odd, because you realize that, by then, he was just over forty years old. We also discover that he has an inordinate interest in health, diet, exercise, and the general maintenance of his uncommonly youthful appearance. His linguistic attainments include a faultless command of English and French, along with Arabic, of course, as any man trafficking in his line of goods must have. Not much to go on by way of description, I fear."

"Not much."

"Again Mr. Strange disappears from sight. And two years ago, The Cloisters is launched in London, with Maximilian Strange at the helm of this fire ship. There you have him, Dr. Hemlock. Your adversary. Certainly a worthy opponent."

"His worthiness doesn't interest me. I'd much rather he was a fool. I'm neither a sportsman nor a hunter."

"Yes, I suppose there is a subtle difference between being a hunter and being a killer."

Jonathan let it pass. "Knowing what you do about Strange, you could certainly put a stop to his operation. I assume he is in the country illegally."

"I have tried to impress upon you the scope of the disaster that would derive from the slightest leakage of these films, or the activities they record. Neither the police nor any other agency of law enforcement must be brought in on this. Our police—like your own—are not distinguished by competence and discretion. And you may wonder why we don't just buy these films back, ransom them, so to speak. Well, Loo frankly doesn't have that kind of money in its war chest, and we must get the film back without alerting persons in the government who must not become involved in this delicate matter—that's part of why MI-5 commissioned us to act for them. We could, of course, dispatch some of our Loo actives to visit The Cloisters and leave no living beings behind them. But what if they failed to locate the films? What if Maximilian Strange has protected himself by leaving the films with someone who would publish them the moment something happened to him? No. No. This must be done delicately. And finally. And that is where you come in."

"Why me?"

"The late Parnell-Greene was able to pass on one further bit of information before his cover fell and he made his unfortunate visit to St. Martin's-In-The-Fields. He heard your name mentioned by Mr. Strange."

"My name?" Jonathan leapt over a ditch and scrambled up a muddy bank. "You certainly don't think I'm implicated in The Cloisters."

"Certainly not." The Vicar braced himself against the wind and pressed on, shouting over his shoulder, "If we thought that for an instant, we would be entertaining you at another of our facilities."

"The Feeding Station?" The wind tore the words from Jonathan's mouth and flung them at the Vicar, who stopped in his tracks, astonished at Jonathan's knowledge of their operation. But again he was pleased with this ability to secure information quickly.

He nodded to himself and strode on. "We ran a thorough check on you, including communication with our colleagues in Moscow, Paris, and Washington. After assuring ourselves that The Cloisters was not a front from your Mr. Dragon and CII mucking about in our affairs, as that aggressive organization is wont to do, we counted it a stroke of rare good luck that a trained professional such as yourself was somehow involved in all this. Oh goodness! I *am* sorry! But you really should be more careful where you tread in a cow pasture. Rather like Paris streets, in that respect. May I give you a hand up?" He winked uncontrollably.

"No!"

"Oh my, oh my. What a pity."

"Forget it. I'm not particularly fond of this jacket anyway."

"It does seem odd, if I may say so, that a man who was once a ranking mountain climber should find a little walk in the country so fraught with difficulty."

"Eagles don't become members of the Audubon Society."

"I beg your pardon?"

Jonathan was becoming angry with himself for allowing the droning civility of this vicar to erode his cool. "Listen. Exactly how did I get implicated in all this?"

"I haven't the foggiest. We only know what Parnell-Greene was able to pass on before his death. There are two threads connecting you to The Cloisters. We know that Maximilian Strange is very interested in you indeed."

"But—"

"We don't know why. Indeed, I had rather hoped you would be able to tell us. You have not, by chance, dealt with him at one time or another?"

"No idea."

"Pity. It might have been a starting point. The other thread linking you to The Cloisters is more direct. What you might call a friend-of-a-friend relationship. On two occasions Parnell-Greene met Miss Vanessa Dyke on the premises."

That stopped Jonathan.

"This might have been totally coincidental," the Vicar continued, "but it does constitute an intertangency between you and Mr. Strange. At all events, it is clear that your best path into The Cloisters is through Miss Dyke. Permit me to hold this barbed wire up for you. Oh, well. You said you were not particularly fond of that jacket. Let's take the shortcut back through the fields. Yes, Dr. Hemlock, I cannot adequately express my regret at having to ring you in on this business. We had no original intention to, you know, even after Parnell-Greene first reported that The Cloisters people were interested in you. He was doing an admirable job of penetrating their organization, and we had no immediate use for you, although we took the precaution of planting our Miss Coyne with your rather seedy friend, Mac-Taint. Just in case."

"And when they hit this Parnell-Greene, you decided to bring me in as his replacement."

"Precisely. Their manner of disposing of poor Parnell-Greene will give you some idea of the kind of men you are up against. He was found impaled on a wooden stake in the belfry of St. Martins's-In-The-Fields."

"Baroque."

"Baroque, yes. But very modern at the same time. A bit of advertising that any public-relations man would approve. When one considers the extra danger involved in setting up so spectacular an assassination, one must come to the view that they were doing more than simply removing a potential danger. They were giving public notice to any who might attempt to interfere with their affairs, notice that was both efficient and darkly creative."

"Creative?"

"Just so. And with a diabolic sense of irony. I have alluded to Parnell-Greene's sexual deviation. He was a pederast; specifically his tastes ran to the passive role. Ergo, a certain grisly flair involved in the choice of anal impalement as a method of execution, don't you think, Dr. Hemlock?"

Jonathan trudged on in heavy silence for several minutes until, breaking through a thorn hedge, they were once again in the Vicar's garden.

"You'll want some brisk hot tea to ward off the cold. Let's go into the den, and I'll have it brought."

The rain swept in over the vicarage with full vigor. After the tea tray had been delivered by one of the young men with flared suit and broad bright tie, Jonathan said, "Why don't you just tell me what you want me to do?"

"That must be obvious. We want the films. And we want them quickly, before they can do whatever they have in mind with them." He winked twice.

"And what about this Maximilian Strange and his people?"

"I assume their number will be reduced by those who have the misfortune of standing between you and the films."

"And that will be the end of The Cloisters?"

The Vicar pursed his lips. "Not really. After consideration, I have decided that closing The Cloisters would have no effect on the appetites that maintain it. They would simply seek elsewhere. So, when all this is over, The Cloisters will continue its services. But under new management."

"It will become a Loo operation?"

"I think that would be best, don't you? The possession of the films together with data we collect in the operation of the establishment will bring effective control of the government under an organization that has the best interests of the nation at heart, together with the background and education to know what those best interests are. More tea?"

"That would make Loo totally antonomous, wouldn't it?"

"Why yes." The Vicar's eyes opened wide with ingenuous frankness. "I believe it will. Just as the information your CII has collected concerning the fiscal and sexual irregularities of your political leaders has long rendered it independent. But I can assure you *we* shall never use our autonomy to undertake ill-conceived invasions of neighboring islands, or to cover up bungling attempts to spy on political headquarters. However . . ." His eyes softened as he envisioned the future. ". . . Such power might enable us to effect a final solution to the Irish Problem."

"You'll understand if I find little real difference between the Loo and The Cloisters."

"Ah, but so far as you are concerned, there is one most salient difference. *We* can put you into prison for thirty years for murder."

"*They* can kill me."

The Vicar shrugged. "Well, if it comes to that . . . but really! Our chat has taken an unnecessarily nasty turn." He winked.

"All right. For nuts and bolts, what kind of support can I expect in getting the films?"

"From the police, none. We cannot run the smallest risk of this affair becoming public. Loo will continue its researches, and you will be advised of any new developments through Yank, who will operate as your contact with us. We are also pursuing another line of entry into The Cloisters, partially in support of you, partially as a second line of defense, should some misfortune befall you. Do not be surprised should you meet Miss Coyne within the walls of that evil establishment. For the rest, you are on your own. You will, of course, have my earnest prayers to support you. And you must never underestimate the power of prayer, Dr. Hemlock."

Rain rattled against the windows of the snug little den with its damp wood fire releasing bluish flames that lapped lambently at the wrought-iron grate. The rainwater had stopped dripping from Jonathan's hair down his collar, and the room was becoming close and steamy with the drying of their clothes. Jonathan cleared his throat. "Listen. I want you to let Miss Coyne out of this. She's done her bit by ringing me in on it."

"Oh? Do I hear the sound of affection? A romance perhaps? How charming!"

"Never mind the crap. Just let her out of it."

"But, my dear man, where would she go? I have no doubt she told you her distressing story. Were it not for us, she would this moment be sitting in a Belfast prison. And were it not for our continuing protection, she might be picked up in the streets at any time. Where is she to go? Do you intend to become responsible for her?" He winked.

"No. I don't."

"Well, there you have it. In point of fact, she came to me this morning and asked to be allowed to help you. Perhaps she's feeling a little guilty, eh? May I offer you one of these biscuits? They're digestives, and I can particularly recommend them."

Jonathan shivered and drew his wet jacket around him. "I'd better be getting back to the inn."

"I do hope you haven't caught a cold. Nasty things at this time of year." He rose and accompanied Jonathan to the door. "You can work out particulars with Yank, who has been instructed to assist you in every way. This afternoon you will receive a little training from The Sergeant."

"Training? From The Sergeant?"

"Yes. You are with Loo now. Drawing the Queen's shilling, as it were. And there are certain regulations to which you will have to conform. From your CII records it appears you are a bit short of formal training in hand-to-hand combat. And The Sergeant—an expert in such matters—has offered to brush you up. In fact, he leaped at the opportunity."

"I'll bet."

"I shall not have a chance to see you again before you go, so let me leave this with you: Be very careful in your dealings with Maximilian Strange. He is a clever man. And be particularly wary of the man called 'The Mute.' "

"Who is that?"

"He works for Strange, he undertakes such physical punishments as Strange considers necessary. We're quite sure he was the one who did for Parnell-Greene. Evidently he does such things for pleasure. So do be careful, there's a good fellow."

"What on earth happened to you?" Maggie's surprise converted into laughter, which she suppressed as soon as Jonathan's eyes told her he had no intention of being a good sport about his condition. "Do leave your shoes outside. I'll ask one of the boys to clean them." The corners of her mouth curled. "If he can find them, that is."

Jonathan stopped cold in the act of prying his shoes off while trying to avoid the cakes of mud and grass. He drew a very deep sigh of self-control, then continued. His fingers slipped, and he came up with a handful of mud.

Maggie did not laugh. Pointedly. "Come along up. I'll draw you a nice hot bath."

He growled.

His eyes closed, his elbows floating loose, he soaked in the large old-fashioned tub, only his mouth and nose out of the steaming water. But it was some time before the heat penetrated to his frozen marrow. Maggie perched on the edge of the tub, attending to him with a blend of maternity and laughter in her gamin face.

"What shall we do with these trousers?" she asked, holding them at arm's length between thumb and forefinger before letting them drop to the floor with a squishing sound.

He heard the reverberating rumble of her speech from under the water, but he could not make out the words. "What?" he asked, lifting his ears above surface.

"I was just asking ... oh, never mind."

"You seem to be taking my condition rather lightheartedly."

"No. No."

"People die of exposure, you know."

"I'll fetch you a towel."

"Exposure to the elements. Do you still think this is funny?"

She shook her head.

"Why have you turned your back to me? Can't you look me in the face and tell me you don't think this is funny?"

She shook her head again.

"All right, lady. You have a count of five, at the end of which in you come to join me."

"I'm all dressed!"

"Two."

"What happened to one?"

"Four."

"You wouldn't . . .!"

The sere, middle-aged cleaning woman looked up from her sweeping and gasped. Approaching her down the hall were Jonathan and Maggie wrapped in towels, she with her dripping clothes over her arm, and he his torn and muddy ones. For the benefit of their round-eyed spectator, he shook Maggie's hand and thanked her for a delightful time. She asked if he would care to drop into her room for a while before lunch, and he said yes, he thought that might be fun. Then he turned to the chambermaid. "Would you care to join us?"

Horrified, speechless, she backed against the wall and held the broom handle protectively before her chest. It was perfectly adequate coverage. He shrugged, said something about ships passing in the night, and followed Maggie to her room.

"How are you going to dress?" Maggie asked as soon as the door was closed.

"I'll go to my own room as soon as I think the maid has left. I wouldn't want to spoil her orgy of outrage." He lay on her bed and stretched his body to get the kinks out. "Were you able to find out anything about the Feeding Station?"

"Hm-m, yes. Rather more than I'd care to know, really. It's a ghastly business."

"Tell me."

"Well . . . that man—the one in your bathroom the other night. He was a product of the Feeding Station. Yank told me all about it. He didn't want to at first, but once he started, it came gushing out, like something he needed to be rid of."

He leaned up on one elbow. Her tone told him she was finding it difficult to talk about it.

She slipped into a bathrobe and sat on the bed beside him. "Evidently the concept of the Feeding Station is a result of the two problems faced by MI-5 and 6 and Loo. The first is the problem of defection and treachery within their ranks. These aren't very common, but they are dealt with vigorously. In fact, the defectors are assassinated. You do the same in the United States, I believe."

"Yes. The assassinations are called 'sanctions' if the target is someone outside the CII, and 'maximum demotes' if the target is one of their own men."

"Well, it seems that these assassinations were often difficult and awkward. There were bodies to dispose of; the police nosing about; and the Loo man who performed the assassination had to surface to award the punishment, maybe thereby stripping his cover for some more important task. So this was the first problem: the difficulty of performing assassinations."

"The second problem?"

"Corpses. Recently dead bodies are at a premium. They are used by the various branches of intelligence for setups, like the one you were victim of. And it seems they also use them as the ultimate deep cover for an active who has to go underground. Rather than simply disappear, the agent dies, or seems to. And there is no better cover than being dead and buried. They also use corpses to leak misguiding information to the other side—whoever that may be at the moment."

"How do they do that?"

"Evidently, a man is found in his hotel room dead of a heart attack, or perhaps he dies in a fatal traffic accident. And he has certain information on him that identifies him as a courier, together with some false data Loo wants implanted. In Lisbon or Athens—wherever the police are for sale—the other side ends up with the false information. They never imagine that a man would give his life just to fob off a bit of rot on them, so they always take it at face value."

"I see. So the Vicar put one and one together and decided to use the bodies of men written off for assassination to fulfill the Loo's need for fresh corpses. I assume they kidnap them and bring them to the Feeding Station to hold until they're needed."

"I don't know. I suppose so. I do know that bodies from the Feeding Station are always in short supply in relation to the needs of the services. The fact that the Vicar used one to rope you in gives you some idea of the importance of this affair, and of your importance to its success."

"I'm flattered. But why is the establishment called the 'Feeding Station'?"

"Well . . ." She rose and lit a cigarette. "That's the really grisly part of the matter—the part that upsets Yank so. It seems they are kept all doped up at a small farm back in the country near here. And they are fed . . . oh, lord."

"Go on."

". . . and they are fed on special diets. You see, Loo discovered that the first thing the Russians do when they have a corpse in want of identification is to pump its stomach and check the contents. And it wouldn't do for a supposed Greek to produce the remnants of steak-and-kidney pie. So, along with matters of proper clothing, the right dust in the trouser cuffs, and all that sort of business, they have to be sure the right food is . . ." She shrugged.

"Thus: the Feeding Station. They're quite a bunch, these Loo people."

"I feel sorry for Yank, though. His reaction to the whole thing is so violent, you forget for a moment that he's part of it."

"Yeah, he's an odd one to find in this business. Of course, they're all odd ones in this business, come to think of it."

"But we're involved in this. We're not odd."

"No! Christ, no. Come over here."

Jonathan was resting in his room after lunch when Yank knocked and entered. "Greetings, Gate. I've just come from the Guv. He laid everything out for me. How do you feel about our working together on this gig?" He sat in the overstuffed chair and put his feet up on the dresser.

Jonathan had been shielding his eyes from the light, his arm thrown across his face, and Yank's potpourri of slang gleaned from a span of thirty years evoked the image of a bearded and sandaled man wearing a zoot suit and a porkpie hat. Jonathan lifted his arm and squinted at Yank. "I can dig it," he said, getting into the spirit of the thing.

"First thing, of course, you'll need a gun." Yank's tone was heavily serious. He'd been around. He knew about these things.

Jonathan dropped his arm back over his eyes and sighed. It was just like working again for CII. A kind of inefficient, rural CII. Each event had a lived-in feeling. "Right. Of course. The gun. I don't want to carry it. But it should be in my flat when I return."

"Gotcha. The Mayfair flat, or the one on Baker Street?"

"Baker Street. And I'll need *two* guns. One in the bottom of my shirt drawer, covered by three or four shirts and surrounded by rolled-up socks. The second above it, covered by only one shirt."

"Whatever you say, man. You snap the whip; we'll make the trip. But why two guns hidden in the same place?" Then it dawned. "Oh, I get it! If they search the room, they'll find the top gun and not look further for the other one. Now *that* is what cool is all about!"

Jonathan lifted his arm and looked at Yank to ascertain if he was real.

"What kind of guns will you be wanting? Our MI–6 lads run to Italian automatics."

"I know they do. They're deadly as far as you can throw them. I want American-made .45 revolvers—five cartridges in, and the hammer down on an empty."

"Not an automatic?"

"No. If there's a misfire, I want something coming up."

"They're awfully bulky, you know." Yank blushed involuntarily. "But then, of course, you know."

Jonathan sighed and sat up. "Listen, when I bring the guns along, I won't be going to a party. And I won't care if the handles match my cummerbund. I am not MI–6."

"Yes. Of course. Sorry." The American accent had disappeared again.

Jonathan lay back and rubbed his temples. "Another thing. Have someone who knows his business dumdum the bullets."

Yank's sporting sense was offended.

"Tell whoever does it that I want to be able to spin a man around if I only hit him in the hand. Lead slugs without jackets. Points both scooped out and crosshatched."

"Yes," Yank said coldly. "I quite understand."

Jonathan smiled to himself. Yank really had no stomach for his job. The romance and peekaboo of being a government agent doubtless appealed to him, but, as his reaction to the Feeding Station had shown, the grisly "wet work" of the business upset him.

But he recovered quickly. "When you get back to your pad, you'll find everything A-okay. I suppose you'll want a box of cartridges? Taped under the toilet top, maybe," he added helpfully.

Jonathan laughed aloud. If he couldn't do it with ten shots, it would be because he was too dead.

"OK. So much for the gun. After tea, you'll be having a little brushup with The Sergeant. He's a top man in both judo and karate. Marine champion in his day. You could learn a lot from him."

Jonathan nodded absently.

Yank swung his feet down from the dresser. "Right. See you later, alligator."

As he left, Jonathan returned to rubbing his temples. "After a while . . . ," he mumbled.

Jonathan and Maggie took tea together in a corner of the phony Tudor dining room beneath a window. She was quiet and distant, and he assumed she was thinking about her role as an inside person at The Cloisters. He was willing to let the silence lie over them. They no longer needed to touch or to talk.

Briefly, a warm sun penetrated the hanging clouds and touched her cupric hair. The light was vagrant and indirect, seeming to come from within the hair, as gloamings seem to rise from the ground. She was looking down, and her eyes were half hidden by her soft lashes.

"You're a beautiful woman, Maggie Coyne," he said matter-of-factly.

She looked up at him, the bottle green eyes caught in a triangle of sunlight.

The light dimmed out as the sun disappeared into a wrap of misty clouds.

Then Yank arrived. "We gotta get to gettin'," he said brightly. "The Sergeant's waiting on you in the exercise room."

Jonathan smiled good-bye to Maggie and followed Yank out of the dining room. As they passed through the lounge, he picked up a back copy of *Punch* and started thumbing through it idly as they mounted the stairs.

From within the exercise room came the sound of guttural grunts, a shouted open vowel, then, as they entered, the splatting thud of a man being slammed down on the mats.

The room was a converted library with its paneled walls incongruously covered with hanging tumbling mats, as was the parqueted floor. It was directly above the pub, and there was a faint odor of stale beer rising from the floor and mixing with the saline smell of sweat. Henry was just rising from the mats slowly and painfully while another Loo man was kicking at a mat-wrapped beam, his toes curled to take the impact on the balls of his feet. He shouted with each blow as he shifted his practice from a front attack to a lateral one.

In the center of the room, large and hulking in his loosely bound judo jacket, was The Sergeant, his heavy frame oddly graceful as he shuffled toward Henry who was crouched in a defensive posture. Jonathan knew that The Sergeant had seen them enter and would do something to impress him, and he mildly pitied Henry.

Yank leaned against the padded wall and watched in silent admiration as The Sergeant stalked his prey, not bothering to feint and grunt. He carried his hands a bit too high. Bait for the trap, Jonathan thought. Henry feinted at The Sergeant, then went in to take advantage of the high guard. A clutch at the jacket, a sweeping kick, and Henry was in the air.

He was not able to lay out fully and achieve the flat, wide distribution fall that would absorb most of the impact, and he came down on one shoulder with a liquid nasal grunt.

Stepping over Henry, and pretending to see them for the first time, The Sergeant said, "Well, bless me if it isn't the American doctor." He was confident and at his ease, for this was *his* ground.

Jonathan's face was bland. "That was amazing," he said, and The Sergeant thought he detected a hint of nervousness in the way he fingered the magazine.

"Just training, mate. Well, let's get to it. What's your pleasure? Judo? Karate?"

Jonathan looked around helplessly at the other men in the room, who were watching him with much interest and some amusement. The Sergeant had been talking about this encounter all day. "Well, actually, neither one. I suppose you've read my records from CII." He laughed hollowly. "Everyone else seems to have."

The Sergeant closed the distance between them and stood looking down at Jonathan from a three-inch height advantage, his thumbs hooked in his loosely tied black belt. "I looked over the part the Guv give me. But I couldn't make no sense of it. Where it should read 'level of competence,' it said something odd."

"Yes." Jonathan walked past The Sergeant and sat down at a little library table in a protected alcove, set back out of the way of the combatants. The chair he selected left the only vacant one in the corner of the room. "I believe the records said 'not qualified, but passed.'"

"Right. That was it. Now, what the bloody hell is that supposed to mean?"

Jonathan shrugged and looked up at him with diffident, wide eyes. "Well, it's a peculiar thing. It means that I've never qualified myself in any hand-to-hand sport. Boxing, judo, karate—none of them. But the instructors—men like you—saw fit to pass me anyway."

The Sergeant crossed and stood over him. "Well, you'll not find anything slipshod like that in Loo. If I pass you, you're damned right qualified."

"I suppose you know what's best. But I'd like to explain something to you." Jonathan searched hard for the right words, and as he did so, he stared absentmindedly at The Sergeant's crotch. Growing uncomfortable, The Sergeant shuffled for a moment, then sat down in the corner chair opposite Jonathan.

Jonathan's demeanor was uncertain. "Well, if I explain this weird thing to you, perhaps you can give me some pointers that will help me improve my tactics."

"That's what I'm here for, mate."

"You see. Although I have never learned much about formal methods of fighting, I almost always win. Isn't that odd?"

The Sergeant regarded the slim body across from him. "I'd say you were bloody jammy."

"Perhaps," Jonathan admitted openly. "But there's more to it than that. You see, when I was a boy, I knocked around on the streets. And I was fairly lightweight then too. But I had to find some way to stay in one piece when it came to Fist City." He smiled wanly. "As it did from time to time."

Yank made mental note of the term "Fist City." He would use it someday.

"And how did you manage that?" The Sergeant asked, obviously bored with this talk and eager to get on with it.

"Well, for one thing, I seem to be able to lull the other man into a sense of security. Then, too, I learned that no fight has to last more than five seconds, and the man who lands the first two blows inevitably wins, if he is not bound to conventions of sportsmanship, or to the effete nonsense of any given technique."

The Sergeant wasn't sure, but he felt that there was a knock at his trade in that somewhere. His shoulders squared perceptibly.

Jonathan treated him to the gentle clouded smile that other men had recalled in retrospect. "You see, there's a period of warming up in any fight. The bowing and shuffling of judo; the angry words before a barroom brawl. And I learned that I could do best by attacking with whatever weapon was handy while the other fellow was still pumping himself up for the fight."

The Sergeant snorted, "That's all very well and good, *if* there's a weapon handy."

Jonathan shrugged. "Oh, there's always a weapon handy. A brick, a belt, a pencil—"

"A pencil!" The Sergeant roared with laughter, then addressed the small audience. "You 'ear this? The yank here toughs up his opponents by tappin' 'em on the head with a pencil! Must take a while!"

Jonathan recalled an incident in Yokohama in which his assailant had ended with a Ticonderoga #3 driven in four inches between his ribs. But he grinned sheepishly at The Sergeant's derision.

For his part The Sergeant no longer felt anger toward Jonathan. It was now scorn. He had seen this kind before. All lip and sass until it came down to the mats.

"No, now really, Sergeant. There must be a dozen useful weapons in this room," Jonathan protested through the light laughter of the lookers-on.

"Like *what*, for instance?"

Jonathan looked around almost helplessly. "Well, like ... I don't know ... like this magazine, for instance."

The Sergeant looked disdainfully at the *Punch* on the table between them. "And what would you do with that? Read him the jokes and make him laugh himself to death?" He was pleased with himself for getting off a good one.

"Well, you could ... well, look. If I rolled it up tight, like this. See? Now, wait. You have to get it tight. And when it's compact it weighs more than a stick of wood of the same size. And you know how sharp the edges of paper are. The end here could really cut a fellow up."

"Could it just? Well—"

Eight seconds later he was on his back in a litter of table and chairs, and Jonathan stood over him, the back of an inverted chair crushing hard against his larnyx. Blood oozed from The Sergeant's eye socket, where the end of the magazine had been jabbed home with a cutting, twisting motion. The thrust into his stomach had brought The Sergeant's hands down and had left his nose undefended for the crunching upward smash of the magazine that broke it with pain that eddied to his gut and the back of his throat. The flat-handed cymbals slap on his ears had punctured the eardrums with air implosion, so he could barely hear what Jonathan growled at him from between clenched teeth.

"What are you going to do now, Sergeant?"

The Sergeant couldn't answer. He was gagging under the pressure of the chair in his throat, and his temples throbbed with the pulse of blocked blood.

"What are you going to do now?" Jonathan's voice was guttural and subhuman. He was in the white fury necessary to key himself to put bigger men away so totally that they never thought of coming back after him.

The Sergeant managed a strangled sound. He couldn't see well through the blood, but he caught a terrifying glimpse of Jonathan's glassy, gray green eyes.

Jonathan closed his eyes for a second and breathed deeply, calming himself from within. The adrenaline rush was still a lump in his stomach.

He spoke quietly. "I could have done that with half the punishment. But I figured the apologetic little man in my bathroom owed you something."

He released the pressure and set the chair aside. As he pulled down his cuffs so that the proper one-half inch protruded from his jacket, he said, "I'll bet I know the words you're looking for, Sergeant: not qualified, but passed. Right?"

Jonathan was sitting alone in the hotel bar, sipping a double Laphroaig when Yank joined him.

"Oh, brother! You really whipped his pudding for him. Had it coming, I reckon."

171

Jonathan finished his drink. "You reckon that, do you?"

Yank slid onto the barstool next to him. "I guess you'll be going back to London in the morning. When you get to your flat, you'll find a list of telephone numbers there—one for each day. You can use them to keep me informed of your progress, and I'll pass the good word on to the Guv. Any questions?"

None small enough for Yank to handle.

"Oh, yeah," Yank said. "About this Vanessa Dyke. I suppose you'll be getting in contact with her to get an angle on entrée into The Cloisters. Do you want me to have her watched until you get there?"

"Christ, no."

"But the Guv said that she—"

"She probably met your Parnell-Greene by coincidence."

"Maybe. But she was the last person he reported having met before we found him dead. Of course, you could be right. Maybe it was just a case of two queers getting together to compare notes. Right?"

Jonathan tilted his head back and looked at him coldly. "Miss Dyke is an old friend."

"Sure, but—"

"Get out of here."

"Now, wait a minute. I have—"

"Out. Out."

Yank shuffled nervously for a moment, then he cleared his throat and tried to make an exit without loss of face. "OK, then. I'll be getting back to the city." He made a slow fanning gesture with the fingers of one hand. "Later, sweet patater."

Yank had gone back to London, and Henry had taken The Sergeant to a doctor in the village to attend to his nose and eye, and to see if anything could be done about his hearing, so Jonathan and Maggie had the dining room to themselves. A heavy rain had descended with the evening, enveloping the inn in the white noise of frying bacon. A draft fluttered the candle between them, and she rubbed her upper arms as though she were cold. She wore the muted green paisley gown she had worn on their first evening together—only three nights ago, was it?

Despite moments of laughter and animation, their contact was uncertain and frail, and several times he realized that they had been silent for rather a long time, each in his own thoughts. With a little effort he would pick it up again, but the chat invariably thinned into silence again.

"... they tend to be blue this time of year, don't they?"

He had been staring at the rain streaks on the window. "What? Pardon me?"

"Tangerines."

"Oh. Yes." He looked out the window again, then he frowned and looked back to her. "Blue?"

She laughed. "You were miles away."

"True. I'm sorry."

"You're leaving in the morning?"

"Hm-m."

"Going to take up this line of contact through your friend ... ah?"

"Vanessa Dyke. Yes, I suppose so. It seems the only angle we've got on getting me into The Cloisters. I can't believe she really has anything to do with all this, though."

173

"I hope not. I mean, if she's a friend of yours, I hope not."

"Me too." He tilted back his head and looked at her for a moment. "The Vicar told me you were to be placed inside The Cloisters."

She nodded, then she examined the cheese board with sudden discretionary interest. He realized that she was trying to pass over the thing, make it seem less important than it was. "Yes," she said. "They've found a way to locate me inside by tomorrow night. Would you like a little of this Brie? It's Brie de Meaux, I think."

"Brie de Melun, actually. It'll be dangerous inside there, you know."

"You know, I'm as bad at cheese as I am at wine."

"The Vicar said you volunteered to work inside."

"Did he?" Her arched eyebrows and playful green eyes slowly dissolved to a calmer, less protected gaze, then she lowered her lashes and looked at the cheese knife, which she aimlessly pushed back and forth with her finger. "I guess I lack great moral strength. I can't carry such burdens as guilt and shame very far. By helping you now, I hope I'll be able to convince myself that I've made up for getting you into this thing. Because . . ." She looked up at him and smiled. "Because . . . I've grown a little fond of you, sir." The saccharinity of this last was diluted by her broad comic brogue.

Her hand was available for pressing, but that was hardly the kind of thing Jonathan would do.

They got through coffee and cognac without any need for conversation. The rain had stopped, and the enveloping sound that had gone unnoticed was

174

palpable in its absence. The new, denser silence contributed to the emptiness of the drafty dining room and the dimming of candle flames drowning in melted wax to produce a voided, autumnal ambience.

"They've put a car at my disposal," Jonathan said, voicing the last step of a thought pattern. "I suppose I could go into London tonight. Get my mind sorted out against tomorrow."

"Yes. You could."

"Then I'd be able to call on Vanessa first thing in the morning."

"Shall I come help you pack?"

"Do you think that's wise?"

"No."

"Come help me pack."

It was early dawn when he loaded his suitcase into the yellow Lotus, pressing the boot closed so as not to disturb the misty silence. His hands came up wet from the coating of dew that smoked the car. A bird sounded a tentative note, as though seeking avian support for his suspicion that this grudging gray might be morning. No confirmation was forthcoming. There was no sky.

"Yes," he muttered to himself, "but what about the early worm?"

The interior of the car was coldly humid, and it smelled new. He turned on the wipers to clear the windscreen of condensation, then he looked up toward the window of her room before pressing the stiff gearbox into reverse and easing back over the crunching gravel.

He had untangled himself from her carefully and eased out of bed so as not to disturb her. Her position had not changed when he returned from the bathroom, dressed and shaven. He had looked up at her with a wince when the locks of his suitcase snapped too loudly, but she didn't move. As he eased the door open, she said in a voice so clear he knew she had been awake for some time.

"Keep well."

"You too, Maggie."

Putney

The Lotus was tight and the roads were clear that early in the morning, so Jonathan pulled into the parking area of the Baker Street Hotel far too early to telephone Vanessa, who was a constitutionally nocturnal animal. He bought a few newspapers in the lobby and ordered breakfast sent up to his penthouse flat, and an hour later he was sitting before an untidy tray, newspapers littered around him. Time passed torpidly, and he found himself staring through the page of print, his mind on the unknown persona of Maximilian Strange. With sudden decision, he rose and located Sir Wilfred Pyles's number in his rotary file. After a sequence of guardian secretaries at the U.K. Cultural Commission, Sir Wilfred's hearty and gruffly civil voice said, "Jon! How good of you to call so early in the morning."

"Yes, I'm sorry about that."

"Quite all right. Coincidentally, I just opened a letter from that academic wallah—whatshisname, the Welshman?"

"fforbes-Ffitch?"

"That's the one. Seems he has a plot to send you

off to Sweden on some kind of lecture series. Asked me to use my good offices to persuade you to go."

"He doesn't give up easily."

"Hm-m. National trait of the Welsh. They call it laudable determination; others see it as obtuse bull-headedness. Still, one becomes used to it. Teachers and baritones constitute the major exports of Wales, and one can't blame them for trying to be rid of both. But look here, if you are determined to scatter gems of insight on the saline soil of the Vikings, you can count on the commission's support."

"That's not what I called you about."

"Ah-ha."

"I need a bit of information."

"If it's within my power."

"How are your contacts at MI-5?"

"Oh." There was a prolonged pause at the other end of the line. "*That* kind of information, is it? As I told you, I've been on the beach for several years."

"But surely your contacts haven't dried up."

"Oh, I suppose I still have some of that influence that accompanies the loss of power. But before we go further, Jon ... you're not up to any nastiness, are you?"

"Fred!"

"Hm-m. I warn you, Jon—"

"Just a background check—maybe with an Interpol input."

"I see." Sir Wilfred was capable of subarctic tones.

"I want you to run down a name for me. Will you do it?"

"You are absolutely sure you're not engaged in

anything that will bring discomfort to the government."

"I could mention times when we were working together and *you* were strung out."

"Please spare me. All right. The name?"

"Maximilian Strange. Any bells?"

"A faint tinkle. But it's been years since I've been involved in all that. Very well. I'll call you later this afternoon."

"I'd better call you. I can't be sure of my schedule."

"I'll need a little time. About five?"

"About five."

"Now I have your word, haven't I, that you're not up to anything detrimental to our side? Because if you are, Jon, I shall be actively against you."

"Don't worry. I'm working for the White Hats. And if anything were to blow, you could rely on 'maximum deniability.' "

Sir Wilfred laughed. They had always made fun of the advertising agency argot that riddled CII communications.

"If any questions come up, Fred, just pass the buck to me."

"Precisely what I had intended to do, old man."

"You're a good person."

"I've always felt that. Ciao, Jon."

"Tchüss."

After waiting another long half hour, Jonathan dialed Vanessa Dyke's number. He arranged to drop over for a cup of tea and a chat. She seemed a little reluctant to meet him, but their friendship of years turned the trick. After he hung up, he spent a few minutes looking out his window over Regent's Park, sorting himself out. Two things had bothered him about the conversation with Van. Her speech had been blurred, as though she had been drinking. And the first question she had asked was: "Are you all right, Jon?"

He had never visited Vanessa in London, and the minute he stepped from the Underground station, he felt that this part of Putney was an odd setting for her vivacious, pungent personality. The high street was typical of the urban concentrations south of the river, its modest Victorian charm scabbed over by false fronts of enameled aluminum and glass brick; short rows of derelict town houses stared blind through uncurtained and broken windows, awaiting destruction and replacement by shopping centers; the visual richness of decay was diluted here and there by the mute cube of a modern bank; and there were several cheap cafes featuring yawning waitresses and permanent table decorations of crumbs and spills.

Clouds and smoke hung in umber compound close above the housetops, and a dirty drizzle made the pavements oily. Every woman pushed a pram containing a shopping bag, a laundry bag, and, presumably, a baby; and every man shuffled along with his head down.

Monserrat Street was a double row of shabby brick row houses, built with a certain architectural nostalgia for Victorian comfort and permanence, but with the cheaper materials and sloppier craftsmanship of the 1920s. The shallow gardens were tarnished and scruffy, the occasional autumn flower dulled by soot, and all looking as though they were maintained by the aged and the indifferent. An abnormal number of houses were vacant and placarded for sale, an indication that West Indians were approaching the neighborhood.

The garden at #46 was a pleasant contrast to the rest. Even this late in the season, and even in this color-sucking weather, there was an arresting balance and control that used the limited space comfortably. The hydrangeas were particularly consonant with the district and the mood of the climate; moist and subtle in mauve, blue, and tarnished white.

"Tragedy struck the life of noted art critic and scholar when his swinging, ballsy image was abruptly shattered yesterday afternoon." Van stood at her door, leaning against the bright green frame, a glass of whiskey and a cigarette in the same hand.

"Hello, Van."

". . . Bystanders report having observed this internationally notorious purveyor of manly charm engaged in the mundane and middle-class activity of admiring hydrangeas."

"OK. OK."

". . . Reports differ as to the exact hue of the flowers under question. Dr. Hemlock refuses comment, but his reticence is taken by many to be a tacit admission that he is becoming older, mellower, and—so far as this reporter can see—wetter with each minute he stands out there. Why don't you come in?"

He followed her into a dark overfurnished parlor, its Victorian fittings, beaded lampshades, antimacassars, and velvet drapes the antithesis of the black-and-white enamel, ultramodern apartment that had been hers when first they met in New York fifteen years earlier. Only the Swiss typewriter on a spool table by the window and a tousled stack of notes on the sill gave evidence of her profession. It was difficult to imagine that her regular flow of journalistic art criticism, with its insight and acid, had its source in this quaint and comfortable room.

"Want a drink, Jon?"

"No, thank you."

"Why not? Somewhere on the high seas at this moment, the sun is over the yardarm."

"No, thanks."

She dropped into a wing chair. "So? To what do I owe the honor?"

Jonathan toyed with a vase of cut hydrangeas on the court cupboard. "Why are you trying to make me feel uncomfortable, Van?"

She ignored his question. "I hate hydrangeas. You know that? They smell like women's swimming caps. Similarly, I hate flowery oriental teas. They smell like actresses' handbags. You'll notice I didn't say 'purses.' That's because I abhor sexual imagery. It's also because I eschew olfactory inaccuracy." She leaned back against the wing of the chair and looked at him for a second. "You're right. I'm feeling nasty, and I'm sorry if I'm making you uncomfortable. 'Cause we're old friends, pal-buddy-pal. You know what? You are the only straight in the world with soul."

Jonathan sat opposite her in a floral armchair, not because he felt like sitting, but because it seemed unfair to stand over her when she was so obviously distressed and off-balance. He had never heard her throw up so thick a haze of words to hide in. Her back was to the window, and its wet, diffused light illuminated her face with unkind surgical accuracy. The short black hair, semé with gray, looked lifeless, and the lines etched in her thin face constituted a hieroglyphic biography of wit and bitterness, laughter and intelligence—accomplishment without fulfillment.

"How are the Christians treating you, madam?" he asked, recalling the opening cue of a habitual pattern of banter from the old days.

She didn't pick up the cue. "Oh, Jon, Jon. We grow old, Father Jonathan, lude sing goddamn. Well, to hell with them all, darling. A pestilence on their shanties—wattles, clay, and all. And the lues take their virgin daughters." She lit a cigarette from the stub of the last. "Let's get to your business. I suppose it's about that guy I introduced you to at Tomlinson's? The guy with the Marini Horse?"

"No. Matter of fact, I'd forgotten all about him."

"He hasn't contacted you again since that evening?"

"No."

He could see the tension drain from her face. "I'm glad, Jon. He's a good person to avoid. A real bad actor."

"He pays well, though."

"Faust could have said that. Well then! If it's not the Marini Horse, what impels you to break in on my matronly solitude?"

He paused and collected himself before launching into what was sure to be an imposition on an old friendship. "I'm in some trouble, Van."

She laughed. "Don't worry about it. These days, it's no worse than a bad cold."

"I have to get into The Cloisters."

For a moment, she was suspended in mid-gesture, reaching for her glass. Then she looked him flat in the eyes, shifting her glance from one pupil to the other, her eyes narrowed in her attempt to analyze his intent. She sat back deep in her chair and sipped her drink in cold silence.

After a time she said, "Why The Cloisters? That isn't your kind of action. Too baroque."

"We grow old, Mother Vanessa. We need help."

"Oh, bullshit!"

"OK. I told you I was in trouble. Explaining will deepen my trouble. And it might give you some. I'm mixed up with some nasty people, and they'll do old Jonathan in, unless he can get into The Cloisters and accomplish something for them."

"And you came here to cash in old debts of friendship."

"Yes."

"Dirty bastard."

"Yes."

She stood up and wiped the haze off a pane of the window, and for a while she stared out past the garden and rain to the dull brick façades across the street. She ran her fingers through her cropped hair and tugged hard at a handful. Then she turned to him. "Now I *insist* you have a drink with me."

"Done."

She poured out a good tot of Laphroaig and passed him the glass. Then she perched herself up on the wide windowsill and spoke while looking out on the rain, squinting one eye against the smoke that curled up from the cigarette in the corner of her mouth. "I'd better tell you first off that you're in more trouble than you know. I mean ... Jon, I don't know how much pressure these people can bring to bear on you to force you to try to get into The Cloisters, but it better be pretty big league. Because The Cloisters people are maximal bad asses. They could kill you, Jon. Honest to God."

"I know."

"Do you? I wonder. You remember reading about this Parnell-Greene? The one in the tower of St. Martin's? The Cloisters people did that. And think of *how* they did it, Jon. That wasn't just a killing. That was an advertisement. A warning in good ol' Chicago gangland style."

"I've been filled in on Maximilian Strange's response to intruders."

She drew a very long oral breath. "Maximilian Strange. Jon, you're in worse trouble than I thought. I wish I could tell you. But if I did, I'd run a fair risk of being killed. I know that I've often described my life as a pile of shit." She smiled wanly. "But it's the only pile of shit I've got."

Jonathan leaned forward and took her hand. "Van, I'm very sorry you're in this thing at all. I'm not asking you to get me into The Cloisters yourself, because I know they could trace it back to you. Just put me onto someone who can. You know it's important, or I wouldn't ask."

She stood and set her glass aside. "Let me think about it while I make us a pot of tea. We'll drink tea and watch the rain."

"Sounds fine. I'd like that."

As he glanced over the titles of some of her books, she made tea in the kitchen, talking to him all the while in a heightened voice. "You know, scruffy and middle class though it is, I really love this house, Jonathan. I bought it, and fixed it up, and painted it, and swore at the plumbing—all by myself. And I love it. Especially at night when I'm working by the window and I can watch nameless people shuffle by in the rain. Or on days like this, drinking tea."

"It's a great place, Van."

"Yeah. You're about the only person from the old New York bunch who would understand that. The little row house, the antimacassars, the mauve hydrangeas—all pretty far from the image I used to cut."

"True. Even the other evening at Tomlinson's you were still playing it for superbutch."

"I know it's silly. I just feel impelled to be the first to say it. You know what I mean?"

"I know.

"What?"

"I know!"

"Still. This is the real me. Little lady peeking through lace curtains. Cup of tea in hand. Brilliant statement taking form on my typewriter. Gas fire hissing in hearth. Christ, I'll be glad when I get so old I'm never horny. Being on the hunt makes you act such a fool." She came in with a small pot under a cozy and two Spode cups, and pulled her chair up close to his and poured. "I used to fear the thought of becoming an ugly old woman. But now that I'm there, I can tell you this: It beats hell out of being an ugly young girl."

Jonathan raised his cup. "Cheers."

"Cheers, Jon."

They drank in silence as the rain stiffened against the window.

"Grace," she said at last.

"Madam?"

"The person who can get you into The Cloisters. A really beautiful black woman who owns a club in Chelsea. She's very close to Strange."

"Her name is Grace?"

"Yes. Amazing Grace. Kind of a stage name, I suppose. A nom de guerre. Her club is superposh with expensive drinks and cute little black hookers with tiny waists and fine wide asses. But she's the real attraction herself."

"Beautiful?"

"Oh Christ yes!"

"Amazing Grace. Great name."

"Great chick. Her place is called the Cellar d'Or. It doesn't open until midnight."

Jonathan finished his tea and put down the cup. "I better get a lot of sleep before I go over there. It may be a long night."

Vanessa walked him to the door. "Listen, old friend and aging stud, you'll take real care of yourself, won't you?"

"I will. Now, let's think about you. Is there somewhere you could go for a few days? Somewhere well away from here?"

"I see your point. There's a woman I know in Devon. She writes mysteries."

". . . and she lives in a cottage, keeps a Siamese cat, and drinks red wine."

Her eyebrows lifted.

"No, I don't know her, Van. It's just that people love to play out their stereotypes."

"Even you?"

"Probably. But it's hard to recognize. I'm a typical example of a species of which there is only one living specimen."

"Blowhard bastard."

"Right family, but what's the genus?"

"Wiseass?"

"I didn't know you were up on animal taxonomy. But seriously, Van. You will get out of town, won't you?"

"Yes, I will."

"This afternoon?"

"I have a little work to do. I'll get through it as soon as I can."

"Make sure you do."

She smiled. "For a cold-blooded bastard, you're not a bad guy. Come, give us a big hug."

They embraced firmly.

Halfway down the walk, he stopped to smell the wet hydrangeas again. "I've got a problem," he told Vanessa who was leaning against the bright green door, the Gauloise dangling from her lips. "I can't remember what bathing caps smell like."

"Like hydrangeas," Van said.

Back in the gaudy Baker Street flat, he stretched full length on the bed he and Maggie had used a few days before. Beyond the windows, a cold wet evening had already descended, and he lay in the growing gloom, alone and unmoving, putting himself together for whatever lay ahead at the Cellar d'Or.

Amazing Grace. Outlandish name, but somehow consonant with this whole bizarre business. This was not at all like his sanction experiences with CII.

Those had been simple mechanical affairs. He had taken an assignment only when he really needed the money, and had gone to Berne or Montreal or Rome, met a Search agent who had already done all the background work, and received the complete tout on the target: his habits, the layout of his home or office, his daily routine. And after working it out, he had walked in, performed the sanction, and walked away. They were never real people; only faceless beings, most of them examples of the humanoid fungus that populates the world of espionage—scabs and pus pots the world was better rid of.

And there had been very little personal danger for him. He traveled freely under his professional role of art historian. He had no motive, no personal relation to the target. He didn't even have fingerprints. CII had seen to that. When he became a sanction active, his fingerprints disappeared from all government, police, and army files.

But this Loo business was different. He hated this job, and he was afraid of it. He had quit working for Search and Sanction because his nerves had become frayed, and because his tolerance for working with well-meaning patriotic monsters had worn thin. And now he was older, and the task was more complicated. And there was Maggie to look after. The ingredients of disaster.

Shit!

But they had him. Loo and that damned vicar had him against the wall. And he wasn't going to prison for murder, even if it meant killing a dozen Maximilian Stranges.

He ran a shallow meditation unit and got some

189

rest that way, slightly under the surface of the still pond he projected on the back of his eyelids.

He snapped out of it. It was time to call Sir Wilfred Pyles.

"Don't speak," Sir Wilfred said directly they were connected. "Fifteen minutes. This number." He gave Jonathan a number, then hung up.

During the fifteen minutes before he dialed, Jonathan sat hunched over the instrument, realizing that something had tumbled. Sir Wilfred obviously couldn't use his own phone for fear of a tap and he had doubtless moved to a public phone to await the call.

The phone was picked up on the first ring. "Jon?"

"Yes."

"I assume you have the picture?"

"Yes."

"Rather like old times, eh?"

"I'm afraid so. I take it something tumbled."

"Indeed it did! You're into something very hot, Jon. I rang up an old chum in MI–5 and asked him to run a little check for me. They often do it for old boys who want to sort out a business acquaintance, or a call girl. He said he'd be delighted to. It seemed a piece of cake. But when I mentioned the name of your Maximilian Strange, he froze up and asked me to hold the line. Next thing you know, one of those intense young spy wallahs was talking to me, demanding to know details. Well, I fobbed him off as best I could, but I'm sure he saw right through me."

"So you weren't able to find out anything."

"Well, nothing directly. But their reactions speak volumes. If that constitutionally lethargic lot in MI–5 were stirred to action by the mere mention of your fellow's name, he must be top drawer. You haven't gotten to Bormann by any chance?"

"No, nothing like that."

"I'm afraid I've done you a disservice, Jon. MI–5 is on to you."

"You told them my name?"

"Of course. Surely you haven't forgotten the code of our line of work: every man for himself."

". . . and fuck the hindmost."

"You must be thinking of the Greek secret service. Well, tchüss, Jon."

"Ciao, buddy."

Jonathan raked his fingers through his hair, and took several deep oral breaths before lying back on the bed.

Shit. Shit. Shit!

He lay there for hours, forcing himself to doze occasionally. Eventually, he swung out of bed and prowled around the house for something to eat. He was not really hungry; he had taken care of that before coming up to his flat, eating a large meal of slow-burning protein; treating his body, as he used to in his mountain-climbing days, as a machine requiring the right fuel, the proper amount of rest, the correct exercise. He had eaten correctly. If there was any action tonight, it would come between midnight and three o'clock. The protein would be in mid-burn by then, and he would have consumed two or three drinks—just the right amount of fast-burning alcohol.

A goddamn machine!

It was only to fill the time and distract his mind that he looked around for food. As usual, wherever he lived, the only food in the place was a chaotic tesserae of exotic bits. He had always had a fascination for rare foods, and he enjoyed wandering about in the gourmet sections of large department stores, picking up whatever struck his fancy. His search of the kitchen produced a small jar of macadamia nuts, a tin of truffles in brine, preserved ginger, and a half bottle of Greek raisin wine. He ate the lot.

As he wandered through his flat, turning off lights behind him, it occurred to him to check the guns he had asked Yank to stash for him. His directions for concealment had been followed exactly. He took one out and examined it. The bulky blue steel .45 revolver felt heavy and cold in his hand as he snapped out the cylinder and checked the load. The slugs were scooped and a deep cross had been cut into the head of each. No range. No accuracy to speak of. The bullet would begin to tumble five yards from the barrel. But when it hit, it would splat as wide and thin as a piece of tinfoil, and a nick in the forearm would slam the victim down as though he had been struck by a train. Good professional job of dumdumming.

He considered taking one of the guns with him to Chelsea. Then he decided against it. It was impossible to conceal a howitzer like this, and a pat down would tip him before he had come within striking distance of The Cloisters and Maximilian Strange. He'd just have to be careful.

He flicked the cylinder back and replaced the gun. The phone rang.

"What's up, Doc?"

"Why are you calling, Yank?"

"Oh, I got a couple of things up my sleeve. My

arm, for one. No laugh? Oh, well. Then tell me this: How did things go with Miss Dyke?"

"I had a pleasant visit."

"And?"

"And I got a possible lead to The Cloisters."

"Oh? What was it?"

"I'll tell you about it if it works out."

"No, you'd better tell me about it now. The Vicar wants to know what you're up to at every moment. He wouldn't want to have to start back at square one if something were to happen to you. Or if you were to do something foolish."

"Like?"

"Like try to run off. Or sell out. Or something like that. Not that I really think you would. Having met the Vicar, I think you have a pretty good idea of what he would do to anyone who tried to do the dirty on him."

"Ship me off to the Feeding Station?" Jonathan brought that up on purpose.

After a swallow: "Something like that. So tell me. What is your lead to The Cloisters?"

"A woman named Grace. Amazing Grace. She runs a place called the Cellar d'Or. Mean anything to you?"

"Are you sure it's a woman?"

"What do you mean?"

"Amazing Grace is a hymn, after all. Get it?"

"Oh, for Christ's sake!"

"Sorry. No, I never heard of the woman. But I'll check through the Loo files for you. Anything else?"

"Yes. Do you have a tail on me?"

"Pardon?"

"A man's been following me all day. Out to Vanessa's and back. Is he one of yours?"

"I don't know what you mean."

"Medium build, blue raincoat, one hundred and sixty pounds, glasses, left-handed, rubbers over his shoes. He's probably standing down in the street right now, wondering how to appear to be reading his newspaper in the dark. If he's not yours, he's MI–5's. Too fucking amateur to be anything else."

"How could he be MI–5? They're not in on this."

"They are now. I made a mistake."

"The Vicar's not going to like that."

"Hard shit. Can you get in contact with MI–5 and pull this guy off? There are probably three of them, the other two out on the flanks. That's normal shadow procedure for your people."

"It could be they're only trying to help."

"Help from MI–5 is like military advice from the Egyptian army. If you don't get rid of them, I'll do it myself, and that will hurt them. I don't want them blowing my scant cover. Remember, I'm the only man you've got in the game."

"Not quite. We've managed to situate Miss Coyne."

"Oh?"

Yank was instantly aware that he had breached security. "More about that later, when we get together with the Vicar for a final briefing. Meanwhile, good hunting tonight. See you in the funny papers."

Jonathan hung up and crossed to the window to look down on the man who had followed him from Vanessa's. Christ, he was getting sick of British espionage. Sick of this whole thing. He indulged his anger for a while, then brought it under control by taking shallow breaths. Calm. Calm. You make mistakes when you're angry. Calm.

Chelsea

As Jonathan stepped from the Underground train at Sloane Square, he was still being followed by the fool in the blue raincoat who had been with him since Vanessa's. Presumably, Yank had not been able to get through to MI-5 and give them the word to discontinue surveillance. Jonathan decided to let him hover out there on his flank. At least he could keep an eye on him until the time came to shake him off, should the shadowing seem to endanger his cover.

Halfway up the tiled exit tunnel he passed an American girl sitting on a parka. Flotsam of the flower tide. She abused a cheap guitar and whined a Guthrie lament, having chosen a spot where the echo would enrich her thin voice with bathroom resonances and allow her to slide off miscalculated notes under the cover of reverberation. She was barefoot, and there was a large rip in the stomach of her tugged and shapeless khaki sweater. The surface of the parka was salted with small coins to invite passersby to contribute to maintenance.

Jonathan dropped no coin, nor did the man following in the blue raincoat.

Once away from the square, he closed into himself as he walked along seeking the address Vanessa had given him. He had no desire to come into contact with the jostling crowds of street people. It had been fifteen years since last he had been in Chelsea. In those days, a few of the young people who chatted in pubs or made single cups of cappuccino last two hours eventually went home to paint or write. But not these youngsters. They neither produced nor supported. Chelsea had always been self-consciously artsy, but now it had become younger, less attractive, more American. Head shops crowded up against the Safeway, and jeans were to be had in a thousand varieties. Discotheques. Whiskey a go-gos. Boutiques with scented candles and merchandise of green stamp quality. Shops vied for obscure names. Tall girls with hunched shoulders clopped along the pavement, and peacock boys swaggered in flared suits of plum velvet, cuffs flapping with dysfunctional bells. Rancorous music bled from doorways. People in satchel-assed jeans stared sullenly at him, an obvious representative of "the establishment," that despised class that oppressed them and paid their doles.

He had hoped the young would spare Chelsea the humiliation they had inflicted on San Francisco, Greenwich Village, the Left Bank. And he was angry that they had not.

But after all, he mused, one had to be fair-minded. These youngsters had their virtues. They were doubtless more content than his generation, hooked as it was on the compulsion to achieve. And these young people were more at peace with life; more alert to ecological dangers; more disgusted by war; more socially conscious.

Useless snots.

He turned off into a side street, past a couple of antique shops, and continued along a row of private houses behind black iron fences. Each had a steep stone stairway leading down to a basement. And one of these descending caves was illuminated by a dim red light. This was the Cellar d'Or.

He sat watching the action from his nook at the back of one of the artificial plaster grottoes that constituted the Cellar d'Or's decor. The light was dim and the carpets jet black, and the uninitiated had to be careful of their footing. The fake stone grottoes were inset with chunks of fool's gold, and all the other surfaces, the tables, the bar, were clear plastic in which bits of sequins and gold metal were entrapped. The glow lighting came from within these plastic surfaces, illuminating faces from beneath. And the air between objects was black.

He sipped at his second, very wet Laphroaig served, as were all the drinks in the club, in a small gold metal chalice. The most insistent feature of the club's bizarre interior was a large photographic transparency that revolved in the center of the room. It was lit from within, and every eye was drawn frequently to the woman who smiled from the full-length photograph. She stood beside what appeared to be a very high marble fireplace, her steady, mildly mischievous gaze directed at the camera and, therefore, at each man in the room, no matter where he sat. She was nude, and her body was extraordinary. A mulatto with café au lait skin, her breasts were

conical and impertinent, her waist slight, her hips
wide, and perfectly molded legs drew the eye to
small, well-formed feet, the toes of which were
slightly splayed, like those of a yawning cat. The
black triangle of her écu appeared cotton soft, but it
was something about the muscles and those splayed
toes that held Jonathan's attention. Stomach, arm,
leg, and hip, there was a look of lean, hard muscle
under the powdery brown skin—steel cable under
silk.

That would be Amazing Grace.

The Cellar d'Or was essentially a whorehouse.
And a rather good one. All the help—the chippies,
the barmen, the waiters—were West Indian, and the
music, its volume so low it seemed to fade when
one's attention strayed from it, was also West Indian. Despite the general air of ease and rest, the
place was moving a fair amount of traffic. Men
would arrive, and during their first drink they would
be joined by one of the girls who sat in twos and
threes at the most distant tables. Another drink or
two and some light chat, and the couple would disappear. The girl would return, usually alone, within
a half hour. And all this action was presided over by
a smiling giant of a majordomo who stood by the
door or at the end of the bar and watched over the
patrons and the whores with a broad benevolent
smile, his jet black head shaved and glistening with
reflections of gold. Nothing in his manner, save the
feline control of his walk, gave him the look of the
professional bouncer, but Jonathan could imagine
the cooling effect he would have on the occasional
troublemaker, descending on him like a smiling machine of fate and disposing of him with a single

rapid gesture that most insouciant lookers-on would mistake for a friendly pat on the shoulder. The giant wore a close-fitting white turtlenecked jersey that displayed a pattern of muscles so marked that, even at rest, he appeared to be wearing a Roman breastplate under his shirt. In age, he could have been anywhere from thirty to fifty.

One of the girls detached herself from a co-worker and approached Jonathan's table. She was the second to do so, and she looked very nice indeed as she crossed the floor: full-busted, long-legged, and an ass that moved hydraulically.

"You would care to buy me a drink?" she asked, her accent and phrasing revealing that she was a recent immigrant.

Jonathan smiled good-naturedly. "I'd be delighted to buy you a drink. But I'd rather you drank it back at your own table."

"You don't like me?"

"Of course I like you. I've liked you ever since we first met. It's just that . . ." He took her hand and assumed his most tragic expression. "It's just . . . you see, I had this nasty accident while I was driving golf balls in my shower and . . ." He turned his head aside and looked down.

"You are joking me," she said, not completely sure.

"In fact, I am. But I do have some serious advice for you. Did you see that fellow who came in here after I did? The one with the blue raincoat?"

She looked over toward the far corner, then wrinkled her nose.

"Oh, I know," Jonathan said, "he's not as pretty as I am. But he's loaded with money, and he came

199

here because he's shy with women. When you first approach him, he'll pretend he doesn't want anything to do with you. But that's just a front. Just a game he plays. You keep at him, and by morning you'll have enough money to buy your man a suit."

She gave him a sidelong glance of doubt.

"Why would I lie to you?" Jonathan said, offering his palms.

"You sure?"

He closed his eyes and nodded his head, tucking down the corners of his mouth.

She left him and, after a compulsory pause at the bar so as not to seem to be flitting from one fish to another, she patted her hair down and made her way to the far corner. Jonathan smiled to himself in congratulation, sipped at his Laphroaig, and let his eyes wander over the photograph of Amazing Grace. Lovely girl. But time was passing, and he would have to make some kind of move soon if he was going to meet her.

Oh-oh. Maybe not. Here he comes.

Like everything else about the giant, his smile was large. "May I buy you a drink, sir?" Quiet though it was, his voice had a basso rumble you could feel through the table.

"That's very good of you," Jonathan said.

The giant made a gesture to the waiter, then sat down, not across from Jonathan as though to engage him in conversation, but beside him, so they were looking out on the scene together, like old friends. "This is the first time you have visited us, is it not, sir?"

"Yes. Nice place you've got here."

"It is pleasant. I am called P'tit Noel." The giant

offered a hand so large that Jonathan felt like a child shaking it.

"Jonathan Hemlock. But you're not West Indian."

P'tit Noel laughed, a warm chocolate sound. "What am I then?"

"Haitian, from your accent. Although your education has spoiled some of that."

"Very good, sir! You are observant. Actually, my mother was Haitian; my father Jamaican. She was a whore, and he a thief. Later, he went into politics and she into the hotel business."

"You might say they swapped professions."

He laughed again. "You might at that, sir. Although I was schooled in this country, I suppose something of the patois will always be with me. Now, you know everything about me. Tell me everything about yourself."

Jonathan had to smile at the disregard for subtlety. "Ah, here come the drinks."

The waiter had not needed an order. He knew what Jonathan was drinking, and evidently P'tit Noel always drank the same thing, a chalice of neat rum.

Jonathan raised his glass to the large transparency of Amazing Grace. "To the lady."

"Oh, yes. I am always glad to drink to her." He drew off the rum in two swallows and set the goblet down on the gold table.

"Beautiful woman," Jonathan said.

P'tit Noel nodded. "I am happy to know you are interested in women, sir. I was beginning to doubt. But if you are holding out for her, you waste your time. She does not go with patrons." He looked again at the photograph. "But yes. She is a beautiful woman. Actually, she is the most beautiful woman in the world." He said this last with the hint of a shrug, as though it were obvious to anyone.

"I'd like to meet her," Jonathan said as casually as possible.

"Oh, sir?" There was an almost imperceptible tensing of the pectoral muscles.

"Yes, I would. Does she ever come in?"

"Two or three times each evening. Her apartments are above."

"And when she comes, is she dressed like that?" he indicated the transparency.

"Exactly like that, sir. She is proud of her body."

"As she should be."

P'tit Noel's smile returned. "It is very good for business, of course. She comes. She takes a drink at the bar. She wanders among the tables and greets the patrons. And you would be surprised how business picks up for the girls the moment she leaves."

"I wouldn't be surprised at all, P'tit Noel."

"Ah. You pronounce my name correctly. It is obvious you are not English."

"I'm an American. I'm surprised you couldn't tell from my accent."

P'tit Noel shrugged. "All pinks sound alike."

They both laughed. But Jonathan only shallowly. "I want to meet her," he said while P'tit Noel's laugh was still playing itself out.

It stopped instantly.

"You have the eyes of a sage man, sir. Why seek pain?" He smiled, and with a sense of comradeship Jonathan noticed that the smile did not come from within. It was a coiled, defensive crinkle in the cor-

ners of the eyes. Precisely the gentle combat smile
that Jonathan assumed to put the victim off pace.

"Why are you so tight?" Jonathan asked. "Surely
many men come in here and express interest in the
lady there."

"True, sir. But such men have only love on their
minds."

"How do you know *I'm* not sperm-blind?"

P'tit Noel shook his head. "I feel it. We Haitians
have a sense for these things. We are a superstitious
people, sir. The moment you came in, I sensed that
you were trouble for Mam'selle Grace."

"And you intend to protect her."

"Oh yes, sir. With my life, if need be. Or with
yours, should it sadly come to that."

"No doubt about how it would go, is there?"
Jonathan said, skipping unnecessary steps in the
conversation.

"Actually, none at all, sir."

"There's an expression in the hill country of the
United States."

"How does it go, sir?"

"While you're gettin' dinner, I'll get a sandwich."

"Ah! The idiom is clear. And I believe you, sir.
But the fact remains that you would lose any battle
between us."

"Probably. But you would not escape pain."

"Probably."

"I'll make you a deal."

"Ah! *Now* I recognize you to be an American."

"Just tell the lady that I want to talk to her."

"She knows you then?"

"No. Tell her I want to talk about The Cloisters

203

and Maximilian Strange." Jonathan looked for the effect of the words upon P'tit Noel. There was none.

"And if she will not see you?"

"Then I'll leave."

"Oh, I *know* that, sir. I am asking if you will leave without disturbance."

Jonathan had to smile. "Without disturbance."

P'tit Noel nodded and left the table.

Five minutes later he returned. "Mam'selle Grace will see you. But not now. In one hour. You may sit and drink if you wish. I shall tell the girls that you are not a fish." His formal and clipped tone revealed that he was not pleased that Amazing Grace had deigned to receive the visitor.

Jonathan decided not to wait in the club. He told P'tit Noel that he would take a walk and return in an hour.

"As you wish, sir. But be careful on the streets. It is late, and there are *apache* about." There was as much threat in this as warning.

Jonathan walked through the tangle of back streets slowly, his hands plunged deep into his pockets. Fog churned lazily around the streetlamps of the deserted lanes. He had made a pawn gambit, and it had been passed. He had lost nothing, but his position had become passive. They now made the moves and he reacted. An hour was a long time. Time enough for Amazing Grace to contact The Cloisters. Time enough for Strange to decide. Time enough to send men. Perhaps he had made an error in not bringing a gun.

On the other hand, the Vicar had said The Cloisters people were seeking him out for some reason,

and they had been doing so even before Loo had involved him in this thing. If Strange needed him, why
would he seek to harm him? Unless they knew he
was working for Loo. And how would they know
that?

It was a goddamn merry-go-round.

Near a corner, he found a telephone kiosk. His
primary reason for leaving the Cellar d'Or had been
to phone Vanessa and make sure she was off in Devon and out of the line of fire. As the unanswered
phone double-buzzed, his eyes wandered over hastily
penned and scratched messages: doodles, telephone
numbers, an announcement that one Betty Kerney
was devoted to an exotic protein diet. There was a
sad graffito penned in a precise, cramped hand:
"Mature person seeks company of young man.
Strolls in the country and fishing. Mostly
friendship." No meeting time; no telephone number.
Just a need shared with a wall. After the phone had
rung many times, Jonathan hung up. He was relieved to know that Vanessa was out of it.

It was nearly time to return to the Cellar d'Or,
and he had seen nothing of the man in the blue raincoat since he had left him trying to disentangle himself from the coyly persistent Jamaican whore, pay
for his drink, and collect his raincoat. All this without arousing undue attention. They were an incompetent bunch. Just like the CII.

During his quiet stroll through the fog, he had decided how he would play this thing with Amazing
Grace. There were two possibilities. On the one
hand, Strange might only have her try to sound him
out—discover his reason for seeking him. In that
case Jonathan would let Grace know that he was

aware of the activities at The Cloisters and of the fact that Maximilian Strange wanted to contact him for some reason. He would tell her he was interested in anything that might prove profitable, if it was safe enough. On the other hand, Strange might have decided to send men to pick Jonathan up and bring him to The Cloisters. In this case it would be important not to seem eager to get inside. He would have to put up some resistance, enough to make it look good. He would have to hurt some of them, while he tried to avoid hurt to himself. Once inside The Cloisters, he would have to play it by ear. It would be a narrow thing.

Damn. If only he knew why Strange was trying to contact him.

He paused for a second beneath a streetlight to get his bearings back to the Cellar d'Or. The blind alley leading to the side entrance was only a block or two from here. There was a shuffling sound down the street, and he turned in time to see a figure jump from the pool of light two streetlamps away.

The blue raincoat. The last thing he needed was this MI-5 ass tagging along. It would make him appear to be bait, and he'd never talk his way out of that.

There was a second of elastic silence, then Jonathan heard another sound, borne on the fog from across the street. There were two more of them.

He ran.

He had only twenty-five yards on them as he broke into the blind mews behind the club and banged loudly at the back door. The noise echoed through the brick cavern, but there was no response. From the dustbins and garbage cans that littered the alley, he found a champagne bottle, which he clutched by the neck, thankful for the weight of the dimpled bottom as he pressed back into a shadowy niche behind a projecting corner of damp brick. The three figures appeared, strung out across the entrance of the alley. Backlit by a streetlight, their long shadows falling before them on the wet cobblestones, they looked like extras from a Carol Reed film. Jonathan could see their featureless silhouettes, mat black in a nimbus of silver phosphorescent fog. He remained motionless, his heart beating in his temples from the effort of his run and from anger at being endangered by these bungling government serfs.

They stopped halfway down the alley and exchanged some muttered words. One seemed to want to go away, another thought they should enter the Cellar d'Or and investigate. After a moment of vacillation, they decided to enter the club. Jonathan pressed back against the wall as they neared. Getting all three was going to be difficult. As they came abreast him, he brought the bottle down on the head of one with a satisfyingly solid crack. The other two jumped away, then rushed at him with well-schooled reactions. Hands clutched at him, a fist hit him on the shoulder; a shoe cracked into his shin. He jerked away with a broad backhand sweep with the bottle that made them dodge back for an instant. One grabbed up a bottle from a dustbin and hurled it. He ducked as it exploded into fragments behind him.

A shaft of light fell upon the scene as the door behind Jonathan opened and the dominating bulk of P'tit Noel filled the frame.

"Thank God," Jonathan said.

Together they waded into the hooligans, and it

was over in five seconds. Jonathan used his bottle on one; P'tit Noel struck the other with the flat palms of his open hands, loud concussing blows that splatted against his head and slammed him against the wall.

One of the men was still conscious, sitting against the brick wall, blood streaming from his nose and mouth where P'tit Noel's palm had flattened them. Another was moaning in semiconsciousness. The last was a silent heap among the garbage cans.

P'tit Noel dragged each up in turn by his lapels and held him against the wall with one hand while he opened the man's eyelids with his fingers, professionally checking the set and dilation of the pupils. "They'll live," he said, as a matter of information.

"Pity."

P'tit Noel wiped his palms on the shirt of one of the downed men. "Why don't you step in and brush yourself off, sir," he said over his shoulder. "Mam'selle Grace will see you now."

"What about these yahoos?"

"Oh, I think they will be gone by morning."

P'tit Noel conducted Jonathan to his small living quarters behind the club and offered him the use of his bathroom to clean up. He wasn't really hurt. There was some stiffness in one shoulder, his trousers stuck to his shin where the kick had brought blood, and he was experiencing the mild nausea of adrenaline recession, but he would be fine. As he stepped from the bathroom, P'tit Noel greeted him with a glass of rum, hot and soothing going down.

"You took your time answering the door."

"Actually, I did not hear you knock, sir."

"Then how come you turned up? For which, by the way, much thanks."

"Intuition. Premonition. As I told you, I am Haitian."

"Voodoo and all?"

"You know voodoo, sir?"

"Not really. No."

P'tit Noel smiled. "It exists. I passed some time studying the legal implications of crime committed under its influence. Because of the limits of my British education, I was prone to scoff at first."

"Which limitations are those?"

"The limitations of logic and evidence. Of European sequential thought."

"You were a student in Jamaica?"

"No, I was a lawyer, sir."

Jonathan admired the cool way he laid that on him. "You know, P'tit Noel, you've developed a magnificent way of saying 'sir.' When you use the word, it sounds like an arrogant insult."

"Yes, I know, sir."

P'tit Noel led him up a narrow staircase to the first floor where the ambience was that of the well-appointed town house—totally alien to the gaudy glitter of the club. They passed down a hallway and stopped before a double door of dark oak. P'tit Noel tapped lightly.

"I shall leave you now, sir. You may go in."

Jonathan thanked him again for his intervention, opened the door, and stepped into a lavishly furnished room of crimson damask and Italian marble.

Grace was indeed amazing.

She stood in the middle of the room, wearing a transparent peignoir of a white diaphanous material. Poised, her fine body was even more seductive when covered with a mist of fabric through which the circles of her brown nipples and the triangle of her écu were a dim freehand geometry. But it was her stature that gave Jonathan pause. Little wonder the marble mantel in the photograph had seemed uncommonly high. Amazing Grace was only four feet six inches tall.

"Good evening, Grace," he said, settling his smiling gaze on her large oriental eyes.

Her nose wrinkled up and she laughed hoarsely. "Well, you handled that just fine, Dr. Hemlock."

"I'm unflappable. Particularly when I'm stunned."

"Is that so." She turned away and walked over the thick red carpet toward a little grouping of furniture before the fireplace. The splayed toes of her bare feet seemed to grip the rug. "Don't just stand there, boy. Come on over here and have a drink with me." She lifted a decanter of clear liquid and filled two sherry glasses, then she arranged herself on a small chaise longue, taking up all the space in an unprovocative way that denied the possibility of his joining her on it.

He took his glass and sat across from her and near the crackling wood fire.

"Happy times," she said, lifting her glass and draining it.

"Cheers." He swallowed—then he swallowed again several times to get it down. His eyes were damp and his voice thin when he spoke. "You drink neat Everclear?"

"Honey bun, I don't drink for flavor."

"I see." Jonathan had been surprised by her accent from the first. He had assumed that she, like her staff, was West Indian. But she was American.

"Omaha," she explained.

"You're kidding."

"Sweety, people don't kid about coming from Omaha. That's like bragging about having syphilis. Pour yourself another."

"No. No—thank you. It's *good*. But no thank you."

She laughed again, a rich brawling sound that was infectious. "Hey, tell me. No shit now. How can a swinging type like you be a doctor? You don't look like you'd waste time jamming nurses behind screens."

"I'm not that kind of doctor. What about yourself? How did you end up in the flesh trade?"

"Oh, just answered an advertisement. 'Positions wanted.'" She hooted a laugh. "But seriously, I did a couple years in Vegas working at a joint that specialized in uncommon meat. My being tiny makes tiny men feel big. Then I decided that management was more fun than labor, so I saved up my money and . . ." She made an inclusive sweep of her hand.

"It looks like you're doing very well."

"I'll probably make it through the winter." Instantly the shine in her eyes dimmed. "Is that enough?"

"Enough?"

"Small talk, honey bun."

Jonathan smiled. "Almost. One more question. P'tit Noel. Is he your lover? I only ask out of a sense of self-preservation."

"Are you kidding, man? I mean, he's nuts about me and all, that goes without saying. I imagine he'd eat half a mile of my shit just to see where it came from. But we don't fuck. I'm a little girl, and he is a big man. He'd puncture my lungs."

The flood of earthy imagery made Jonathan laugh.

"Besides," she continued, refilling her glass, "I don't use men anymore. When I need it, I have a girl in. Women know where the bits are and what they want. They're more efficient."

"Like the Everclear."

"Right."

He shook his head. "You're amazing, Grace."

She drank off half the glass. "So? What did you want to see me about?"

"I want to see Maximilian Strange."

"Why?"

"I believe he wants to see me."

"Why?"

"I'll ask him when I see him."

"What brought you here?"

Jonathan sighed. "Please, lady. That will slow us down a lot."

"All right. No peekaboo. Tell me why you want to see Max. We're partners. Or didn't you know that?"

Jonathan's eyebrows raised. "Partners? *Equal* partners?"

She finished her drink and poured another. "No, Max doesn't have any equals. He's one of a kind. The most beautiful man; the most cruel man. He holds all the patents on excitement."

"It sounds like you feel about Strange the way P'tit Noel feels about you."

"That's not far wrong."

Jonathan rose and looked around. "Grace?

212

There's something I want to do. And you can help me."

"Yeah?"

"I've got this problem. How can I tell you this without offending you? Honey, I've got to piss."

"Nut!" She laughed. "It's back there. Through the bedroom."

When he returned she had taken off her peignoir and was standing with her back to the fire, rubbing her bare buttocks and stretching to her tiptoes in the warmth.

"Do you know that you're nude, madam?"

"I like to walk around bare-assed. I feel free. And it turns men on, and I get a kick out of that. 'Cause they ain't going to get nothin'." She said this last in a low-down Ras accent.

"Well, you keep flashing that fine body around, you'll get yourself raped one of these days."

"By you?" she asked with taunting scorn.

"No, I've given up rape. The pillow talk is too limited."

She frowned seriously. "You know, if some stud decided to rape me, I don't think I'd fight it. I'd let him in. Then I'd tighten up the old sphincter and cut it right off."

"What a lesson that would be for him." But her taut, cabled muscles under smooth skin gave the image credibility, and he couldn't help a quick local wince.

His trip to the bathroom had been profitable. There was a window giving out onto a flat metal roof. He had left it open. If they came for him, he'd be able to give them a chase that would prevent any-

one from thinking he was overeager to get into The
Cloisters.

"Tell me, Grace. When you talked to Strange on
the phone, did he give you any idea when he'd like
to meet me?"

"What makes you think I called him?"

"You called me Dr. Hemlock. P'tit Noel didn't
know my title."

Her feline composure faded perceptibly. "I guess
I screwed up, right?"

"A little. But I won't mention it to Strange."

She was relieved, and he realized that Maximilian
Strange did not tolerate error—even from partners.
"When does he want to meet me?"

"They'll be here any minute now to pick you up."

"Uh-huh. Well, I don't think I can make it
tonight. Let's set something up for tomorrow."

She smiled at the thought of anyone thinking
about changing Max's plans. "No. He said tonight.
He'll be pissed if you're not here."

"He may have to live with that."

At that moment there was the sound of footfalls
outside the door. Several men.

She smiled at him and lifted her arms in an exaggerated shrug. "Too late, honey bun."

"Maybe not. You just stand there warming your
ass, and don't try to stop me. I'm a real terror
against girls of your size." He ran to the bathroom
and scrambled out the window onto the metal roof.
As he did, he could hear her opening the door and
talking rapidly to the men. There were barked orders, and one of the men rushed through the flat
toward the bathroom, as the others ran back down
the stairs.

Jonathan flattened out against the brick wall beside the bathroom window. A big head came poking out, and he hit it with his fist just behind the ear. The face slapped down against the stone sill with the click of breaking teeth, and the head slid back inside with a moan and a sigh.

His eyes not yet accustomed to the dark, Jonathan crept along the top of the roof on all fours. He came blank up against a brick wall and felt his way along it to a corner. By then his eyes had dilated and he could see dimly. Below him was a narrow gap, a cut of black between two windowless brick buildings. It didn't seem to lead anywhere, so he decided to climb upward, toward the dirty, city-glow smear of fog. The gap was only about four feet wide. He slipped off his shoes and, falling back on his mountain experience, eased out over the void and jammed himself between the two brick walls, his back against one, his feet flat against the other. He executed a scrambling chimney climb, holding himself into the fissure by the pressure of his feet against the opposite wall and inching up at the expense of his suit jacket and a quantity of palm skin. The building before him went up beyond his vision, but the one at his back was only three stories tall. When he got to the lip of the flat roof, he shot himself over with a final thrust with his legs, and he lay panting on the wet seamed metal. He crawled across the roof and looked down. Below was a cobblestone alley strewn with garbage cans, and it appeared to give out onto a street. There was light from a distant streetlamp, and he could see to negotiate a heavy, cast-iron drainpipe that led from the roof to the floor of the alley. From afar, he could hear a call and an answering shout, but he couldn't make out the direction. The descent was fairly easy, but when he landed a piece of broken glass went through his sock into the sole of his foot.

Jesus Christ! The same fucking alley!

He pulled the triangle of glass out and gingerly made his way through the shattered bottles.

It occurred to him how ironic it would be if, in attempting to avoid appearing anxious to get into The Cloisters, he had evaded them altogether.

But no worry on that score. There was a shout. Footfalls. And there they were, two of them in the gap, blocking his exit, their forms punctuating the glowing nimbus of fog. They moved toward him slowly.

"All right, gentlemen. I give up. You win."

But they didn't answer, and by their slow inexorable advance he took it that they wanted some revenge for their toughed-up mate above.

Just then a door opened behind him and he was caught in a shaft of light. It was P'tit Noel.

"Thank God," Jonathan said. He heard the explosive sound of P'tit Noel's openhanded slap to the back of his head, but he didn't feel it. He seemed to float away horizontally, and later he remembered hoping he wouldn't land in the broken glass.

Hampstead

Before opening his eyes or moving, he waited until full consciousness had gradually replaced the spinning nightmare vertigo. He was aware of the rocking motion of the automobile and the harsh drag of the floor carpeting against his cheek each time they turned a corner. He was cramped and stiff, but there was no pain in his head, as there ought to have been. The sick dream of it all was intensified by the dark, so he opened his eyes, and he found himself looking strabismally at the glossy tips of a pair of patent leather shoes not four inches from his nose. Light came and went in raking flashes as they passed by lights.

It was as he tried to sit up that the pain came—a vast swooning lump of it, as though someone were forcing a sharp fragment of ice through the arteries of his brain. His eyes teared involuntarily with the pain, but when it passed, it passed completely, not even leaving behind the throb of a headache. He struggled to a sitting position. They were in a taxi. The three men with him watched his efforts dully, without speaking or offering help. He got to his knees, pulled down the jump seat, and sat on it heavily. There were two men across from him on the back seat, and a third beside him on the other jump seat. The streaked drops of rain on the windows glittered with each passing streetlamp.

He looked down. There was no registration number for the cab in the usual frame between the jump seats. They had evidently taken a leaf from the Chicago gangs, using a private taxi for basic transportation because its vehicular anonymity allowed it to prowl the streets at any hour of the night without arousing undue attention.

The driver, unmoving on his side of the glass partition, was undoubtedly one of them. There were neither door nor window handles on the inside of the passenger compartment. Very professional. Unaided, the driver could deliver a man without additional guard.

Jonathan took stock of the men with him. He could forget the driver. Drivers are never leaders. The man on the jump seat lifted his hand to his swollen, discolored mouth from time to time, gingerly touching the split upper lip. That must be the one who had the misfortune to stick his head out the bathroom window. He inadvertently inhaled orally, and winced with pain as the cold air touched the exposed nerves of his broken front teeth. Jonathan was glad he wasn't alone with this one. The owner of the patent leather shoes who sat facing him was a furtive little man with nervous eyes and a tentative moustache. A diagonal scar, more like a brand than a cut, ran in a glairy groove from the right cheek to the left point of his chin, intersecting his lips and moustache, and giving him the appearance of having two mouths. He sat well over against his armrest to make room for the third man, whose great bulk was arranged in an expansive sprawl. That would be the leader of this little squad. Jonathan addressed him.

"I assume we're going to The Cloisters?"

Viscously, the big man brought his heavy-lidded eyes to rest on Jonathan's face where they settled without recognition, not even shifting from eye to eye. The broad face was dominated by an overhanging brow, and his slab cheeks flanked an oval mouth, the thick, kidney-colored lips of which were always moist. So extreme was the droop of his eyelids that he tilted back his head to see, exposing only the bottom half of his pupils. Jonathan recognized the psychological type. He had met them occasionally when working for CII. They were used in low priority sanctions because they were effective, cheap, and expendable. Often they would do "wet work" without pay. Violence was a pleasurable outlet for them.

Attempts at conversation were not going to be fruitful, so Jonathan set to examining his condition. He explored the base of his skull with his fingers and found it only a little tender. The nose was clear, and he could focus his eyes rapidly, so there hadn't been any concussion. The openhanded slap to the back of the neck with which P'tit Noel had put him away is one of the premiere blows in the repertory of violence. It can kill without a bruise and is undetectable without an autopsy to reveal blood clots and ruptured capillaries in the brain. But to use the blow in its middle ranges requires a fine touch. Jonathan had to admire P'tit Noel's skill. Not bad ... for a lawyer.

Despite the Haitian's professional art, Jonathan was a mess. His trousers were torn and filthy, his jacket was scuffed from the chimney climb up the brick wall, and he had no shoes. For his meeting with Maximilian Strange, he would lack the social poise and sartorial one-upmanship he usually enjoyed. Even among these goons, he felt awkward.

"Sorry about those teeth of yours, pal," he said unkindly. "You're really going to make a haul when the Tooth Fairy comes around."

The man on the jump seat produced a compound of growl and sneer, which he instantly regretted as the in-suck of air made him twist his head in pain.

The taxi was easing down a steep cobble street, past what appeared through the streaked windows to be large villas of the late eighteenth century. But then they passed an anachronous modern shopping plaza that looked like a project by a first-year design student in a polytechnic. It seemed carved in soap, and the dissonance it obtruded into the fashionable district spoke eloquently of the truism that the modern Englishman deserves his architectural heritage as much as the modern Italian merits the Roman heritage of efficiency and military prowess. Then they turned and reentered an area of fine old houses. Jonathan recognized the district as Hampstead: Tory homes amid Labour inconveniences.

The taxi turned up through open iron gates and into a driveway that curved past the front entrance. They continued around and to the back of the sprawling stone house and pulled up at the rear. The driver stepped out and opened the door for them.

Directed by small unnecessary nudges from behind, Jonathan was conducted into a dimly lit waiting room where two of them stood guard over him while the kidney-lipped hulk passed on upstairs, ostensibly to announce their arrival. Jonathan used this time to sort himself out. Alone, unarmed, rumpled, and off pace, he had to ready himself for whatever turns and twists this evening might take. He stood with his back against a wall and his knees locked to support his weight. Closing his eyes, he ignored his guards as he touched his palms together, the thumbs beneath his chin, the forefingers pressed against his lips. He exhaled completely and breathed very shallowly, using only the bottom of his lungs, sharply reducing his intake of oxygen. Holding the image of the still pool in his mind, he brought his face ever closer to its surface, until he was under.

"All right! You! Let's go!" The dapper little man with two mouths touched Jonathan's shoulder. "Let's go!"

Jonathan opened his eyes slowly. Ten or fifteen minutes had passed, but he was refreshed and his mind was quiet and controlled.

They led him up a narrow staircase and through a door.

He winced and held up his hand to screen away the painfully bright light.

"Here," Two-mouths said, "put these on." He passed Jonathan a pair of round dark glasses that cupped into the eye sockets and had an elastic cord to go around the head.

Six sunlamps on stands were the source of the painful ultraviolet light, and on one of the low exercise tables between the banks of lamps was a man, nude save for a scanty posing pouch, doing sit-ups as a flabby masseur held his ankles for leverage.

Everyone in the room wore the dark green eyecups. Looking around, Jonathan was put in mind of photographs he had seen of Biafran victims with their eyes shot out.

"Welcome ..." The exerciser grunted with his sit-up, and he swung forward to touch his forehead to his knees, then lay back again. "Welcome to the Emerald City, Dr. Hemlock. How many is that, Claudio?"

"Seventy-two, sir."

Jonathan recognized the voice just an instant before he recalled the face behind the green eyecups. It was the classically beautiful Renaissance man he had met with Vanessa Dyke at Tomlinson's Galleries. The man with the Marini Horse.

"I assume you're Maximilian Strange?" Jonathan said.

"All right, Claudio. That will be enough." Strange sat on the edge of the padded exercise table and pulled off the eye guards as the ultraviolet lamps were turned off. Taking his glasses off, Jonathan found the normal light in the room oddly cold and feeble in contrast to the glare of the lamps in the hotter end of the spectrum. "I regret your having to wait downstairs while I finished my exercise, Dr. Hemlock. But routine is routine." Strange lay down on the table, and Claudio started to cover him with a thick, cream-colored grease, beginning with the face and neck and working downward. "There is a popular myth, Dr. Hemlock, that exposure to the sun ages one's skin and causes wrinkles. Actually, it's the loss of skin oils that sins against the complexion. An immediate treatment with pure lanolin will replace them adequately. You said you *assumed*

I was Maximilian Strange. Didn't you really *know*?"

"No. How could I?"

"How indeed? Do you take good care of your body?"

"No particular care. I try to keep it from being stabbed and clubbed and suchlike. But that's all."

"You make a common mistake there. Men tend to consider indifference to their appearance to be a mark of rugged virility. Personally, I celebrate beauty, and therefore, of course, I celebrate artifice. Growing old is neither attractive nor inevitable. The mind is always young. The challenge resides in keeping the body also young." There it was again: that slight jamming of sentence structure that hinted of Strange's German origins. The only other clue was his pronunciation, neither exactly British nor exactly American. A kind of midatlantic sound that one found only on the American stage. "Exercise, sun, diet, and taking one's excesses in moderation," he continued. "That is all that is required to keep the face and body. How old do you think I am?"

"I can only guess. I'd say you were about . . . fifty-one."

Strange stopped the masseur's hand and turned to look at Jonathan closely for the first time. "Well, now. That is remarkable. For a guess."

"I'd go on to guess that you were born in Munich in 1922." It was showing off, but it was the right thing to do. Jonathan was pleased with the way it was going so far. He was giving the appearance of holding nothing back, not even the fact that he had background knowledge about Strange.

Strange looked at him flatly for a moment. "Very good. I see you intend to be frank." Then he broke into a deep laugh. "Good God, man! What happened to your clothes?"

"I fell down the side of a brick wall."

"How exhibitionistic. Did you have trouble with Leonard?"

"Is Leonard this droopy-eyed ass here?"

"The very man. But your taunts will go unanswered. Poor Leonard is incapable of banter. He is a mute."

Leonard watched Jonathan glassily from beneath heavy-lidded eyes. His meaty face seemed incapable of subtle expression, its heavy-hanging muscles responding only to broad, basic emotions.

Strange climbed from the exercise table and picked up a thick towel. "Will you join me in a steam bath, Dr. Hemlock?"

"Do I have a choice?"

"No, of course not. And you could use a wash anyway." He led the way. "Few people know the proper way to use lanolin, Dr. Hemlock. It must be applied thickly just after your sunbath. Then you allow the steam to melt off the excess. The pores of the skin retain what is necessary for moisture." He stopped and turned to make his next point. "Soap should never be used on the face."

"You'll forgive me, Mr. Strange, if I find this concern for beauty and youth a little grotesque in a man of your age."

"Certainly not. Why should I forgive you?"

Leonard accompanied the two of them to the tiled dressing room that separated the steam bath from the exercise area. As Jonathan stripped down and wrapped a towel around his waist, Strange informed him that his stay at The Cloisters might be a prolonged one, so they had taken the precaution of having his room broken into and some of his clothes brought back.

"And while you were searching for my clothes, you had a chance to take a more general look around."

"Just so."

"And you found?"

"Just clothes. You use a very good tailor, Dr. Hemlock. How do you manage that on a professor's salary?"

"I take bag lunches."

"I see. Ah, but of course, you are doing well on your books—popular art criticism for the masses. How dreary that must be for you."

The three men passed into the steam room, Leonard looking grotesquely comic with only a towel to hide his powerful but inelegant primate body. Not once, not even while undressing, had his hooded eyes left Jonathan, and when they sat on the scrubbed pine benches of the steam room, he positioned himself in the corner, protectively between Jonathan and Strange.

The jets had been open for some time, and now the room was filled with swirling steam that eddied and echoed their movements; the temperature was in the mid-nineties. But Jonathan found no relaxation in the heat and steam. During the introductory badinage, he had recovered from his surprise at discovering that Strange and the Renaissance man were one, and now he had begun to model a cover story for himself. It covered the ground thinly, but he had no time to test it for fissures.

Strange closed his eyes and rested back, soaking

up the steam, his confidence in Leonard's protection absolute. "You realize, of course, that this Dantesque room may be your last living memory."

Jonathan did in fact realize this.

Strange continued, his voice a lazy drone. "You sought to impress me just now by dropping information concerning my past. What more do you know?"

"Not much. I've been trying to track you down, and in the course of it I discovered that you were in the whorehouse business—if I may simplify."

Strange waved an indifferent hand.

"I also discovered you are in the country illegally, and that you have been in one aspect or another of the flesh trade as far back as my sources go."

"What are these sources?"

"That's my affair."

"I think I can guess at them. You were in CII. You were an assassin—or, to be polite, a counterassassin. It is my opinion that you found out what you wanted to know about me from old contacts in that service."

"I'm impressed you know that much about me."

"I'm an impressive man, Dr. Hemlock. So tell me. Why were you seeking me out?"

"The Marini Horse."

"What is that to you? I know something of your financial condition. Surely you don't expect to be able to buy the Horse."

"I don't even particularly care for Marini, nor for any of the moderns for that matter."

"Then what is your interest?"

"I need money. And I thought I might turn a buck out of it."

"How?"

"You have to admit there were some bizarre aspects to our meeting at Tomlinson's. You intend to sell the Horse, and evidently for more money than one would have considered possible. I naturally began to think about that and wonder what I might do to turn it to my fiscal advantage."

"Go on." Strange did not open his eyes.

"Well, my public evaluation of the statue could increase its value by a great deal. Just at this barren moment in art criticism, things tend to be worth whatever I say they're worth."

"Yes, I'm aware of your singular position. A one-eyed man among the blind, if you ask me."

"I thought you might be willing to share some of the excess profit with me."

"Not an unreasonable thought." Strange rose and crossed through the thickening steam to a large earthenware jar of cold water. He poured several dipperfuls over his head and rubbed his chest vigorously. "Good for toning the skin. Care for some?"

"No, thanks. I don't want to be refreshed. I want to relax and get some sleep."

"Later perhaps. If all goes well, we shall take supper together, after which you may wish to sample our amenities here, the most modest of which is a comfortable bed. What would you say if I told you that, while you were seeking to contact me about the Marini Horse, I was bending every effort to contact you?"

"Frankly, I would doubt you. Coincidences make me uncomfortable."

"Hm-m. They make me uncomfortable too, Dr. Hemlock. It seems we have that in common. And yet there are coincidences here. And discomfort. Could it be that it is not particularly coincidental for two such men as we to see profit in the same thing?"

"That could be." This was the narrow bit. The only story Jonathan had been able to put together quickly was Strange's own. He knew he'd be driving up the same street Strange was driving down, and he knew the coincidence of it would loom large, but at least he had been able to mention it first. He rose to get some cold water after all, and with his first movement, Leonard sprang to his feet with surprising alacrity for a man of his bulk and interposed his body between Jonathan and Strange. "Oh, relax, dummy!"

"Sit down, Leonard. I think Dr. Hemlock is aware of the impossibility of his getting out of here without my permission. And I think he realizes how quickly and vigorously an attempt to do me harm would be punished. You must forgive Leonard his passion for duty, Dr. Hemlock. He has been at my side for—oh, fifteen years now, it must be. I'm really very fond of him. His canine devotion and extraordinary strength make him useful. And he has other gifts. For instance, he has an enormous tolerance for pain. Not his own, of course. When it is necessary to discipline one of the young people working for me here, I simply award him or her to Leonard for a night of pleasure. For a few days afterward, the poor thing is of little use in my business, and occasionally he requires medical attention for hemorrhage or some such, but it is amazing how sincerely he regrets his misdeeds and how rigidly he subsequently conforms to our rules of performance." Strange looked at Jonathan, his pale eyes without expression. "I tell you this, of course, by way of threat. But it is perfectly true, I assure you."

"I don't doubt it for a moment. Does he also do your killing for you?"

Strange returned to the pine bench, sat down, and closed his eyes. "When that is necessary. And only when he's been especially good and deserving of reward. When did you leave CII? And why?"

"Four years ago," Jonathan said, as immediately as possible. So that was to be Strange's interrogation style, was it? The rapid question following non sequitur upon less direct chat. Jonathan would have to field the balls quickly and offhandedly. It was a most one-down way to play the game.

"And why?"

"I'd had enough. I had grown up. At least, I'd gotten older." That would be the best way to stay even. Tell trivial truths.

"Four years ago, you say. Good. Good. That tallies with the information I have concerning you. When first it occurred to me that you might be of use in my little project for selling the Marini Horse, I took the trouble to look into your affairs. I have friends . . . debtors, really . . . at Interpol/Vienna, and they did a bit of research on you. I cannot tell you how my confidence increased when I discovered that you had been a thief, or at least a receiver, of stolen paintings. But my friends in Vienna said that you had not purchased a painting for four years. That would seem to coincide with the time you left the lucrative company of CII. Why did you work for them?"

"Money."

"No slight tug of patriotism?"

"My sin was greed, not stupidity."

"Good. Good. I approve of that."

Jonathan noticed that Strange never raised an eyebrow, or smiled, or frowned. He had trained his face to remain an expressionless mask. Doubtless to prevent the development of wrinkles.

"I think that is enough steam, don't you?" Strange said, rising and leading the way back to the exercise room where the man with two mouths was waiting with a glass of cold goat's milk, which Strange drank down before he and Jonathan lay out on exercise tables to be rubbed down. The masseur scrubbed Jonathan with a rough warm towel before beginning to knead his shoulders and back, while Leonard performed the same service for Strange.

Strange turned his head toward Jonathan, his cheek on the back of his hands, and looked at him casually when he asked, "Who is it you visit in Covent Garden?"

Jonathan laughed while he thought quickly. "How long have I been under surveillance?"

"From the evening we met at Tomlinson's. My man lost track of you for a while there. Traffic jam. He waited for you at your apartment."

"Which apartment?"

"Ah, precisely. At that time we didn't know about the Baker Street residence. You use it very seldom. My people waited for some time at your Mayfair flat before further inquiry revealed the existence of the Baker Street penthouse. By the time we arrived there, you had left, but the flat was not empty. There was a man in your bathroom. A dead man. But you had disappeared."

"Hey! Watch it!" Jonathan shouted.

"What's wrong?"

"This steel-clawed son of a bitch is pulling my tendons out."

"Be gentle with the doctor, Claudio. He's a guest. Yes, we quite lost sight of you until, a couple of hours ago, I received a call from Grace. Dear Grace is a colleague of mine. A close and honored friend."

"So?"

"So I would like some explanation that puts these odd bits together. And I do hope it's convincing. I would enjoy an evening of civilized chat."

"Well, I told you I was trying to gain entrée to your place here. I had no idea you were also looking for me, so I tried through Amazing Grace."

"Yes, but how did you know about Grace?"

"You said it yourself. I still have some CII connections. Hey! Take it easy, you ham-handed bastard!" Jonathan sat up and pushed the masseur away.

"Oh, very well," Strange said with some irritation. "I'd rather cut my massage short than listen to you complain about yours. But you should really establish a routine for keeping fit. Look at me. I'm ten years older than you, and I look ten years younger."

"We have different life priorities."

Strange led the way into a lavish dressing room, the walls of which were covered with mirrors set in bronze. The reflections of the three men echoed in infinite redundancy, and Jonathan found himself a principal in a finely synchronized sartorial ballet performed by scores of Hemlocks and scores of Stranges, while scores of droopy-lidded Leonards looked on, their faces impassive, their heads tilted back on thick necks.

When he saw his clothes laid out, Jonathan felt a pulse of relief. He had wondered why Strange had not mentioned finding at least one of the revolvers when his men had picked up his clothes. But these came from his Mayfair flat, not the Baker Street one. Luck was with him. But still he was walking a razor's edge, reactive and imbalanced from the start, never sure how much truth he had to surrender to neutralize the facts already in Strange's possession. He had done well enough so far, but he had had to turn the flow of inquisition away from time to time, with inconsequential small talk or complaining about the masseur, to give himself time to collect his balance and pick a direction. So far, he had been plausible, if not overwhelmingly convincing. But there were big holes—like the dead man on his toilet—that Strange would surely probe. And one link was still open. To close it might expose Vanessa Dyke.

"... but it is a terrible mistake not to give the body the work and diet necessary to keep it young and attractive," Strange was saying. "I know the routines are strenuous and the restrictions irritating, but nothing worth having is ever cheap."

"That's funny. I clearly remember being assured by a song of the Depression that the best things in life were free."

"Opiate hogwash. Self-delusions with which the congenital have-nots seek to excuse their life failures and make less of the accomplishments of others. As I recall, that insipid song suggests that Love, in particular, is free. My dear sir, my life's work is founded on the knowledge that love—technically

232

competent and interesting love—is extraordinarily expensive."

"Perhaps the song was using the word differently."

"Oh, I know the kind of love it meant. Fictions of the fourteenth-century jongleur. Friendship run riot. Pointless nestlings; sharings of tacky dreams and tawdry aspirations; promises of emotional dependency that pass for constancy; fumbling manipulations in the backs of cars; the sweat of the connubial bed. *That* kind of love may be thought free, and considered dear at the price. But in fact it is not free at all. One pays endlessly for the shabby amateurism of romantic love. One enters into eternal contractual obligations under the terms of which the partners pledge to erode one another forever with their infinite dullness. Still, I suppose they lack the merit to deserve more, and probably the imagination to desire more. Should I open the doors of The Cloisters to one of this ilk for a night, he would blunder about, *asinus ad lyram*, until he found, down in the kitchens, some sweating cook or stringy scullery maid who could be a soul mate and who would understand and care for him for all time. There we are! Dressed and civilized. Shall we take a little refreshment?"

"If you wish."

"Good. There are one or two points that want clarifying."

"Personally, I'd like to get around to the topic of the sale of the Marini Horse. Focusing our attention particularly on what profit I can expect from it."

Strange laughed. "In due course. After all, we're

still not absolutely sure that you are going to survive this interrogation, are we? Come along."

The center mirror hinged open like a door, swilling the scores of reflected images around the room in a blurred rush. They passed into a small sitting room about the size and shape of a projection booth, dimly lit, its walls made of glass. Three sides looked out onto the principal salon of The Cloisters: a large, brilliantly illuminated room in the Art Deco style. Glass beads, mechanical foliage, repetitious angular motifs, rainbow and sunrise patterns pressed into buffed aluminum wall panels.

The patrons were dressed in extravagant costumes provided by the management; and shepherdesses, devils, inquisitors, cavaliers, and Mickey Mouses lounged about, chatting, drinking, laughing. But all this panoply was in pantomime; the glass walls were soundproof.

Moving among the patrons were half a dozen hostesses dressed in flapper style: long loops of beads, cloche-bobbed hair, bound breasts under silk frocks, rolled-down hose exposing rouged and dimpled knees. With their artificial lashes of the stiff "surprise" style, their beauty spots, and their bee-stung lips, they looked like mannequins in back issues of high fashion magazines as they served drinks and exotic canapés, or bent over patrons in teasing, flirtatious conversation.

One of the patrons, a Catherine de Medici of uncertain years, with face skin tight from cosmetic surgery that had not included her wattle, approached the glass wall and stared in unabashedly. She moistened the tip of her little finger with the tip of her tongue and made a minute adjustment in her eye liner, then she patted the back of her hair, turned and took a long appreciative sideways glance into the room before pivoting away to greet an approaching highwayman with the boneless face, whimpering smile, and lank hair of his class.

"One-way mirrors," Strange said unnecessarily as he settled into a deep leather chair after carefully hitching up the crease of his trousers. "The decor was Grace's idea. There is something fundamentally evil about the New People of the 1920s that seems to liberate our customers."

Jonathan stood near the one-way glass wall and looked out, his arms folded on his chest. "Art Deco was a monstrous moment in art. When the flamboyant decay of Art Nouveau percolated down to the masses, through the intermediary of machine reproduction, it was unavoidable that the half-trained, ungifted, self-indulgent artists would proclaim the resultant hodgepodge a new art form. After all, here was something even *they* could do. In my view, the recent revival of interest in Art Deco indicts the modern artist and the modern critic—people who communicate and communicate, yet remain inarticulate."

"Oh, I am terribly sorry that our taste doesn't please you. But, *de gustibus* . . ."

"Nonsense. It's the only thing really worth disputing."

Strange laughed shallowly. Laughter was his substitute for smiling, preferred because it did not necessitate creasing the cheeks. And there were as many tones to his laughter as there are nuances in other people's smiles. "At all events, I enjoy this little chamber here. We call it the Aquarium. But it's an aquarium in reverse. The fish are out there in the salon, and the amused observers here in the bowl. And it is charming to realize that that room out there contains a good fifty percent of the real governmental power in Britain."

"All gathered here to find respite from the heavy burdens of leadership by losing themselves in the ecstasy of your contrived orgies?"

"You shouldn't sneer at the exoticism of our offerings. Quite naturally, our patrons expect something out of the ordinary: prenubile girls, catamites, fellatio—that sort of thing. One cannot blame them. Coming here for common garden variety sex would be like ordering sausage, chips, and two veg at Maxim's. But what is really amusing is that half the silly asses out there don't even know what goes on in our splendid cloaca. They believe The Cloisters is only a fashionable, bizarre, and exclusive club with excellent food and wine and charming hostesses."

"Oh? The flapper types aren't hookers?"

"Oh, no. Young models, aspiring actresses, university girls—just window dressing. The costuming goes with the decor. The more enterprising and promising graduate to the more lucrative activities upstairs, but most of them stay with us only a month or so, then pass on to duller activities: careers, marriages, such like. We're constantly replacing hostesses. But I am forgetting my duties as host. I have promised you refreshment. May I suggest brewer's yeast in fresh tangerine juice?"

"It's tempting. But I think I'll have scotch. Do you have Laphroaig?"

Strange turned the question to the dapper, two-mouthed minion who stood behind them, having accompanied them into the Aquarium while Leonard was dressing.

"I'll see, sir." But he did not depart until Leonard came in to relieve him.

"I'm afraid I'm not up on the finer points of scotch," Strange said. "I never drink alcohol. By the way, tell me about the man we found dead in your bathroom. Who was he?"

"I don't know," Jonathan said as smoothly as possible. He had been anticipating this tactic of the sudden question.

"Who killed him?"

"I did."

Strange looked at Jonathan with frank admiration at the immediacy of the answer. "Go on," he said, after a nod of approval.

"It was because of that man that I came looking for you. You've discovered that I used to work for CII in counterassassination. The work was not so dangerous as one might think. Since my targets were men who had assassinated CII agents, they typically came from a level of society neither lamented nor avenged—not by the various law enforcement agencies, at any rate. And, because I took random assignments, I could never be tied to the death by motive. Typically, I never met the mark before the moment of the hit. But . . . but because society is not yet prepared to counter the problem of overpopulation by sterilizing and terminating rotten and unproductive genetic stock, my targets were not without relatives.

"From the few babbled words he got out before I shot him, it appears that he was the brother of some forgotten mark. He had come to retrieve the family honor, such as it was."

"But you shot him first."

"Just so."

"And left him in your *bathroom*?"

"I didn't pick the meeting ground. Bathrooms have tile floors that are easily cleaned up."

Strange nodded appreciatively. "I see."

Leonard entered from behind and replaced Two-mouths, who went off to fetch the drinks.

"You certainly got rid of the body quickly. Our men returned to your rooms a few hours after first discovering the corpse, and it was gone. How did you manage that?"

"I'll make you a deal. I won't ask you how to run a whorehouse, and you don't ask me about assassination."

"That seems fair enough. You mentioned that this business in your bathroom was linked in some way to your desire to penetrate The Cloisters. Would you amplify that a bit?"

"While that poor ass was babbling about how he had been on my trail for years, he let slip the name of the person who had fingered me. He was waving a gun in my face, and I suppose he imagined I would not live to benefit from the information."

"By the way, how did you kill this man?"

"With his own gun."

"How did you get it from him?"

"How do you keep your girls from getting clap?"

Strange laughed. "All right, all right. Go on."

"The informant was a man highly placed in CII. A man who never liked me because I could not pass up opportunities to point out the more blatant stupidities of that asinine and bungling organization. I have every reason to believe that he will continue putting the finger on me. And someday, someone may get lucky."

"Why don't you kill this man?"

"He knows me. I'd never get close enough to him. So I have to hire the job done. And for that, I need a lot of money. And that is why the deal with the Marini Horse attracted me."

"And so you began to seek me out?"

"And so I began to seek you out." That was it. His story was improvised and thin, just covering the major events with little of that extraneous fabric that fills out the good lie. There was nothing to do now but sit and see how it went down.

Strange was silent for a time, his pale eyes looking phlegmatically out onto the salon scene playing mutely before him. Then he nodded slowly. "It is possible. Both your recent actions and my research into your past would seem to bear your story out. The only thing that disturbs me is the coincidence of it all. But then ... I suppose coincidence exists." He turned to Jonathan and rested his pale eyes on him. "Why don't you take supper with Grace and me this evening. We can talk over the details of the Marini sale. Assuming all goes well, you might care to sample our exotic entertainments later. By way of a nightcap."

"I've had a hard day."

Strange laughed. "If it weren't so late and the streets weren't empty, I would tempt your fatigued appetite by sending a couple of my men out in a van to pick up something from the streets for you—fresh from the garden, you might say. A schoolgirl on her way home, perhaps, or a nun just back from confessional?"

"Don't you have some trouble with cooperation from those you abduct?"

"Oh . . . not if they're properly prepared. We use a concoction of hallucinogens and cantharis that seems to be effective—Oh, my dear Dr. Hemlock! I wish you could have seen the cloud of disgust that just swept over your face! I would have thought you had a more leathery conscience than that."

"It's not conscience. Just taste."

"In this business only the bizarre is profitable. The basic components of sex are so mundane: a little heat, a little friction, a little lubrication. One must dress up such cheap raw materials considerably if he hopes to vend them at high profit. Packaging is everything. But, ah . . . here we are at last."

Two-mouths entered through the mirror door bearing a tray with two glasses. Jonathan could not repress a surge of repulsion when he looked at Strange's glass, the gray-tan yeast powder already settling in the tangerine juice and collecting at the bottom. Strange sipped off some of the liquid, then swirled the remainder to carry the yeast back into temporary suspension while he drank it.

"Looks ghastly," Jonathan commented.

"You get used to it. In fact, one comes to rather like it."

Jonathan turned away in gastronomic self-defense. Out in the salon, one of the flapper hostesses caught his eye. As she chatted with a costumed customer, she brushed aside a vagrant wisp of amber hair with the back of her hand. She was only a few feet from the wall of one-way mirrors, and he could see the bottle green of her eyes.

"What interests you so much out there?" Strange asked, joining him at the glass wall.

"Your clients," Jonathan said, indicating a group of men chatting with supercilious gravity, blithely ignorant of the risible effect of their outlandish costumes.

"Hm-m. Silly asses. Look at them, playing out their dumb show of authority and power. Pompously going through the motions of statecraft. They are finished as a people, the English, but they haven't sense to know it. There was a time when Darwinian laws applied to nations as well as to individuals— when the weak and incapable disappeared. If it hadn't been for the sentiment of other nations— yours particularly, Dr. Hemlock—1950 would have marked the end of this effete social organism. I enjoy making them dress up like that, and they take great delight in doing it. It's a national trait—pageantry, make-believe. A nation of people who thirst to be what they are not. That probably accounts for their production of so many gifted actors."

"You despise the British, then?"

"More scorn, I should say."

"But I thought the Germans rather admired and imitated them."

"Oh, we have much in common. Our weaknesses, to be specific. Our army organizations were modeled after theirs. It was the British, you know, who first experimented with the concentration camp as a vehicle for the final solution to genetic problems."

"No, I didn't know that."

"Oh, yes. In the Boer War. Twenty-six thousand

women and children died of disease, malnutrition, and neglect. Vitriol in their sugar; small metal hooks implanted in their meat—that sort of business. Oh yes, the British have been world leaders in many things. But no longer. Now they inflict themselves on the Common Market and become the economic sick man of Europe. In fifteen years only Spain and Portugal will boast a lower standard of living. And it's their own fault. With myopic management and the laziest, least competent workmen in Europe, they suffer from congenital inefficiency. Not the placid, happy inefficiency of the Latins, with their mañana mentalities and hedonistic lassitude. No, the British brand of incompetence is involute and labored. It's a bustling, nervous inefficiency that fails to make up in charm and quality of life what it sacrifices in productivity. The Briton has become a compromise between the Continental, whom he used to despise out of contempt, and the American, whom he now despises out of envy. His is a land of Old World technology and New World beauty. And that's all there is to say about the British."

Jonathan was going to protest against this gratuitous attack on their hosts when Strange continued, "You know, during the war there used to be a riddle in contempt of the Belgian army. One used to ask, 'What would you do if a Belgian soldier threw a hand grenade at you?' And the answer was, 'Pull out the pin, and throw it back.' If the question were asked of the British soldier, it would be totally academic because the hand grenades would arrive six months after the promised date of delivery, the workmanship would be faulty, and the army would be on strike anyway."

"If they disgust you so, why are you here?"

"The police, old man! It is a popular myth that British criminals are Europe's most clever, just barely kept in rein by the brain-children of Conan Doyle and Ian Fleming. These people glory in their train robbers and confidence men, their Robin Hoods from Stepney Green. It is typical of their blinkered Weltanschauung that it never occurs to them that it is not the dash and cleverness of their petty hoodlums that win the day, it is the monumental incompetence of their police. For a man in my profession, the British police are the most comfortable in Europe, just as the Dutch are the least. Of course, if you were interested in civil liberties, it would be quite the other way around. Surely the table is laid for supper by now. You must be looking forward to meeting Amazing Grace again."

Conversation in the small paneled dining room was light and oblique, never touching on the matter of the Marini Horse, nor indeed on the events that had led to this peculiar early morning supper. Amazing Grace conducted the chat with the skill of a geisha, giving both men opportunities to display wit, and leavening all with her personal touch of ribald earthiness. As was her preference in social moments, she was nude, and so the room was kept warm and cozy by a gas fire set in a fireplace of curiously wrought iron. While she and Jonathan dined on rack of lamb, Strange went through a series of dishes featuring pallid substances with mealy aromas. In place of the wine they enjoyed, he drank goat's milk. It was only with the fruit and cheese that his diet and theirs converged. The cheese board bore many cheeses, yet only one. There was Danish blue, Roquefort, Gorgonzola, and Stilton. Strange explained that, next to yogurt, the blue-veined cheeses were best for digestion. The fruits were all organically grown and free from insecticides, and there were no bananas which, it seemed, were eatable only in the tropics where they were allowed to ripen naturally.

Jonathan admired the way in which Amazing Grace excelled as hostess, enthroned on her special elevated chair, and he remarked in passing that she had all the social graces of a parson's daughter, together with some of the traditionally suspected appetites.

"But I *was* a parson's daughter," she said with a rich laugh. "Not that all that many people have heard of The First Evangelical Synagogue of the Blessed Lord and All His Works."

Two-mouths brought in the brandy and coffee on a tray, then joined Leonard against the wall in silent vigil.

"There's a certain social advantage to eating in the destructive way you two seem to enjoy," Strange said. "The arrival of brandy is the accepted signal for talk of business. And, as I have none of my own, may I use yours for that purpose?"

"Well, if things are going to get serious," Grace said, "I'll slip into a robe. I wouldn't want my bobbing little boobies distracting anyone."

Jonathan said that was a thoughtful gesture.

"All right," Strange began, flicking an imaginary bit of lint from his sleeve. "As you know, I intend to turn the Marini Horse into liquid money. The other evening, when I broached that possibility to you,

you said that the five million pounds I was expecting to get would cause some comment in art circles."

"More like a riot, I'd say."

"Even if the figure were arrived at in public auction at Sotheby's?"

"Particularly then. Marini is still alive; his work lacks the fiscal kudos of his death. And after all, the man is a Modern."

"Yes, I am aware of your reactionary preferences in art. I've read a couple of your books by way of trying to understand your personality. But the abstract artistic value of the casting is not to the point here. What I am interested in is getting the price I want without undue public notice. More specifically, Dr. Hemlock, I want forty-eight hours from the time of the sale before there is any official reaction. Can you arrange that?"

"At a price."

"That's my kind of man!" Grace interjected.

"What price?" Strange asked.

"Well, naturally, I would like to get whatever the market will bear. But I'm afraid my native greed will have to give way to a very real interest in survival. I told you that I have to hire a man to put that CII official away before he fingers me again. I estimate that that will cost me about fifty thousand dollars."

"So much?"

"He's a deep man, hard to get at."

"Very well, fifty thousand then."

"A little more, I'm afraid. To pull this off, I shall need baksheesh to spread around among the local critics and newspaper people—mostly indirect baksheesh, of course."

"Give me a total," Strange said curtly.

"Thirty thousand pounds."

Strange and Grace exchanged glances. "Your services are dear," Strange said.

"Oh, please. If you're pulling in five million, then—"

"Yes. All right. Thirty thousand then. But let me impress on you, as a gesture of friendship, how foolish it would be for you to try to double-cross me on this."

"You would sic the dummy there on me, right?"

"Indeed I would. And I have a feeling that Leonard is none too fond of you as it is, after the dental damage you inflicted on his mate."

"If you're through flexing your muscles, there are some things I have to know if I'm to do this business for you."

"Such as?"

"Is the Marini legally yours?"

"Oh yes. Bill of sale and all."

"I assume you will deliver it to Sotheby's for the auction?"

"The morning of that day, yes."

"Where is it now?"

Strange turned to him slowly, like a casemate gun swinging onto a target. "That is none of your business. It is perfectly safe, and it can be produced quite quickly, at my volition. Anything more?"

"One thing. How much time do I have to prepare the way?"

"The auction is Wednesday morning."

"Four days? I only have four days?"

"That will have to be enough. Grace and I cannot afford to linger about. And, anyway, my affection for the British is not without limits. I shall be glad to see the last of this narrow little island."

Grace stood and stretched, her fingers stiff and reflexed in the air, her abbreviated peignoir rising above the taut buttocks, her splayed toes gripping the carpet. "I think I'll go into the Aquarium for a nightcap. Maybe a look at the customers will turn me on." She smiled and left the room, the purling of her tense body under its gossamer gown arresting conversation until she had disappeared.

"Nice little bonbon there," Jonathan commented.

"Oh, yes. I enjoy bringing her pleasure. I arrange complicated little events for her. She's so daring and inventive, it's great fun to plan for her."

"You're a selfless man."

Strange laughed. "My dear man! I never indulge in sexual activity myself."

"Never?"

"Not since I was a boy. I passed my youth in establishments of this kind. As you may know, it is the practice of candy manufacturers to allow their workers to eat to their heart's content when first they are employed. Within a few months, the workers become so cloyed that they make no further inroads on the merchandise."

"And you never—"

"Never. Too draining. Too hard on the body. But I have my own vice. Unfortunately, it's the most expensive vice in the world."

Jonathan pictured Amazing Grace's body. "Wasteful," he couldn't help commenting.

"I have other uses for Grace. A devoted ally, and a decoration without equal. I delight in the effect we create together. She, petite, proud, beautiful, sensuous. And I . . ." He paused and shrugged. "And I am graceful and classically handsome. There is not a jaw that does not tighten with envy when we make an entrance."

He had admitted being handsome so matter-of-factly as to make it almost acceptable. And indeed, he was classically handsome, the most handsome man Jonathan had ever seen outside Greek sculpture.

But he was not attractive. His features were so regular, so smooth, so anticipated that the eye slipped over them, finding nothing to engage it. The face lacked the arresting traction of biographic imprint: there were no creases of concern, no grooves of concentration, no crinkles of laughter. Even the pallid, round eyes kept clear and sparkling with tinted eyedrops were devoid of narrative. The fall of light and shadow over his smoothly tanned features had the uninspired, geometric quality of the novice artist's solution to a problem of chiaroscuro —very accurate, very dull.

"Shall we join Grace for a nightcap?" Jonathan asked, eager to end this evening while he was still ahead.

"By all means. Oh, there *is* one more thing, come to think of it. How did you get on to Grace and the Cellar d'Or establishment?"

For the first time, Jonathan was taken off balance by Strange's technique of the sudden question dropped non sequitur.

Strange laughed. "Miss Dyke must be very fond of you indeed to impart such delicate information."

"I put a little pressure on her," Jonathan said simply. Since they already knew, he confessed offhandedly to glean what advantage seeming honesty had. He was glad she was off with her writer friend with the cats and red wine.

Strange nodded. "It's comforting to know where your loyalties lie."

"With myself, as always."

"The trademark of the successful man." Strange rose. "Do let's join Grace."

When they arrived in the Aquarium, Grace was curled up in the deep leather chair, sipping at a tumbler of Everclear. "May I offer you some?"

"No," Jonathan said quickly. He crossed over and looked out into the salon, as Strange took up a perch on the arm of Grace's chair and, with an absentminded proprietorial gesture, began to roll the nipple of one breast between thumb and forefinger.

"Is everything settled?" she asked.

"I think so. Dr. Hemlock and I share qualities of selfishness and greed that augur well for a profitable cooperation."

In the salon outside, a handful of rather spent clients sat about. Two portly old gentlemen in caps and bells descended the wide Art Deco stairs, looking drained and fragile. They collected their waiting mates and left. Only two hostesses were still on duty, and one of these was leaning against the aluminum wall, her face lax and puffy. "You say the hostesses aren't hookers?" Jonathan asked.

"Do I detect a tone of carnal interest?" Strange said.

"Yes, you do. Tired though I am, I feel a bit like celebrating our agreement."

"Which one turns you on?" Grace asked.

"Looks like there's only two to pick from. I

really don't care. You're the licensed meat inspector here. Which one would you suggest? The blonde?"

Grace sat up and looked over the choices. "I wouldn't say so. That other one—she's got the right muscle arrangement for it. She's an Irish girl. Our model agency sent her over this morning and I interviewed her. She's not really cute, with that ragamuffin face of hers, but there's something about those big green eyes and that hair that I felt was perfect for the flapper look." Grace's professional eye scanned the girl's legs and buttocks. "Yeah," she said sitting back, "she'll give you the better ride."

"If she is willing," Jonathan said.

"Don't worry about that," Strange said. "I'll arrange it for you—a gift to seal our bargain in the Arabic way. A little shot of dream juice, and she will be yours—moist and panting. But you're sure you wouldn't prefer something a bit more—occult?"

"No. She'll do fine. But no cantharis."

"Why not?"

"I'm tired. If I can't make it, I don't want her groaning about and groping at me all night."

Strange laughed. "As you wish. We have a little something that will render her perfectly pliable. She will know what is going on, but she will be without will. But I'm afraid she may babble a bit."

"Better a babbler than a groper."

"Pity the options are so limited." Strange rose. "I'll bid you good night, if I may. It's already seventeen minutes after my bedtime, and, as you may have noted, I am a man of routine. I'll attend to the Irish bit on my way. We'll take breakfast together and discuss details. Is noon too early for you?"

He left without awaiting an answer to this rhetorical question.

Amazing Grace poured herself another drink and sat again in the deep chair, her knees drawn up and her feet on the seat, her furry écu revealed between her heels. "Well, what do you think of Max? Isn't he a beautiful person?"

"I suppose," he said, pressing his eyes with his thumb and forefinger in an effort to relax the tension in his temples. "But there's something hokey and childish in the way he plays it for Mephistopheles. A kind of campish eviler-than-thou."

Out in the salon, Jonathan saw Two-mouths approach Maggie and speak to her. She frowned and followed him toward a back door. Jonathan hoped she wouldn't put up too much of a fight when they put the needle in her.

"You're not trying to tell me that Max didn't impress you, are you, honey bun?"

"Oh, no. He impressed me all right. In fact, he scares the shit out of me."

She laughed. "I really like you, Hemlock. You must have been some kind of bad actor in your day. Only really tough men admit to being scared. Cheers." She emptied her glass, and he could not help swallowing twice sympathetically in a vicarious effort to help her get it down. "But," she continued, "he's a rare and beautiful animal. He's really evil, you know. Black mass sort of thing. Not just nasty or naughty or crotch-happy, like most men who think they're bad. But really *evil*. And there's nothing sexier than that. You have to get past sin, past sacrilege before things get really delicious."

"What does P'tit Noel think about all this?"

"He doesn't even know about The Cloisters. And if he did, it wouldn't matter. He'd do anything in the world for me. Like a puppy dog—like a real big, real fierce puppy dog, that is."

"Hey, would you mind not pointing that thing at me? It makes me nervous."

She laughed and pulled down her peignoir.

"And you don't feel sorry for P'tit Noel?"

"Hell no. I know his type. He likes getting hurt. Big gesture; romantic crash. Like winos who drink because it's so goddamn tragic and attractive to be a wino. You know what I mean?"

"Yes, madam, I do." He ran his fingers through his hair, tugging at the back of it to suppress his fatigue. "May I ask you something, Grace?"

"Shoot."

"I can't understand how Van Dyke got mixed up with you people. I've known her for years, and I can't imagine what Strange could have paid her that would bring her into this."

"He didn't pay her," she said, tickling her lips with the rim of her empty glass and smiling at him. "*I* did."

Jonathan looked down. "I see."

Two-mouths conducted him through the exercise room into the now empty salon, its Art Deco sconces still ablaze. Jonathan looked toward the wall of mirrors behind which he assumed Amazing Grace was sitting, finishing a last Everclear. He waved good night to her, feeling a little foolish as he saw only his reflection wave back.

Up the wide staircase with its aluminum walls buffed in patterns of swirls, and down the long cor-

ridor, Two-mouths kept up a patter of talk to which
Jonathan attended only vaguely.

"You could of knocked me over with a feather,
you could, sir, when Mr. Strange told me to fix up
that hostess for you. I thought you'd be done for
sure, what with how you give such a beating to
Lolly—he's the one what's teeth you cracked off,
Lolly is. She didn't half put up a fight, that little
Mick. Took two of us to get the needle in. Good
thing for her Leonard wasn't there. He'd have done
it right enough, and no fuss either. She wouldn't of
been able to walk for a week, if Leonard had done
it. He doesn't half rip 'em when he gets a chance.
Well, here we are, sir. Pleasant dreams."

Jonathan entered the dark bedroom, and the door
clicked locked behind him. The city glow beyond
the window gave dim illumination, and he could see
a bundled figure on the bed. She turned in her delirium and moaned softly, then she laughed to herself.

It was in rooms like this that the compromising
films of government officials had been taken, and
possibly some of them had been taken in the dark.
Jonathan removed his jacket and checked his shirt
sleeve. The starch gave off none of the phosphorescent glow that would indicate infrared light, so at
least this room was not equipped with cameras and
sniper scope lenses. But it was doubtless bugged and,
under the drugs, she might say something that would
give him away. He had to keep that in mind.

He undressed quickly and approached the bed.
Maggie had been tossed onto it, still dressed in her
flapper frock. One shoe was off and the other dangled from a toe, and a rope of beads had fallen
across her face. In the dim light she opened her eyes

and stared up at him, frowning. She was confused, trying hard to understand what was happening to her. As the needle had entered her, she had reminded herself that she must do nothing to endanger Jonathan's cover, and that thought had gone swirling down with her into the churn and chaos of distorted reality. She had clung to it for a time, then she had forgotten what it was she was clinging to. But it was important. She remembered that much.

"What? ... What ..." She looked at him, her eyes pleading for help. Then she laughed again.

"My name is Jonathan Hemlock," he told her immediately, really speaking for the microphones. It would not do for her to name him out of the blue.

"Jonathan? Jonathan?"

"That's right. But you can call me 'honey.' Come on, let's get your clothes off."

"Are my clothes still on?" She spoke with the clumsy diction of someone whose lip is rubbery from dentist's Novocain. "Isn't that funny?"

"A knee-slapper. Come on. Turn over."

He undressed her as quickly as possible, but with her limp and uncooperative body, it was not easy. Indeed, some bits would have been comic under less dangerous circumstances. She, at least, found it funny.

"Say," she said with the sudden seriousness of a drunk. "Do you really think we should be doing this?"

"Why not? We live in a permissive society."

"But ... here? Isn't it ... isn't it dangerous?"

"I'll be careful."

"What? What? I don't understand, Jonathan."

"You see? You remember my name."

"Yes, of course. Of course I know your name. You're—"

He kissed her. She hummed and drew him down to her.

He was painfully tired, but sleep was evasive. The open microphone was like a living thing in the dark, straining to catch their words, and the presence of it was palpable and uncomfortable. Maggie slept. The drugs had been good for her in one way. They had liberated her even beyond her usual abandoned and inventive lovemaking, and climax had been a total and body-shuddering thing for her, as though the sensation had begun in the small of her back and gushed outward. She had worked hard at it, and then she had slept, curled up on her side, sitting in his lap, his arms around her, completely and safely wrapped up by him.

He did not know she had awakened when she spoke softly. "Jonathan?"

He instantly thought of the bug—probably in the headboard to catch guests' quietest words. "Go to sleep, honey," he said rather harshly.

"I love you, Jonathan." It was a declarative sentence. A matter of fact. She might have said it was Tuesday, or raining.

"Well, that's just great, honey. You're a warm, wonderful, loving person. Now please let me get some sleep, will you?" But the microphone could not transmit the message in the way he hugged her in and buried his cheek in her hair.

He wondered if he would ever get to sleep, get the rest his body demanded. He was still wondering this when he awoke to find it was full day and there was a brilliant bar of sunlight across the bed. He opened his eyes and looked up. Maggie was there, sitting on the edge of the bed. She had been awake for some time, looking at his sleeping face, occasionally touching his hair gently, fearful of disturbing him, but desiring the possessive contact.

"Good morning," he said feebly, and he took her hand, only to find that his grip was too weak to squeeze it. The efforts of the past two days had caught up with him, and he had slept at coma depth.

"Good morning," she said, the brogue dealing carelessly with the vowels. She put her finger to her lips and pointed to the headboard, where a small core of metal shone dully in the center of a carved decoration.

He nodded and brought her with him as he turned around in the bed, lying with their heads at the footboard. They kissed good morning, and he brought his lips into contact with her ear and whispered to her soundlessly. "Play it out. Good girl wakes up in bed with strange man."

"Don't!" she said aloud. "Please don't."

He made a wry face at her histrionics. She shrugged; she had never pretended to be an actress.

"Do you remember last night?" he asked aloud. Then whispering he added, "You were fantastic." The danger of this double-talk was mischievously exciting, and they were in a docilely playful mood.

"Yes, I remember," she said aloud, as though ashamed. "I remember your name and . . . what we did. But how did I get here?"

"You don't recall that?"

"Something . . . a needle. I can't remember all of it." She whispered, "The Vicar wants to see you this

256

evening at his place. Something important has come up."

"Well, don't worry about it, honey," he told the microphone. "I'm sure they'll pay you for your trouble. And it really wasn't all that bad, was it?"

"Was I . . . was I good?" Her voice carried that tone of nuzzling coyness Jonathan associated with sticky mornings after, once the phase of self-recrimination had been passed. He was sorry she knew it.

"Don't worry about it," he said aloud. "You're probably a fine cook."

By way of punishment, she ran the tip of her tongue into his ear.

"Hey!"

"What is it?" she asked aloud, all innocence.

"I just remembered the time. It's late and I have worlds to conquer." He rose from bed and went into the bathroom to bathe and shave.

"Will I see you again?" she asked, enjoying the game of acting for the microphone.

"What?" he shouted from the next room over the rush of water.

"Will I see you again?"

"Certainly. Certainly. I'll look you up!"

"You don't even know my name!"

"That's all right. I'm not nosy!"

"Bastard," she muttered quietly, feeling clever about introducing just the right note of the girl whose innocence has been around.

He arrived for breakfast in the paneled dining room to find that Strange and Grace had finished and were having a last cup of tea—Earl Grey for her, rose hip for him.

"Good morning," Jonathan said cheerily. "Sorry I'm late. Slept like a hammered steer."

"Doubtless the effect of a clear conscience," Strange observed, as he broke off a bit of dry toast and put it into his mouth, rubbing his fingers together lightly to flick off crumbs that might otherwise have dropped onto his spotless white flannels.

Jonathan lifted the covers of serving dishes on the sideboard and found some eggs with chives. "And how are you this morning—or early afternoon?" He addressed Amazing Grace, who was sitting nude in a broad shaft of sunlight, her body stretched out to receive the warmth, her eyes almost closed with feline pleasure. Her tea saucer was balanced on her écu, and from Jonathan's angle it seemed that her crotch was steaming into the sunlight. He crossed to her and cupped one of her conical breasts in his palm. "I'm going to get you one of these days," he warned.

She opened her eyes. "God, you're a horny one. Didn't that Irish bit drain you off a little?"

"She's an hors d'oeuvre type; you, on the other hand, are meat and potatoes."

"You sure got a sweet way with words, honey bun."

Jonathan sat across from Strange and began to eat his eggs with appetite.

"You are in high spirits today, Dr. Hemlock."

"There's been a big load lifted from me."

"You speak of the official in Washington you intend to silence?"

"What else?" He poured himself some coffee. "Say, that girl was an odd one. Do you know what she said to me, right off the bat?"

"That she loved you?" Strange asked, unable to pass up the opportunity to show off.

Jonathan set his cup down and looked up in surprise, "Yes. How did you . . .?" Then he laughed. "The room was bugged. Of course."

"They all are. I listened to your tapes this morning as I went over my accounts. A kind of Muzak to lighten my labors."

"I'll be damned. That should have occurred to me. How do you think the girl will take being jabbed full of junk, then drilled by a stranger?"

"The process differs from romantic love only in degree and efficiency. She's a modern young lady. I judge she'll be satisfied with a handsome bonus. By the way, she called you a bastard while you were in the shower."

"Is that right? And I thought I had her by the heart. Just goes to show how vulnerable the congenital romantic can be. Would you pass the toast?"

Breakfast progressed with small talk of the kind designed to cover meaning. It was not until Grace left to dress and return to the Cellar d'Or that Strange got down to business.

"I assume you have thought about the task before you, Dr. Hemlock?"

"I have some ideas. If things work out just right, we should be able to get your asking price for the Horse without government inquiry. But I'll have to play it largely by ear, and I'll need your permission to use a free hand in making the arrangements."

Strange glanced at him. "What kind of arrangements?"

"I'm not sure yet. But I'll have to do something bold—some grand gesture that will blind them with its obviousness. By the way, I'll need some of that money for grease and baksheesh."

"How much?"

"All of it?"

Strange laughed. "Really, Dr. Hemlock!"

"Just thought I'd try. I suppose ten thousand pounds would do it."

Strange's pale eyes evaluated Jonathan for a long moment. "Very well. The money will be ready for you when you leave."

"Good."

"Ah-h, Dr. Hemlock ... Don't think of doing anything foolhardy. Please remember that unfortunate fellow who was found impaled in the belfry of St. Martin's-In-The-Fields."

"I get the picture. Is there more coffee?"

"Certainly. Leonard did that business at my request, not that the impulsive devil didn't get pleasure from it on his own. The informer was drugged and brought to the church, where the stake had earlier been set in place. They lifted the fellow to just above it, the point lightly touching his anus. Then Leonard jumped down and swung his weight from his ankles, driving him well on. Gravity did the rest. But with that unhurried pace characteristic of natural forces." Strange laid his hand on Jonathan's arm and squeezed it paternally. "I hope you understand why I am burdening you with the lurid details."

"Yes, I understand."

"Good. Good." He patted the arm and withdrew his hand.

Jonathan's eyes were clouded with his gentle combat smile when he said, "Tell me. Would you mind passing the marmalade?"

Covent Garden/ Brook Street/ The Vicarage

The lone painter who worked with tunnel concentration before a vast canvas in MacTaint's converted fruit warehouse was the ragged, furious man with long skinny arms who had come to assume over the years that the space, the stove, and the tea were his by squatter's right. He snapped his head around angrily as Jonathan pushed open the corrugated metal door, allowing a gust of wind to enter with him. The painter continued to fix Jonathan with a wild stare until the door had been slid to, guillotining the offending shaft of blue daylight that had intruded on the yellow pool of tungsten light from the naked bulb hanging from a long frayed cord.

Jonathan's light greeting was parried by a rasping growl as the painter used the interruption as an opportunity to heap another shovelful of coal into the large potbellied stove. As a final gesture of impa-

261

tience, he kicked the stove door closed violently, almost immediately regretting that he was not wearing shoes.

Receiving no answer to his light knock on the inner door, but hearing a voice from within, Jonathan pushed the door open and looked in. Lilla was sprawled in a deep wing chair before the television, a half-empty glass of gin dangling from her pudgy hand and the crumbs of some earlier feast decorating the front of her feathered dressing gown. In a self-satisfied drone of BBC English, a commentator was summing up the industrial situation which, it appeared, was not so bad as it might be. True, the gas workers were on strike, as were the train drivers, the teachers, the hospital workers, the automotive workers, and the truckers; but the dockers might soon return to work, and there was a chance that the threatened strikes of the civil servants, the electricians, the printers, the construction workers, and the miners might be delayed if the government conceded to their demands.

"Hello?"

She turned her head and peered in his general direction, her eyes watery and uncertain. "Now, don't tell me, young man. I never forget a face."

"Is MacTaint around?"

"He's gone beyond. To relieve his bladder, as we used to say in the theatre. Come in. Entrez. I was just havin' my mid-afternoon pick-me-up. Care to join me?" She gestured toward the bar with her half-full glass of gin, slopping the contents in a discrete arc.

"No, thank you , Lilla. I just wanted to see—"

"You know my name! So we *have* met before. I

told you I never forget a face. It was in the theatre, of course. Now let me see . . ."

Just then MacTaint came shuffling in, wearing his long overcoat and mumbling to himself. "Ah, Jonathan! Good to see you!"

"The gentleman and I was just havin' a chat about the old days in the business, if you don't mind."

"What business was that?"

"The theatre, as you know perfectly well."

"Oh yes, I remember now. You used to sell chocolates in the aisle and your ass in the alley out back. The chocolates went better, as I recall."

"Here! That will be enough of that, you stinking old fart." She turned her wobbling head to Jonathan. "Do excuse the diction."

"Right, now get along with you. We have business to talk over."

"Don't exercise that tone of voice in my presence, you dinky-cocked son of a bitch!"

"Slam a bung in it, you ha'penny flop, and get your dripping hole upstairs!"

"Really!" Lilla drew herself up, fixed MacTaint's general area with a stare of quivering disdain, and swept to her exit.

MacTaint scratched at his scruffy beard, his lower teeth bared in painful pleasure. "Sorry about her, lad. Of late she's been nervy as a cat shitting razor blades. But she's a good old bitch, even if she does take a sip now and then."

"I could use a drink, if there's any left."

"Done." Eddies of ancient sweat were almost overcoming as MacTaint brushed past on his way to the bar, moving with his characteristic shambling half trot. He returned with two glasses of Scotch and handed one to Jonathan, then he sprawled heavily in a fainting couch of rosewood, one ragged boot up on the damask upholstery, his chin buried in the collar of his amorphic overcoat. "Well, here's to sin." He swilled it off with a great smacking of lips. "Now! I suppose you're needing your two hundred quid."

"No. You keep it. For your trouble."

"That's very good of you. But holding it's been no trouble."

"I'm talking about future trouble."

"I was afraid you might be." The old man's eyes glittered beneath his antennal eyebrows. "What future trouble?"

"I'm still not in the clear, Mac."

"Sorry to hear that."

"I need help."

MacTaint pursued an itch from his cheek to his shoulder, then down his back inside the greatcoat, but it seemed just out of reach to his fingertips. "What kind of help?" he asked after scratching his back against the chair.

Jonathan sipped his whiskey. "The theft of the Chardin. Is it still on?"

Instantly Mac's voice was flat and tentative, and the leprechaun façade fell away. "It is, yes."

"And it's still scheduled for Tuesday night?"

"Yes. Why do you ask?"

"I want to go with you." Jonathan placed his glass carefully on the parqueted side table.

MacTaint examined a new tear in his canvas trousers with close interest. "Why?"

"Can't tell you, Mac. But it's tied up with the trouble I'm in."

"I see. Why didn't you lie and make up some convincing story?"

"I would never do that, Mac."

"Because we're such great friends?"

"No. Because you'd see through it."

MacTaint enjoyed a good laugh, then a short choke, then a long racking cough that ended with his spitting on the carpet. "You're a proper villain, Jonathan Hemlock. That's why I like you. You con a man by admitting you're conning a man. That's very fine." He wiped his eyes with his fist and changed tone. "Tell me this. Will taking you along screw up my work?"

"I don't see why. You only need a couple of minutes, using your technique."

"Ah, then you know what my technique is?"

"I've had a couple of days to figure it out. Only one possibility. You get a good fake. You mutilate it, break in, and swap it for the original. Everyone assumes there's been an act of vandalism—not a theft. The fake is repaired with care, and if anyone ever notices a blemish, it's put down to the repair job."

"Precisely, my son! And, though I say it who shouldn't, there's a touch of genius in it. I nicked my share of paintings in the past ten years this way."

"And that accounts for the rash of vandalism in British museums."

"Not quite. In one case a real vandal broke in and damaged a painting, the heartless son of a bitch!"

Jonathan waited a moment before asking, "Well? Can I go with you?"

MacTaint clawed meditatively at the scruff on his scalp. "I suppose so. But mind you, if there's trouble, it's devil take the hindmost. I love you like a son, Jon. But I wouldn't do porridge even for a son."

"Great. What time do I meet you on Tuesday night?"

"About ten, I suppose. That will give us time for a few short ones before we go."

"You're a good man, MacTaint."

"True enough. True enough."

Because it was handier, Jonathan went to his Mayfair flat to make a pattern of calls to selected art reviews and critics who create British taste. His approach differed slightly, but only slightly, as he covered the range from *The Guardian* to *Time and Tide*. In each case he introduced himself, and there was the inevitable catch in the conversation as the person on the other end of the line realized to whom he was speaking. Jonathan began by assuming the critic had heard that a Marini Horse was in the country and was going up for auction within a week. He smiled as the critic inevitably responded that he had indeed heard something of this. What he was seeking, Jonathan said, was reliable verification of the rumor that the Horse would bring between three and five million in the bidding. After a pause, the critic said he wouldn't be surprised—not a bit surprised. Their initial flush of pleasure at being consulted by Jonathan Hemlock inevitably gave way to the public school whine of superior knowledge. Jonathan knew the type and expected their self-esteem to expand to fill any space he left for it.

He made a point of mentioning each time that the mossbacks of the National Gallery had pulled off quite a coup in securing the Marini Horse for a one-day exhibition just before it went off to the auction room, but he assumed the critic already knew all about that. The critic knew all about that, and several of them intimated that they had had some modest part in the arrangements. Each conversation ended with pleasantries and regrets for not having got together for lunch—a social hiatus Jonathan intended to fill in at the first opportunity.

As he dialed each new number, Jonathan pictured the last man hastily thumbing through reference volumes, taking rapid notes and frowning importantly.

In his mind Jonathan could see the prototypical article, some version of which would appear in a score of major and minor papers the day after tomorrow. "It has long been the opinion of this writer that the innovative work of Marini has suffered from a lack of study and recognition in England. But it is to be hoped that this gap will be closed by a forthcoming landmark event that I have been following closely: the public auction of one of Marini's characteristic bronze Horses. Unless I miss my guess, the Horse will bring something in the neighborhood of five million, and although this figure may surprise the reader (and some of my colleagues, I am sorry to say), it is no surprise at all to the few who have followed the work of this modern sculptor whose genius is only now coming into full recognition.

"It is particularly telling that the National Gallery, not distinguished by its innovative imagination, has arranged to place the Marini Horse on display for one day before it is sold and—who knows—possibly lost to England forever. Etc. Etc."

Jonathan's finger was tender with dialing by the

time he had finished his list of two-step opinion leaders. But he made one further call, this one to fforbes-Ffitch at the Royal College of Art.

"Jonathan! How good of you to call! Just a moment. Let me clear the decks here, so I can talk to you." fforbes-Ffitch held the telephone away from his mouth to tell his secretary that he would continue his dictation later.

"Now then, Jonathan! Good Lord! I'm up to my ears. No rest for the wicked, eh?"

"Nor for the poorly organized."

"What? Oh. Oh, yes." He laughed heavily at the jest, to prove he had gotten it. "One thing is certain: The men higher up certainly cleave to the adage that the only way to get a job done is to give it to a busy man. My desk's awash with things that have to be done yesterday. Oh, say! So sorry I didn't see you after that lecture here the other day. A smashing success. Sorry about the mix-up in topics. But I think you landed on your feet. And I have to admit that it was a bit of a feather in the cap to get you there. Never hurts to know who to know, right?"

"It was about feathers and caps that I wanted to talk."

"Oh?"

"You've been after me to do that series of lectures in Stockholm."

"I have indeed! Don't tell me you're weakening?"

"Yes. That is the quid. And there's a quo. You're a trustee of the National Gallery, aren't you?"

"Yes. Youngest ever. Something to do with the government attempting to project a 'with-it' image. Does what you want have something to do with the Gallery?"

"Let's get together and talk about it this afternoon."

"Lord, Jonathan. Don't know that I can. Calendar bulging, you know. Here, let's see what I can do." Holding the phone only a little away from his mouth, fforbes-Ffitch clicked on his intercom. "Miss Plimsol? What do I look like for this afternoon? Over."

A voice told him he had a conference coming up in ten minutes, then he had arranged to take a business drink with Sir Wilfred Pyles at the club.

"A drink with Sir Wilfred?" fforbes-Ffitch repeated, in case Jonathan had not heard. "What time is that? Over."

"Four o'clock, sir."

"Sixteen hundred hours, eh? Right. Over and out. Jonathan? What do you say to a drink at my club at sixteen forty-five hours?"

"Fine."

"You know the club, don't you?"

"Yes, I know it."

"Right, then. See you there. Been grand chatting with you. Let's hope everyone benefits. Ta-ta."

Just as Jonathan set the phone back on its cradle, it rang under his hand, and the effect of the coincidence was a little rattling.

"Jonathan Hemlock."

"Hey, long time no see, man. Until Miss Coyne checked in with me a couple of hours ago, we didn't know what had happened to you."

"I'm fine, Yank. Why are you calling?"

"I've been trying to get you for two hours. But your line was always busy. What's up, doc?"

"You can tell the Vicar that things are moving along."

"Great. But you can tell him yourself. Tonight. Things are coming to a head. He wants to have a little confab with you. Can do?"

"Miss Coyne mentioned that to me. Where?"

"At the Vicarage."

"All right. I'll drive out. Probably get there six or seven in the evening."

"Roger-dodger. Oh, by the way. Sorry I wasn't able to get through to those MI–5 guys in time."

"That's all right. I took care of them."

"Yes, I know. The man at MI–5 had me on the carpet. Two of the guys are still in hospital."

"They probably need the rest."

"I thought it would be best if we didn't mention this to the Vicar. No use getting his bowels in an uproar. You dig?"

"Whatever."

"Okeydoke. Hang in there."

Jonathan hung up. Talking to Yank always filled him with bone-deep fatigue—like the prospect of going shopping with a woman.

Then one oblique consolation to all this occurred to him. Whatever happened, he had ten thousand pounds from Strange—about twenty-five thousand dollars made at the cost of a few hours of telephoning. The trick was, living to spend it.

fforbes-Ffitch's club was only a short walk up from Claridge's, not far from Jonathan's Mayfair flat. It was typically clubby: a good address for taking lunch; a large and comfortable dining room with stiff linen and conversation, where one was served by nanny waitresses with skins the color and texture of the Yorkshire puddings they foisted upon you; the carafe wine was decent; and there were heavy comfortable leather chairs in the lounge for taking coffee and brandy, and for being seen chatting with people who wanted to be seen chatting with you. As an institution, it shared the catholic British problem of not being what it used to be. There simply wasn't the money floating about to support such monuments to gentle leisure since British socialism, failing in its efforts to share the wealth, had devoted itself to sharing the poverty.

The ostensible criteria for club membership were relations with the world of art and letters, but there were more critics than painters, more publishers than writers, more teachers than practitioners. Typically correct in bulk and shoddy in detail, it was the kind of place that prided itself on an excellent Stilton soaked in port, but served white pepper. The members wore suits, the fine material and careless fitting of which bespoke London's better tailors, but they wore short socks that displayed rather a lot of shiny, pallid shin as they sat sprawled in the lounge.

fforbes-Ffitch was just saying good-bye to Sir Wilfred when the part-French hostess conducted Jonathan into their company.

"Ah! There you are, Jonathan. Sir Wilfred, may I present Jonathan Hemlock? He's the man I was just mentioning—"

"Hello, Jon."

"Fred."

"Damned if it doesn't seem that everybody in London is devoted to the task of introducing us.

271

Makes me wonder if there was something faulty in our first acquaintance."

"Oh." fforbes-Ffitch was crestfallen. "You've met, then."

"Rather often, really," Sir Wilfred said. "We've just been chatting, fforbes-Ffitch and I, about your going to Stockholm to do that series of lectures for him. You will have my commission's fiscal support. Delighted you have decided to do it, Jon."

"It isn't settled yet."

"Oh?" Sir Wilfred raised his eyebrows at fforbes-Ffitch. "I'd rather got the impression it was."

"I'm sure we'll be able to work it out," f-F said quickly, with an offhand gesture.

"Say, may I have a word with you, Jon? You wouldn't mind, would you?"

"Not at all," fforbes-Ffitch said. He stood smiling politely at the silent men, then with a sudden catch he said, "Oh! Oh, I see. Yes. Well, I'll order a couple of drinks then." He departed for the bar.

Sir Wilfred drew Jonathan toward the deep-set windows that overlooked the street. "Tell me, Jon. Are you quite all right? I am speaking of this Maximilian Strange business, of course."

"Don't worry, Fred. There's nothing going on. It was a false alarm."

Sir Wilfred examined Jonathan's eyes closely. "Well, let's hope so." Then his manner relaxed and brightened. "Well, now I must be off."

"The demands of business?"

"What? Oh. No. The demands of dalliance, actually. Take care."

Jonathan found fforbes-Ffitch sitting rigidly on the front edge of a deep lounge chair in a quiet corner.

He was making much of being a busy man kept waiting, frowning and checking his watch. "You might have told me you knew Sir Wilfred," he complained, as Jonathan sat across from him. "Saved me a touch of embarrassment."

"Nonsense. Embarrassment becomes you."

"Oh? Really? No, you're having me on."

"Look, I don't want to take too much of your valuable time."

fforbes-Ffitch appreciated that. "Right. Got another appointment at seventeen thirty hours."

"Roger. Then let's get to it." Jonathan made his case quickly. ff-F was obviously committed to gaining credit by persuading Jonathan to undertake the lecture series in Sweden. In fact, he had rather overstated Jonathan's willingness to Sir Wilfred. OK. Jonathan would do the lectures if in return ff-F would use his influence as a trustee of the National Gallery to persuade them to display the Marini Horse publicly the day before it was auctioned off.

"Oh, I don't know, Jonathan. A privately owned object in the Nat? Never been done before. Has all the characteristics of a publicity trick. I just don't know if they'll go along with it."

"Oh, I was hoping your influence would be sufficient to swing it." Jonathan's instinct for the jugular proved correct.

"I may be able to, Jonathan. Certainly give it a bash."

"You might mention in your argument that half the art reviewers in England will be mentioning in their papers that the piece will be on display at the Gallery. Your fellow trustees wouldn't want to disappoint the taxpaying public, to say nothing of making fools of the critics, none of whom are too friendly with what they describe as the reactionary practices of that elite group."

"How on earth could the newspapers be saying such a thing?"

Jonathan lifted his palms in an exaggerated shrug. "Who knows where they get their wild ideas?"

fforbes-Ffitch looked long and very slyly at Jonathan. "This is your doing, isn't it?" he accused, shaking a finger.

"You see right through me, don't you? No use trying to con a con."

fforbes-Ffitch nodded conspiratorially. "All right, Jonathan. I think I can assure you that the other trustees will listen to reason. But not without a battle. And in return, you owe me one lecture tour. I know you'll love Stockholm."

True to club routine, the drinks arrived just as they had risen to leave.

Maggie sat on the edge of an oaken bench beside the hearth, unmindful of the glass of port beside her. The focus of her soft unblinking attention was the languets of flame that flickered deep within the log fire, but the attitude of her body and her half-closed eyes indicated that she was looking through the fire into something else. Daydreams, perhaps.

Leaning against a bookcase in the Vicar's study, Jonathan watched the play of light in her fine autumnal hair. The unlit side of her face was toward him, and her profile was modeled by an undulating band of firelight along the forehead and nose. Subtle shifts of color from the flames were amplified in her hair, now accenting the amber, now the copper.

A gust in the stormy night drafted through the chimney, flaring the embers with a bassoon moan, and breaking her fragile concentration. She blinked and inhaled like someone awakening, then she turned and greeted him with a slight smile.

"Boyoboy, it's sure raining cats and dogs," Yank said from across the room where he had been nursing a funk and dealing heavy blows to the Vicar's port supply. He had been set off his feed earlier that evening while they were dining at the Olde Worlde Inn. They had been served lamb couscous, and someone had jokingly mentioned that they owed the feast to governmental indecision. The Feeding Station had been preparing a victim to be found dead in Algiers, but there had been a change in plans. Yank had blanched and left the room. Until this banal meteorological observation, he had been uniquely silent, and the forced energy in his voice indicated that he was not completely over the crisis of disgust.

"Sorry to keep you waiting." The Vicar entered with a drawn and preoccupied air. His gray face and the lifeless hang of his jowls and wattle over his ingrown celluloid dog collar attested to days of tension and strain, as did the intensification of his nervous wink. "At least I see you have found the port. Good." He lowered himself heavily into his reading chair beside the fire. As a passing gust of wind stiffened the tongues of flame and sucked them up the fire step, Jonathan recognized the ironically Dickensian quality of their little grouping.

"Let me say at the outset that I am not very pleased with you, Dr. Hemlock," the Vicar said, winking.

"Oh?"

"No. Not pleased. You have not kept in regular contact with us as you were instructed to do. Indeed, were it not for Miss Coyne's report of this afternoon, we shouldn't even have known that you had gained entrée into The Cloisters."

"I've been busy."

"No doubt. You have also been disobedient. But I shall not dwell on your insubordination."

"That's wonderful of you."

The Vicar stared at Jonathan with heavy reproof. Then he winked. "The situation is grave. Much graver than I could have guessed. As you will recall, we were puzzled over the fact that Maximilian Strange did not seem to be making use of the damaging film for blackmail. Doubts concerning his ultimate motive for collecting the filthy evidence have plagued us almost as much as have the films themselves. And the Loo organization overseas has concentrated all its energies on solving the enigma. Bits and pieces of information have been collected, and they fit together to make a frightening picture. Not to put too fine a point on it, the situation is this: England is for sale." He paused dramatically to allow the significance of this to sink in. "In point of fact, effective control of the British government is to be auctioned off. The power holding those recriminating films will be able to bleed us dry—trade concessions, NATO secrets, North Sea oil—all this will go to the highest bidder."

Jonathan found himself wondering whether it was the fact of the sale or the democratic nature of the bidding that pained him the more deeply.

"At this very moment," the Vicar continued,

"representatives of every major power are congregating in London; gold transfers are being arranged in Switzerland; and secret talks are being conducted in embassies. Not excluding your own embassy, Dr. Hemlock," he added with stern emphasis.

"Who knows? You may enjoy working for Yurasis Dragon when CII takes you over."

"Don't be flip, Hemlock!" He winked angrily. "I promise you that long before such a thing is realized, you will be in the dock facing irrefutable charges of murder. Is that clear?"

"Get off my ass, padre."

"Sir?" He winked three times in rapid succession.

"Your threats are empty. You say the entire Loo organization has been working on this?"

"They have."

"Do they know when the sale is to take place?"

"No, not precisely."

"Do they know where?"

"No, they don't."

"Do they know where the films are now?"

"No!"

"I know all three. So get off my ass, and stop making empty threats."

Maggie smiled into her glass, as the Vicar brought his indignation under professional control. He rose heavily and crossed to his desk, where he shuffled some papers around pointlessly, making thinking time. "Dr. Hemlock, you represent everything I detest in the aggressive American personality."

Jonathan checked his watch.

The Vicar's hands closed into fists. Then they relaxed slowly, and he turned back. "But ... I have learned in my business to admire efficiency, whatever its source. So!" He pressed his eyes closed and took a deep breath. "I assume you have worked out a way to intercept the films and deliver them to me?"

"I have."

"You realize, of course, that you must accomplish this quite on your own. I won't have the police in on this, or the Secret Service. No one must have the slightest hint of the awkward predicament our leaders have gotten themselves into."

"You've made that abundantly clear."

"Good. Good. Now tell me—where are the films?"

"They're inside a bronze casting by Marini."

"How do you know this?"

"Fairly obvious deduction. Maximilian Strange has engaged me to help him sell a Marini Horse at auction for five million pounds—more than a hundred times its market value. It's obvious that the Marini is not the item for sale. The Horse is only the envelope."

"I see. Yes. Where does this auction take place?"

"At Sotheby's, three days from now. The Horse will be on display at the National Gallery the day before the auction, and that's when I get the films."

"You are going to steal from the National Gallery?"

"Yes. I have a friend who is a regular nocturnal visitor there."

"And you are quite sure you can manage this?"

"I have great faith in my friend's ability to get in and out of the National Gallery at will. I shall be going with him on this occasion."

"He knows about the films?"

"No."

"Good. Good." The Vicar mulled over the information for a time, winking to himself. "Tell me. How did the films get inside the statue in the first place?"

"This particular Marini is known as the Dallas Horse. It was broken by a careless Texan, then brazed together. The story is widely known in art circles. It was a simple matter to cut it open along the braze, deposit the films, then braze it over again."

"I see. And you are absolutely sure the films are there?"

"I'm satisfied they are. Maximilian Strange detests England. It's his only passion. If he were only selling a bronze statue, there would be no reason to do so from London. In fact, the statue was brought over here from the States. Clearly it's the films that are the homegrown product."

The Vicar returned to his reading chair and mused for several minutes, slight noddings of his head accompanying his location of each piece in its place. "Yes, I'm sure you're right," he said at last. "It's so like Strange. An open auction at Sotheby's!" He chuckled. "Brazen and amazing man. A worthy foe."

"You told me earlier that you considered Strange to be the cleverest man in Britain ... which might be considered damning with faint praise."

The Vicar looked up. "Did I? Well, now I am sure I was right." He turned to Yank, who had been looking on without participating, still heavy with the wine he had been drinking to excess. "Fill the doctor's glass. It appears we have reason to celebrate."

"I'll take the wine, but you shouldn't delude yourself that we're home and dry. I still have to go back into The Cloisters and deal with Strange. You see, he doesn't know that his Horse is going on display in the National Gallery. He won't know that until he reads the newspapers. And I'm not sure how he will react. He's been keeping the Horse somewhere deep, and he won't be pleased to have it in the open, its gut full of films, for twenty-four hours before the auction."

"What might he do?"

"He might smell a rat. If he does, he'll probably go to ground with the films."

"What then?"

"We lose."

"I shouldn't say that so fliply, if I were you, Dr. Hemlock. Remember the dire consequences to your freedom should you fail at this."

Jonathan closed his eyes wearily and shook his head. "I don't think you see the picture. If Strange doesn't buy my story about putting the Horse on display to allay governmental curiosity over the selling price, then his response to me will be vigorous, probably total. And your threat of trial for murder won't matter much."

"You seem to take that rather calmly."

"Cite my alternatives!"

"Yes, I see. My, you *are* in a tight spot, aren't you?"

Jonathan's desire to punch that fat face was great, but he tightened his jaw and held on. "I am going to make one demand of you," he said.

"What would that be?" the Vicar asked civilly.

"Miss Coyne's out of this from here on. In fact, she is out of your organization altogether."

The Vicar looked from him to Maggie. "I see. I had been given to understand that you two were romantically involved—well, physically involved at least. So I suppose this request is to be expected. Are you sure this is what the young lady wants? Perhaps she would prefer to see you through this. Lend some support, if need be. Eh?"

"It's not her choice. I want her out."

The Vicar blew out an oral breath, his heavy cheeks fluttering. "Why not? She has served her purpose. Certainly, my dear. You are free to go. And have no fears about your little flap in Belfast. It will be taken care of." He enjoyed playing Lord Bountiful; it was the churchman in him. "However," he continued, turning to Jonathan, "I do think you would do well to take advantage of the Loo organization and bring a couple of our men along with you to the National Gallery."

Jonathan laughed. "The very last thing I need is the burden of your pack of bunglers. Those men from MI–5 who tailed me to the Cellar d'Or almost blew my cover."

"Yes, Yank told me about that. I was most disturbed. I assure you it won't happen again."

"I wasn't able to contact the guys in time to call them off," Yank explained from his corner.

"I don't care about that. Just keep any Loo people away from me."

"I'm afraid our Loo organization doesn't impress you much, Dr. Hemlock. Indeed, I have a feeling that you share with Strange a certain disdain for things British."

"Don't take it to heart. I arrived during an awkward period for your country. The twentieth century."

The Vicar tapped the desk with his fingertips. "You had better succeed, Hemlock," he said, winking furiously.

The split-reed cry of the wind around the corners of the Olde Worlde Inn slid with the force of the storm from a basso hum to a contralto quiver. Jonathan listened to it in the dark, his eyes wandering over the dim features of the ceiling.

They had not spoken for a long time, but he knew from the character of the current between them that she was awake.

"I have to give the papers time to carry the story about the Marini Horse. There's nothing for me to do tomorrow but keep out of sight."

She turned to him and placed her hand on his stomach in response.

"Do you want to spend the day with me?" he asked.

"Here?"

"Christ, no. We could run down to Brighton."

"Brighton?"

"That's not as mad as it seems. Brighton's interesting in the middle of winter. Desolate piers. Storm swept. The Lanes are empty, and the wind flutes through them. Amusement areas boarded up. There's a melancholy charm to resort areas in the off-season. Strumpets all dressed up with no place to go. Circus clowns standing in the snow."

"You're a perverse man."

"Sure. Do you want to come with me?"

"I don't know."

A metallic tympany of sleet rattled against the window, then the stiff wind backed around, and the room was silent.

"Last night, at The Cloisters . . ." She paused, then decided to press on. "Do you remember what I said?"

Of course he remembered, but he hoped she had been babbling and would forget it all later. "Oh, you were pretty much out of your head with the dope. You were just playing out fantasies."

"Is that what you want to believe?"

He didn't answer. Instead, he patted her arm.

"Don't do that! I'm not a puppy, or a child that's stubbed its toe."

"Sorry."

"I'm sorry too. Sorry the idea of being loved is such a burden to you. I think you're an emotional cripple, Jonathan Hemlock."

"Do you?"

"Yes, I do."

The downward curl of the last vowel made him smile to himself.

"I have a plan," he said after a silence. "When this thing is over, we'll get together and play it out. Gingerly. Week by week. See how it goes."

She had to laugh. "Lord love us, if you haven't found the tertium quid between proposal and proposition."

"Whichever it is, do you accept?"

"Of course I do."

"Good."

"But I don't think I'll go to Brighton with you."

He rose to one elbow and looked down at her face, just visible in the dark. "Why not?"

"There's no point to it. I'm not a masochist. If we went to Brighton together—with its sad piers and rain and ... all of that—we'd end up closer together. We'd laugh and share confidences. Make memories. Then if something happened to you ..."

"Nothing's going to happen to me! I'm a shooter, not a shootee."

"They're shooters too, darling. And worse. I'm frightened. Not only for you. I'm frightened selfishly for myself. I don't want to get all tangled up in you—my life so tangled up in your life that I can't tell which is which. Because if that were to happen, and then you were killed, I would take it very badly. I wouldn't be brave at all. I'd just roll myself into a ball and make sure I never got hurt again. I'd spend the rest of my life looking out through lace curtains and doing crossword puzzles. Or I might end up in a nunnery."

"You'd make a terrible nun."

"No. Now lie down and listen to me. Stop it. Now, here's what I'm going to do. Tomorrow morning I'm going back to my flat, and I'm going to get right into bed with a hot water bottle and a book. And every once in a while, I'll pad out and make myself some tea. And when night comes, I'll take a bunch of pills and sleep without dreaming. And the next day, I'll do the same. I hope it rains all the time, because Sterne goes best with rain. Then Tuesday night, I'll meet you here at the Vicarage. You'll give over the films, and we'll say good-bye to them, and away we'll go. And if you *don't* turn up at the Vicarage. If you ... well then, maybe I'll go down to Brighton alone. Just to see if you're lying about the wind fluting through The Lanes."

"I'll be there, Maggie. And we'll go off to Stockholm together."

"Stockholm?"

"Yes. I didn't tell you. We've agreed to do a month in Sweden. I know a little hotel on the Gamla Stan that's . . ."

"Please don't."

"I'm sorry."

"And please don't telephone me before it's all over. I don't think I could stand waiting for the phone to ring every moment."

He felt very proud of her. She was handling this magnificently. He gave her a robust hug. "Oh, Maggie Coyne! If only you could cook!"

She turned over and looked into his eyes with mock seriousness. "I really can't, you know. I can't cook at all."

Jonathan was relieved. This was much easier on him. Play it out with banter and charm. "You . . . can't . . . cook!"

"Only cornflakes. Also, I hate Eisenstein, I can't type, and I'm not a virgin. Do you still want me?"

Jonathan gasped. "Not . . . not a virgin?"

"I suppose I should have told you earlier. Before you gave your heart away."

"No. No. You were right to conceal it until I had a chance to discover your redeeming qualities. It's just that . . . just give me a little time to get used to the idea. It hurts a little at first. And for God's sake, don't ever tell me his name!"

"*His* name?" she asked with innocent confusion. "Oh! Oh, you mean *their* names."

285

"Oh, God! How can you twist the knife like that?"

"Simple as pie. I just take it by the handle, and—"

"Ouch! You gormless twit!"

Eventually they kissed, then they nestled into what had become their habitual sleeping entwinement. The rain rattled on the window, and the wind exercised the Chinese tonic scale. At last, Jonathan slipped into a deep sleep.

"Jonathan?"

He gasped awake, sitting up, hands defensively before his face. "What?"

"Why do you think I'd make a terrible nun?"

"Good night, Maggie."

"Good night."

Putney

It was midmorning when Jonathan arrived back at the Baker Street penthouse, having driven rapidly up from Brighton with the windows of the Lotus down and the wet wind swirling his hair.

The day spent alone had been good for him. His nerves were settled, and he felt fit and fast. It had rained without letup—a drowning, drenching rain that gushed down drainpipes and frothed into the gutters. He had bought a cap and a scarf and had walked slowly through the deserted Lanes and out onto the blustery piers—his wide raincoat collar the outer boundary of his vision and caring.

It was best that Maggie had not come with him. She was a wise girl.

He had eaten in a cheap cafe, the only customer. The owner had stood by the rain-streaked front window, his hands tucked up under his stained apron, and lamented the high cost of living and the weather, which, he had reason to know, had been changed for the worse by Sputniks and atomic tests.

To keep a low profile, he had stayed at a cheap bed and breakfast place, the energetic, talkative landlady of which recognized his accent and asked if he had ever met Shirley Temple face to face—bless her soul with that good ship Lollypop and that blackie who used to dance up and down the stairs (they can all dance, you have to give them that). Too bad all the picture houses were being made into bingo parlors, but then they don't make movies like that anymore, so maybe it wasn't such a loss. Still . . . the landlady hummed a bit of "Rainbow on the River" to herself. No. He had never met Bobby Breen either. Pity.

That night he had jolted awake—stark awake so suddenly that ugly fragments of a nightmare were caught in the light of memory before they could scurry into the dark of the unconscious. The Cloisters. Strange had not bought his story and was going to kill him. Two-mouths rode on a bronze horse, both of them grinning. Leonard's drooping eyelids revealed only bloodshot whites. He was choking . . . gasping in a mute attempt at laughter. Amazing Grace was there—haughty, nude. He was strapped to an exercise table. An altar. Eccyclemic violence.

Then the images had faded, all sucked down into the vortex of the memory hole. He had smiled at himself, wiped the icy sweat off his face, and gone back to sleep.

As soon as he entered his penthouse flat, before unpacking or even removing his overcoat, he telephoned Vanessa Dyke. All morning he had been uneasy about her, fearing that she would return to London early for some reason. The phone doublebuzzed again and again, and he felt a sense of relief. Then, just as he was going to hang up, there was a click and a male voice said, "Yes?"

Jonathan thought he recognized the voice. "May I speak to Miss Dyke?" he asked, apprehensively.

"No, you cannot. You certainly cannot do that." The voice was mushy with drink, but he now recognized it.

"What are you doing there, Yank?"

"Oh, yes. Dr. Hemlock, I believe. The man who makes jokes about the Feeding Station."

"Pull yourself together, shithead! What are you doing there? Has anything happened to Van?"

It was a different, an empty and weak Yank who responded. "You'd better come over here."

"What is it?"

"You'd better come over."

Goddamnit!

He angrily snapped open the drawer of his chest. Automatically he checked the load of the two .45 revolvers: five double dumdum bullets in each cylinder and the hammer over an empty. He put the guns in the bottom of an attaché case and covered them with the half-dozen newspapers he had purchased outside his hotel, each one carrying an article on the forthcoming auction of the Marini Horse, and the news that it would be on display at the National Gallery today. The papers would provide an excuse for the attaché case when he brought it to The Cloisters.

But first Vanessa.

He stepped from the cab and paid the driver, then he turned up through the open gate and the shallow garden with its tarnished hydrangeas.

Yank opened the door before he knocked, a vagueness of expression and a toppling rigidity of stance indicating that he had been drinking. "The

289

bad guys beat you to it, Jonathan baby. Come on in and make yourself at home."

Jonathan pushed past him into the sitting room where he and Vanessa had taken tea a few days before. It was cold now, and damp. No one had thought to light the fire. The portable typewriter was still on the spool table by the window, and reference books were open upside down beside it. The Spode from which they had drunk was still laid out, the cozy slumped beside the pot, the evaporated lees of tea a dark stain in the bottom of the cups.

She had never left for Devon.

Jonathan glanced around at the quaintly old-womanish furniture, the lace curtains, the antimacassars. Everything accused him.

"Dead?" he asked perfunctorily.

Yank was standing in the doorway, supporting himself against the frame. "She struck out. Dead as a doornail—or was that Marley?"

"Where is she?"

"Yonder." He waved in the direction of the kitchen beyond a closed door. He picked up a bottle of Vanessa's whiskey and poured some into a glass.

"Cloisters?" Jonathan asked, taking the glass from him and setting it aside.

"Who else, amigo? Their modus operandi is a calling card. It was done in the style of the Parnell-Greene murder. I think I'd best sit down." He dropped into an easy chair and let his head rest on the antimacassar as he breathed orally in the short pants of nausea. "There must have been three or four of them. They . . ." He wet his lips and swallowed. "They raped her. Repeatedly. And not just with their . . . with themselves. They used . . .

290

things. Kitchen utensils. She died of hemorrhage. She's in there. You can take a look if you want. I had to, so it's only just that you should." He stood up too quickly, his balance uncertain. "You know? You know what I was thinking? It was probably the only time she ever made love with a man."

Jonathan turned half away, then spun back, driving the heel of his hand into Yank's jaw. He went down in a boneless heap. It was unfair, but he had to hit somebody.

There was a half-filled suitcase on a chair. She must have been packing when they walked in on her. On the carpet was a long cigarette burn. The cigarette had probably been slapped from the corner of her mouth.

He steeled himself and stepped over Yank to enter the kitchen. She was on the kitchen table, covered from face to knees with a raincoat. Yank's. Only the torso was on the table. The bare, unshaven legs hung over the edge. The feet were long and bony, like the Christ of a Mexican crucifix, and their limp, toed-in dangle spoke death louder even than the sweet, thick stink. Needing to accept his share of the punishment, Jonathan pulled down the coat and looked at the face. It was contorted into a snarl that bared the teeth. He looked away.

There had been no bruises on her face. Apparently they had kept her conscious as long as possible. Two or three of them must have held her onto the table while Leonard raped her, before looking through the kitchen drawers to find things to . . .

Leonard! Jonathan said the name aloud to himself.

Yank was back on his feet by the time Jonathan

291

returned to the sitting room, but he was unsteady. And he was weeping.

"I'm getting out of this," Yank said to the wall.

"Sit down. Pull yourself together. You're not all that drunk."

"How can people do this kind of thing? And not only The Cloisters people. How can something like the Feeding Station exist? I don't want any of this. I just want a ranch in Nebraska!"

"Sit down! I'm not impressed by your sudden delicacy in the face of violence. Just remember that I wouldn't be involved in this thing—and Vanessa wouldn't have been—if you people hadn't roped me in with that murder setup. So just shut up! Are the police in on this yet?"

"You're a cold-blooded bastard, aren't you? A real professional."

"How hurt do you want to get?"

"Go ahead! Beat me up!"

Jonathan wanted to. He really wanted to.

But he took a breath and asked, "Have the police been informed?"

Yank drooped his head and held it in his hands. "No," he said quietly. "They'll receive an anonymous call later. After we're out of here."

Jonathan looked around the room. He hadn't given her name to Strange, he had only confirmed it as a token of sincerity. So it wasn't really his fault. And immediately he felt contempt for himself for taking refuge in that thought.

Before leaving, he turned back to Yank. "Don't forget your raincoat."

Yank looked up at him with disbelief and disgust swimming in his bleary eyes. "She was your friend."

Jonathan left. For an hour he walked through the zinc-colored streets of Putney, through the gritty fog, past melancholy brick row houses, some of which had tarnished hydrangeas in their pitiful little front gardens.

Then he caught a cab for The Cloisters.

The Cloisters

". . . Physical beauty is a worthy goal in its own—
unh—right, of course. But there are fringe benefits.
The rituals—unh—it entails are almost—unh—as
valuable as the ends—unh!" Max Strange rested for
a moment at the top of a sit-up. "How many is
that?" he asked his masseur.

"Sixty-eight, sir."

Strange blew out a puff of air and began again.
"Sixty-nine—unh—seventy—unh. For instance, Dr.
Hemlock, I do my best thinking—unh—when I am
sunbathing or exercising, or taking steam." He
dropped back on the exercise table with a grunt.
"That's enough."

As the masseur spread creamy lanolin on
Strange's body, Jonathan looked around the exercise
room, green and dim through the round glasses that
protected his eyes from the ultraviolet rays of the
bank of sun lamps surrounding Strange. Leonard
and Two-mouths stood near him, and three other of
Strange's enforcers leaned against the walls with
studied, sassy languor, among them the scowling fellow with yellowish temporary caps on his front
teeth. The bulging green glasses made the group look

like those man/insect mutants so popular with makers of low budget science fiction films.

Jonathan checked his hate, blanking out the image of Vanessa, closing out Leonard. He had to appear casual and loose.

Strange's face and throat were being massaged with heated lanolin, and his voice was rather constricted as he said, "While I've been taking a little sun and exercise, I've been thinking about you a great deal."

"That's nice," Jonathan said. "I brought along some copies of newspapers. Evidence that I have been busy. After these writeups, no one will question the price the Horse will bring."

"Yes, I've already seen the papers."

"I suppose you're pleased."

"To a degree. But all this about putting the Horse on display at the National Gallery. I don't recall our agreeing on that."

"It was an inspiration of the moment. I told you I would need a certain freedom of movement. After my first couple of contacts, I realized that the critics weren't going to buy my story wholeheartedly without some kind of special kudos. And the idea of lending the authority of the National occurred to me. It cost me most of the ten thousand to arrange it."

"I see." Strange stayed the masseur's hand. "That's enough. You may turn off the lights." He sat up on the edge of the table and took off his protective glasses. "You have a subtle mind, Dr. Hemlock."

"Thank you."

Strange looked at him without expression. "Yes

... a subtle mind. Come along. We'll take a little steam together. Do you a world of good."

"Not just now, thanks."

Strange glanced to the floor. "It's a pity, is it not, that most attempts to phrase politely run the risk of rhetorical ambiguity."

They were an unlikely assortment of form and flesh, the four of them sitting in the billowing steam, towels about their waists. Raw material for Daumier. There was the rotisserie-tanned, classically muscled body of Strange—youngest and oldest of them all; Jonathan's lean, sinewy mountain climber's physique; the thin and brittle frame of the two-mouthed weasel—fish-belly white and hairless, a dried chicken carcass, a xylophone of ribs, one mouth grinning from social discomfort, the other pouting for the same reason; and the primate hulk of Leonard with its thick, short neck and stanchion legs—tufts of hair bristling from the sloping shoulders, his head tilted back, his heavy-lidded eyes ever upon Jonathan.

Until Strange spoke, the silence had been accented by the monotonous hiss of entering steam. "I am displeased with you, Dr. Hemlock. You shouldn't have arranged to put the Horse on public display without my permission."

"Well, there's not much we can do about that now."

"True. Any change in your widely publicized plan would attract attention. I have no choice. And *that* is why I am displeased."

"Don't worry. The security system in the National is among the best in the world."

"That is not the point."

"What the hell *is* the point?"

Strange turned to the thin-chested man with two mouths. "Darling, go fetch that little leather box, there's a good man."

The weaselly serf rose and left the chamber, swirling eddies of vapor in his wake.

"Darling?" Jonathan couldn't help asking.

"His name. Kenneth Darling. I know, I know. Fate delights in her little ironies. But at this moment I am less interested in the deviousness of Fate than I am in yours."

"Any particular deviousness?" Might as well play it out.

Strange leaned his head back against the sweating tile wall and closed his eyes. "Where have you been for the past two days?"

"Arranging for the auction. Contacting critics and reviewers. Setting up the National Gallery display. Earning my money, really."

"Conscientious man."

"Greedy man. What's troubling you, Max?"

"I had you followed from the time you left here."

"Nu?"

"And again, as before, my man lost you in the maze of streets in Covent Garden."

Jonathan shrugged. "I'm sorry your people are incompetent. If I'd known the idiot was following me, I'd have left a trail of bread crumbs."

"For two days, you did not return to either your Baker Street flat or the one in Mayfair. Where were you?"

Jonathan sighed deeply, then spoke slowly and clearly, as though talking to a backward child or a travel agent. "After making the arrangements for the

Horse, I went to ground down in Brighton. Why, you will now ask, did I go to ground? I'll tell you why I went to ground. It seemed wise to maintain as low a profile as possible until the thing was done. What did I do in Brighton? Well, I read a bit. And I took long walks through The Lanes. And one evening, I—"

"Very well!"

"Are you satisfied?"

"Don't talk like one of my employees."

"By the way, where are your employees? When I came in, the place seemed deserted."

"So it is, save for a small staff. The Cloisters is no longer in business."

"That will leave a great gap in the social lives of our betters."

Strange waved off this oblique line of conversation with the back of his hand. "When you returned to London this morning, you went to your Baker Street apartment. From there you took a taxi to Miss Vanessa Dyke's house in Putney."

"Right. Right. The fare was one pound six—one fifty with tip. The driver thought the government ought to ban private cars from the city. Particularly when there is fog—which, by the way, he ascribed to massive ice floes broken off the polar cap in result of recent Apollo moon shots—"

"Please!"

"I don't want you to think I'm holding any details back."

"While in Putney, you undoubtedly discovered the accident that had befallen Miss Dyke."

Jonathan glanced at Leonard. "Accident. Yes."

"It must seem to you," Strange said, stretching his

legs over the pine bench until the muscles stood out, "that our treatment of Miss Dyke was overreactive. After all, she was guilty only of setting you on our path at a time when we were actively seeking you out ourselves. But the years have taught me that violence and terror, if they are to be effective deterrents, must be exercised systematically and inexorably. We propose certain rules of conduct, and we have to enforce them without reference to individual motives. In this we operate as governments do. It is our good fortune to have Leonard here to carry out the punishments. I loose him like an ineluctable Fury, and punishment becomes both automatic and profound. The effect of Miss Dyke's action is of no weight in this. She was punished for her intention."

Cold air entered the steam room, and the vapor undulated as Darling returned carrying a small black leather case.

"Ah!" said Strange. "Here we are. Leonard, will you give Darling a hand?"

Leonard rose and threw his thick arms around Jonathan's chest, locking his hands in front and pinning Jonathan's arms to his sides. After the first automatic reaction, resistance to that python grip was pointless. With fumbling haste, Darling opened the case, took out a syringe, and injected its contents into Jonathan's shoulder.

"You may let him go, Leonard. But if he makes the slightest gesture of aggression toward me, I want you to beat him, hurting him rather a lot." Strange looked obliquely at Jonathan. "It's not that I'm a physical coward, Dr. Hemlock. But it would be a great pity if you were to damage my face. Surely, as a lover of beauty, you understand."

Jonathan breathed as shallowly as possible, fighting to bring his pulse rate down and to clear his mind. "What's going on, Strange?"

Strange laughed. "Oh, do come on! The midnight bell has rung. Time to stop the dance and remove our masks. Don't worry about the hypodermic. It won't kill you. In fact, there will be no effect at all for five or ten minutes. And even then, you'll find it quite pleasant. The little girl you toyed with the other evening was under a similar drug. It relaxes you, calms your aggressive impulses, makes you docile and obedient."

Jonathan felt nothing as yet. "Why are you doing this?"

"Oh, I think you've served your purpose now, don't you? And you should be pleased to know that your plans will go ahead just as you wanted. In an hour the armored van will arrive to carry the Horse to the National Gallery, where it will be the object of attention by the ogling masses. And tomorrow it will be on the floor of Sotheby's. We've known about you all along, of course. About your friends in Loo. About the pompous old vicar."

Did he know about Maggie? That was Jonathan's primary worry.

"Tell me, Jonathan—I feel I may use your first name now—is your mind still clear enough to reason out why I have let you go so long?"

"It's fairly obvious. You had a real problem in arranging the open auction of the films without alerting the British authorities."

"Precisely. And the good Lord sent you along to do it for us—*and* with the benediction of the Loo organization, too! Obviously, you intended to intercept the Marini Horse while it was in the National Gallery. But now you won't have to trouble yourself about that. Tomorrow, a little after noon, the gavel falls. The British government, with all its trade concessions, defense secrets, wealth, and problems, becomes the property of the highest bidder. And Amazing Grace and I disappear."

"But if I don't show up with the films . . ." Jonathan stopped and frowned. That's odd, he thought. He had forgotten what he was going to say.

Strange laughed. "Naturally, I have considered that. Your vicar knows the films are in the Horse, and if you don't bring them, he will be constrained to make other arrangements—loath though he is to bring the police in on this. I have taken that possibility into account, and I have neutralized it. And of course I'm neutralizing you. You won't be going anywhere near the National Gallery."

Jonathan somehow didn't care. The steam felt very good. Caressing. It penetrated his muscles and tingled them pleasantly. There was nothing to be afraid of. Maximilian Strange was a handsome man, a cultured man . . . what did that have to do with anything? "Do I, ah . . ." What was he going to say? "Oh, yes! Do I die?"

"Oh, I imagine so," Strange said with warm concern. "But not just now."

"I see," Jonathan said, recognizing the profound meaning in these words. "And if I don't die now," he reasoned, "then I die later. I mean, everyone dies sooner or later, you know." He felt he had them here. No one could deny that.

"We'll keep you around for a while, just in case

something goes wrong. You may be of some bargaining value."

That was right, Jonathan thought. He should have thought of that himself. That was a very good idea.

"Help him up to his room," the steam said.

"No, that's all right," Jonathan's voice said. "Thank you, but that's all right. I can . . ." But he couldn't. He couldn't stand up. And that was amazingly funny.

No, it was not funny. It was really very serious. And dangerous.

But funny.

A helpful man named Darling—that's funny too—helped Jonathan to his feet. Leonard looked on benevolently.

"Don't dress him," the steam said thoughtfully. "Nudity has a great psychological deterrent. No one is brave when he is nude."

That was wise, really. How could you be a hero with your ass hanging out? Poor Leonard. He couldn't talk. But he had killed Vanessa! Don't forget that. And these other goons, they had held her onto the table. Jonathan would teach them.

"Leonard," he said soapily, tapping his knuckle against the tree-trunk chest, "you're dumb. You know that? You are as dumb as a bullet. You are, in fact, a dumdum."

"Come along, mate." Darling led him out of the steam room.

"It's cold out here, Darling. I need my attaché case to keep me warm." Would they see through that?

"Just come along with me, mate. You're drunk with the dope." Darling's voice had an odd echo.

Then Jonathan realized why. He had two mouths! Naturally, he echoed.

The stairs were very difficult to climb. It was the undulations, of course. The room they led him to was the one he had been in the other evening. With Maggie.

Mustn't mention her name!

Jonathan was guided to the bed, where he lay down slowly, very slowly, deeply.

"Wait a minute!"

Darling answered from everywhere. "What is it?"

"I don't seem to have my attaché case. I need it . . . for a pillow."

"Look, mate. Give over, won't you? I've already been through it and took out the guns. Mr. Strange give 'em to me as a present."

Jonathan was deeply disappointed. "That's too bad. I wanted to shoot you all. You know what I mean?"

Darling laughed dryly. "That's hard lines for you, mate. I guess you struck out. Now you just rest there. I'll be back in a couple of hours to shoot you."

"Oh?"

"With more dope. It only lasts four or five hours."

"Oh, I'm sorry about that. But then, all things are mutable. Except change, of course. I mean . . . change can't be mutable because . . . well, it's like all generalizations being false . . . and angels on the point of a pin. You know what I mean?"

But Darling had left, locking the door behind him.

Jonathan lay nude, spread-eagle on his back, watching with awe and admiration the permutations of the ceiling rectangle into parallelograms and trapezoids. Amazing that he had never noticed that before.

He was cold. Sweating and cold. There were no blankets on the bed. Only one sheet. And the chintzy bastards had taken his clothes!

He pulled the corner of the sheet over his chest and gripped it hard as he felt his body rise, up past the images and ideas above him. He tried to focus on those images and ideas, but they vanished under concentration, like the dim stars that can only be seen in peripheral vision.

It seemed that he had to get out of there. Go to a museum with MacTaint. For some reason . . . for some reason.

It was true what Darling had said. He had well and truly struck out. Struck out. Struck out.

Later—four minutes? four hours?—he tried to get up. Nausea. The floor rippled when he stood on it, so he knelt and put his forehead on the rug, and that was better.

Yes! He had to go with MacTaint to get the films from within the Marini Horse. Of course! But it was cold. His skin was clammy to the touch.

The window.

Then the pattern on the rug caught his attention. Beautiful, brilliant, and in constant subtle motion. Beautiful.

Forget the rug! The window!

He crawled over to it, repeating the word "window" again and again so he wouldn't forget what he was doing. He pulled himself up and looked out.

Fog. Almost evening. He had been out for hours. They would be back soon to shoot him up again.

With both hands he lifted the latch and pushed the window open. He had to wrap his arms around the center post of the casement before he dared to put his head out and look down.

No way. Never. The room was on the top floor. Red tile eaves overhung the window, and below there was a deadfall of three stories to a flagstone terrace. The building was faced with flush-set stone. No cracks, no mortise, no ledges to the window casements.

No way. Even in his prime as a climber, he could not have descended that face without an abseil rope.

Abseil rope. He turned back into the room, almost fainting with the suddenness of the movement.

Nothing. Only the sheet. Too short. That was why they had taken away his bedding.

He was able to walk back to the bed. He reeled, and he had to catch himself on the bedpost, but he had not had to crawl. His mind was clearing. Another half hour, maybe. Then he would be able to move about. He would be able to think. But he didn't have a half hour. They would be back before that.

He lay flat on his back on the bed, shivering with the cold that seemed to come from within his bones. The euphoria had passed, and a dry nausea had replaced it. Now, try to think. How to get rid of the effect quickly when they came back and shot him up again? He had to think it out before they returned, and he again sank into the pleasant, deadly euphoria.

Yes. Burn the dope up! With exercise. As soon as

they left next time, he would start exercising. Make the blood flow quickly. Precipitate the effects and burn them off. That might work! That might give him half an hour to move and think before they returned to give him the third dose.

Oh, but he would forget! Once the crap was in him, he would lie there and groove on the ceiling, forgetting to exercise. He would forget his plan.

He looked around the room desperately. There was a narrow mantelpiece over an ornate hearth that had been blocked up. That would do. He would have four or five clear minutes after they put the dope in him and before it got into his bloodstream. During that time, he would exercise furiously to force the onset of the effects. Then, before he started to trip out, he would climb up on the mantel, where he would do isometrics to keep the heart pumping, to get the crap through him and out. And if his mind wandered, if the dope started to float him away, he would fall from the mantel ledge. That would snap him out of it. And if he could, he would climb back and begin exercising again. Somehow he would force the effects to pass off more quickly. He would gain time before the third needle.

Now relax. Empty your head.

There was a sound down the hall. They were returning.

Relax. Make them think you're still out. He produced the image of a still pond on the backs of his eyelids. This time control mattered. He had to get under quickly.

Darling preceded Leonard into the room. He clicked on the lights, and they advanced on the bed with its still form stretched over a wrinkled puddle of sheet.

"Still out," Darling said, as he opened the black leather case. "Gor, what's this? Look at him! The sweat's fair pouring off him! He's cold! Here. Put your hand on his chest. Feel his heart thumping there. What do you think, Leonard? Maybe he's one of them low tolerance blokes. Another dose might do for him."

But Leonard took the syringe from Darling's hand and, snapping Jonathan over by his arm, drove the needle into the shoulder muscle and squirted home the contents, not caring if there was air in the ampul.

"He didn't even flinch," Darling said. "Took the fun out of it for you, didn't I? I told you he was out. If he dies before Mr. Strange wants, remember that I'm not taking the blame."

They left, turning out the lights and locking the door behind them.

Slowly, Jonathan opened his eyes. He allowed his body's demand for oxygen to take control of his breathing rate. He felt all right; weak but in control. But he knew that the delightful killer was in there, mixing with his blood. He rose from bed as hastily as his sketchy balance would allow and brought the small sheet with him to the open window. After some fumbling, he tied one end of it to the center post, allowing the seven feet of slack to dangle outside. Then he lay down on the floor and began exercising. Sit-ups until his stomach muscles quivered, then push-ups.

For more than a minute, he sensed no effect from the dope. Up. Down. Up. Down. Up—and up, and up. He seemed to rise so slowly, so effortlessly. That's it, he told himself. The exercise was working. He was bringing it on quickly. He decided it was time to get on the mantel. He stood up. But the room was telescoping on him—all the lines rushing into the corners in exaggerated foreshortening.

"God," he muttered. "I waited too long! It's coming too fast!"

The gas hearth was there, way over on the other side of the room. He put his arms out and leaned toward it, hoping he would reel and fall in that direction. But the crash came from behind. He had staggered backward and hit the wall behind him. The room seemed filled with the rasp of his breathing. He was afraid they would hear it.

Can't walk to it. Get down on the floor and crawl. Safer. Beautiful. Beautiful rug. Oh, no! He was alone in an endless sea of floor. He didn't know which direction to go. He could see the mantelpiece when he looked up, but it kept changing directions, and it didn't get any nearer.

He sat on the floor, one foot under him, the other leg stretched out before him, his head hanging down and his chin on his chest, his oral breathing shallow and rapid. He felt weightless. And contented. He was comfortable, and it was too funny—this trying to find a mantel.

No! He ground his teeth together and forced himself to think. Keep crawling. Find a wall. Then crawl along it. Must lead to the hearth eventually.

He crawled on. Once he rested with his face in a corner of the room, and the walls felt soft and comfortable against his cheeks. He wanted so much to sleep. But he snapped himself out of it and crawled on. Then his hand touched marble—beautifully grained, somehow luminescent marble. That was the mantelpiece.

Now climb up on the ledge!

Too high. Too hard.

Climb.

Twice he slipped and fell back to the floor, and it took all his mental strength to resist the desire to stay there and enjoy the ceiling.

At last he stood on the narrow ledge of the mantel, his back against the wall, his arms cruciform, fingers trying to hold onto the flowers in the wallpaper. He was frightened and his heart pounded. The floor, rippling and blurring, was so far down there.

Good. The fear was good. It made his pulse race. It would burn off the dope. Now exercise. Isometric tension . . . release. Tension . . . release.

He had the impression that he could see by means of darkness as other people saw by means of light. And so much darkness was coming in through the open window that he could see details in the room clearly. There were bursting sacs of light behind his eyes. The rug. Beautiful color. It floated up toward him slowly, seductively.

The pain and shock of the fall brought him briefly to his senses. He was lying face down on the rug. He couldn't breathe through his nose. Blood. It didn't hurt. It made him want to sleep.

The climb back up was cerebral. His sense of balance was gone, along with his sense of direction. He had to tell himself that tops tend to be above bottoms. He had to think out the fact that leaning out would cause a fall. Eventually he was on the mantel ledge, on his knees. He could not stand. Kneeling, his chest now against the wall, he began the isometric exercises. Tension . . . release. Tension . . . release.

An infinity of timelessness passed. He needed to sleep. Right now. He rested back on the supporting air.

This time, he slept through the fall and crash.

The cold woke him up. He was sweating and cold. His mouth was dry from oral breathing, and his upper lip was stiff. He touched the stiff lip. It was flaky, gritty. The blood from his nose had congealed. He had been out for some time. But he knew from the nausea and the cold that the hallucinatory effects of the drug had passed. He was weak and dizzy, but he could think and he could move. He got to his hands and knees slowly and looked around the room. Dark shadows, a rectangle of gray city smear at the window. The window. He remembered.

With the help of the bedpost, he got to his feet and reeled to the window. The night air was freezing cold as it flowed over his sweating, naked body. He stood, supporting himself on the casement and sucking in great breaths of damp refreshing air. The sheet was still knotted about the center post.

Looking down, he could just make out the stone terrace three stories below. A mist of light from a room below spilled out over the wet flagstones. He climbed up onto the sill and stood in the frame. Then he gripped the underledge of the eaves and leaned out. And instantly he was overcome by vertigo, drowning in dizziness. Desperately, he scrambled back. Too soon. He would have to wait until the last moment. Just before they came in. Give his mind a chance to get as clear as it would ever be.

Leonard and Darling left their dart game with fellow employees and crossed the deserted Art Deco salon, their reflections following them along the wall of mirrors that hid the Aquarium. They took the long curving stairway two steps at a time because they were a little late for the next scheduled injection. Leonard unlocked the door, and Darling switched on the lights.

"Christ!" Darling ejaculated.

In a rush they checked the closet, the bathroom, and under the bed. Then Leonard noticed the open window and the sheet knotted around the center post. He slammed his fist against the casement in fury.

"The Guv won't half be browned off at this!" Darling said. "He'll have our arses for it!" He looked down to the terrace below. "Can't have got far. That sheet didn't help much. Must of broke both his legs. Come on!"

They ran from the room, Leonard charging down the staircase to examine the grounds, while Darling ran up the corridor to his room, where he snatched up the revolvers he had liberated from Jonathan's attaché case.

Head downward on the steep sloping roof, Jonathan lay tense and still. When he had heard them approaching the door, he had gripped the underedge of the eaves and swung out, tuck-rolling up and over. For a terrible moment, only the lower half of his body was on the slippery roof, his torso and head dangling over. The incline was greater than he had expected, and the sharp overlapping edges of the tiles prevented him from scrambling up. Only his fingertip hold on the underside of the edge prevented him from falling to the terrace below, but the pressure out against his reflexed wrists was agonizing and enervating. He clenched his teeth to keep from screaming with the pain as he pressed against his wrists with all his force, his jaw muscles roped and his head shuddering with the effort as he wriggled up against the sawtoothed set of the rough tile edges, gouging skin from his knees and rib cage and abrading his scrotum. His leverage was spent before he could get his chin past the eaves, and his angle on the roof was such that he could maintain his purchase only by keeping the throbbing wrists locked and by spreading his legs, increasing the area of traction to the maximum. Blood rushed to his head, and his racing pulse thrummed with dry lumps in his ears.

The lights came on in the room below, dimly illuminating the fog around him. He heard Darling say "Christ!," then there was the sound of a search through the room. Would the sheet mislead them? His lungs needed air, and he opened his mouth wide to breathe, so the intake would make less noise. Some of the dope was still in him, making thought slimy and vision uncertain. The strength was leaking out of him, draining from his wrists and shoulders.

He slipped ... only a couple of inches, but he couldn't get it back. Now even more weight over the edge. Vertigo. The dim flagstone terrace so far below. No strength. Wrists winced with pain.

Leonard's head appeared just below him. The Mute snatched at the dangling sheet, then peered down. Jonathan squeezed his eyes shut and concentrated with all his force: Don't look up! Don't look up! The cold of the wet tiles against his nude body was numbing. Again he slipped two inches! But at that second Leonard banged his fist against the casement in fury, covering the sound. Darling said something from within.

They ran out of the room.

A strangled, whimpering groan escaped Jonathan. Getting down would be as dangerous as getting up had been. The pitch of the roof was sharp, and there was a thin coat of greasy dirt on the tiles lubricated by the moisture of the fog. Once he pulled in his legs and let the slip start, there would be no stopping it. With those limp and throbbing wrists, he would have to catch the underedge of the eaves as he slid past and swing back in through the window. If he was off by six inches to either side, he would crash against the building and fall to the flagstones below.

No use thinking about it. No time. No strength left.

He let go.

He was an inch or two off, and as he swung into the room backward, he clipped his head on the center post of the window casement. Dizziness and pain made him reel as he got to his feet, but he drove on, head down, running for the open door.

As Darling started back down the hall with the big revolvers, he heard the crash in Jonathan's room and ran toward it. They collided in the doorway and went down in a jumble in the hall. Jonathan fought blindly and desperately, grappling for Darling's throat and getting it, both thumbs against the larynx. He could feel that there was little strength left in his grip, so he closed his eyes and bared his teeth, pressing desperately as Darling struggled to bring either revolver to bear on Jonathan's naked side. He wriggled like a beached fish as Jonathan squeezed for all he was worth, expecting at any moment to hear the roar of a gun and to have his guts blown out by a flattening dumdum. From nowhere, the thought came to Jonathan of Vanessa struggling on her kitchen table. Darling had probably held her down as Leonard had prodded at her. With a final surge of desperate fury, Jonathan drove his thumbs through, and the larynx crumpled like a papier-mâché pin box. Darling gargled and died.

For a second Jonathan lay there gasping, his forehead on Darling's silent chest. He got to his knees and picked up the revolvers. Keep moving, he ordered himself. He blinked away the large spots of blindness in the center of his eyes and stumbled on, down the wide curving staircase and across the sterile Art Deco salon. He burst into the exercise room, dropping to the floor with both guns up before him. It was empty. But he could hear them now, shouting outside the house. He cocked back both hammers with his thumbs and struggled to his feet. Dizzy. Nausea.

He reeled toward the door to the small paneled dining room and kicked it open with the ball of his foot.

The dope swam in his head, and the scene played out like a dream—a slow-motion ballet. Strange and Grace were dining. She turned toward the opening door, her naked breasts wobbling viscously with the motion. Strange floated to his feet and put out one hand, palm forward as though in a Hindu gesture of blessing. Jonathan raised one gun and fired. The roar reverberated in his head, and even the recoil kick seemed to lift his hand slowly. Like magic, the left side of Strange's face disappeared and in its place was a splash of red gelatin. Grace clutched the air, her face contorted into a scream of horror, but no sound came. Strange sank away under the table, and she fainted.

From too slow, things began to go too fast. Jonathan stumbled back into the exercise room, panting and unsteady. He needed to vomit. The sound of running men was closer. He turned on the bank of sun lamps and directed them toward the outer door. "I'm sick!" he whimpered aloud as he fumbled on the round green glasses haphazardly, one eye squeezed closed by the elastic band.

They burst into the room. Three of them. The broken-toothed one in the lead tried to shield his eyes from the blinding glare, holding his automatic before his face. Jonathan's first shot blew his arm off at the shoulder, and he spun and fell, spraying the other two with his blood. The next dumdum took the one closest to the door in the small of the back as he scrambled to retreat. His body was lifted into the air and slammed against the wall of exercise bars. He did not fall because his arm got tangled in the bars, but his body jerked convulsively.

The third man got off a wild shot in the direction of the lights, and one of them imploded above Jonathan's head, showering him with hot glass. Jonathan's return shot blew away the man's leg at the knee. He stood for a second, surprised. Then he fell to the unsupported side.

The silence rang with the absence of gun roars. The man tangled in the exercise rings slid to the floor, his forehead rattling on each rung. Then it was still.

"I'm sick!" Jonathan told them again, the words thick and muffled.

The tide of vertigo rose within him. The back of his throat was bitter with vomit. Mustn't pass out! Leonard is still out there somewhere! Hold on!

He tugged the green glasses off and staggered over to the door to the dressing room. Mirrors. An infinity of naked men with guns. Blood caked on their faces; their knees and chests scuffed and bleeding. He opened the center mirror and went into the Aquarium.

And there was Leonard. He had a Mauser machine pistol and was fitting on the wooden holster/stock, slowly and deliberately, his hooded eyes expressionless. He was on the other side of the one-way glass, standing alone in the empty Art Deco salon, pressed close to the mirrored wall, waiting for Jonathan to emerge through the exercise room door.

Jonathan's heart pulsed in his temples. He was so tired, so sick. He only wanted to sleep. The mist of dope in his brain cleared for a moment. Vanessa. Leonard and Vanessa—and kitchen utensils. He set his teeth and crept soundlessly to the mirrored panel before him. He raised both guns, their barrels almost touching the glass, and he waited as Leonard on his side inched forward, waited until Leonard's huge body had moved directly in front of the barrels. One gun was pointed at Leonard's neck, the other at his ear.

The mirror exploded and Leonard's headless body surfed over the parqueted floor on a hissing tide of shattered glass. It twitched violently, tinkling and grinding in the glass. Then it stopped.

And Jonathan threw up.

Covent Garden

The driver of taxi #68204 threaded through the tangle of narrow lanes above Hampstead High Street in search of a fare. He accepted philosophically the improbability of making a pickup in that quiet district at that time of night, and he decided to return to center city. As he stopped at a deserted intersection, he began to sing "On the Road to Mandalay" under his breath, shifting keys with liberal insouciance. The back door of his cab opened, and a passenger entered.

"Where to, mate?" the driver asked over his shoulder without turning around.

"Covent Garden."

"Right you are." The driver pulled away, humming his inadvertent variations on the theme of "Roses of Picardy." He vaguely wondered what a man with an American accent wanted in Covent Garden at that time of night. "The market?" he asked over his shoulder.

"What? Oh. Yes. The market will do."

The passenger's voice was faint and confused, and the driver feared that he might have picked up a drunk who would soil the back of his cab. He pulled over to the curb and turned around. "Now. listen, mate. If you're drunk . . . I'll be buggered!" The passenger was nude. "'Ere! Wot's all this!"

"Go to the market. I'll give you directions from there."

The driver was prepared to put a stop to all this rubbish, when he noticed two very large revolvers on the seat beside the passenger. "The market, is it?" He released the hand brake and drove on. Not singing.

They stopped at the entrance to a narrow, unlit alley in the heart of the Garden district. "This it, mate?"

"Yes." The passenger sounded as though he had dropped off during the ride. "Listen, driver, I don't seem to have any money on me . . ."

"Oh, that's all right, mate."

"If you'll just come in with me, I'll—"

"No! No, that's all right. Forget it."

The passenger rubbed the back of his neck and his eyes, as though trying to clear his mind. "I . . . ah . . . I know this must seem irregular to you, driver."

"No, sir. Not at all."

"You're sure you don't want to come in for your money?"

"Oh yes, sir. I'm quite sure. Now, if this is the place you want . . ."

"Right." Jonathan climbed painfully out of the cab, taking his revolvers with him, and the taxi sped off.

The outer workshop of MacTaint's place was empty, save for the gaunt, wild-eyed painter who

320

looked up crossly as Jonathan's entrance brought a gust of cold air with it. He muttered angrily under his breath and returned to the magnum opus he had been working on for eleven years: a huge pointillist rendering of the London docks done with a three-hair brush.

Jonathan strode stiff-legged past him, still unsteady on his feet, and made for the entrance to the back apartment.

The painter returned to his work. Then, after a minute, he raised his emaciated, Christlike face and stared into the distance. There had been something odd about that intruder. Something about his dress.

He steeped sleepily in the deep hot water of the bath, a half-empty tumbler of whiskey dangling loosely from his hand over the edge of the tub. Although the water still stung and located all his abrasions—knees, chest, shoulder, the back of his head where he had cracked it swinging back in through the window—his mind was quite clear. The worst of it was over. All he had to do now was to get the films from within the Marini Horse.

MacTaint entered the bathroom, carrying towels, shuffling along in his shaggy greatcoat, despite the steamy atmosphere of the room. "You didn't half give Lilla a start, coming in like that with blood all over you and your shiny arse hanging out. I thought I was going to have to mop up the floor after her. Got her settled down with a bottle of gin now, though."

"Give her my apologies, as one theatre personage to another."

"I'll do that. Gor, look at you! They gave you a fair bit of stick, didn't they?"

"They got a little stick themselves."

"I'll bet they did." He ogled the bath water with mistrust. "That ain't good for you, Jon. Bathing saps the strength. Dilutes the inner fluids."

"Could I have another pint of milk?"

"Jesus, lad! Is there no end to the harm you're willing to do yourself?" But he went out to fetch the milk, and when he returned he swapped the bottle for the empty glass in Jonathan's hand.

Jonathan pulled off the metal lid and drank half the pint down without taking the bottle from his lips. "Good. I'm feeling a lot better."

"Maybe. But not good enough, my boy. There's no way in the world you could go along with me tonight. Not with your shoulder like that. Say! They got your beak too, did they?"

"No, I did that myself. Falling from a mantel."

". . . a mantel?"

"Yes. I climbed up there to keep awake."

"Oh, yes."

"But I fell off again."

". . . I see. I'll tell you one thing, Jon. I'm glad I'm not in academics. Too demanding by half."

"Look, Mac. You're sure you can get into the Gallery tonight?"

MacTaint looked at him narrowly. "You ain't in no condition to come along, I tell you. And I ain't having you put sand in my tank."

"I know. I recognize that." Jonathan reached over and poured milk into his tumbler, then he put in a good tot of whiskey. "Tell me how you're going to get the Chardin."

MacTaint looked around for a glass for himself and, not finding one, he dumped the toothbrushes out of a cup on the sink and used that. Then he made himself comfortable on the lid of the toilet seat. "I go right up the outside of the building. They got scaffolding up for steam cleaning the façade. All part of 'Keep London Tidy.' And no chance of being seen, what with the canvas flaps they got hung on the scaffolding to keep the dirt and water from getting on blokes below. The window latch is in position, but it doesn't do nothin'. I've had a lad working on it with a file, bit by bit, for the past two months. I just nip up the scaffolding, in through the window, and do the dirty to the national art treasures."

"Guards?"

"Lazy old arseholes waiting for their pensions to come through. It'll only take a couple of seconds to swap my Chardin for theirs."

Jonathan turned on the hot water with his toes and felt the warmth eddy up under his legs, stinging afresh his scuffs and cuts. "Tell me, Mac. How much do you expect to make from the Chardin?"

"Five, maybe seven thousand quid. Why?"

"There's something I want in there. Just one chamber away. I'll give you five thousand for it."

"You've got that much?"

"A man gave me ten thousand to do something for him. I'll split it with you."

"A painting?"

"No. Several reels of film. They're inside a hollow bronze horse by Marini that's on display in the next chamber."

MacTaint scratched at the top of his head, then

studiously regarded a fleck of scruff on his fingernail. "And you were going to get it while you were along with me?"

"Right."

"Even though that might have fucked up my business?"

"That's right."

"You're a proper villain, Jonathan."

"True."

"A bronze horse, you say? How do I get away with it? I mean, I might attract a little attention running through the streets, dragging a bronze horse behind me."

"You'll have to break the horse with a hammer. One big blow will crack it."

"I can't help feeling the guards might hear that."

"I'm sure they will. You'll have to move like hell. That's why I'm offering you so much money."

MacTaint clawed at the flaky whiskers under his chin meditatively. "Five thousand, eh?"

"Five thousand."

"What's on the film?"

Jonathan shook his head.

"Well, I suppose that was a mug's question." He wiped the sweat from his face with the cuff of his overcoat. "It's hot in here."

"Yes, and close too." Jonathan had been trying to breathe only in shallow oral breaths since MacTaint had entered. "Well?"

MacTaint scratched his ear meditatively, then he squished his bulbous, carmine-veined nose about with the palm of his hand. "All right," he said finally. "I'll get your damned film for you."

"That's great, Mac."

"Yes, yes," he growled.

"When will you get back here with it?"

"About an hour and a half. Or, if they catch me, in about eleven years."

"Can you drop the film off at my place in Mayfair?"

"Why not?"

"I'll give you the address. You're a wonderful man, MacTaint."

"A bloody vast fool is what I am." He shuffled off to find some clothes as Jonathan rose to get out of the bath. Jonathan was temporarily arrested by a bolt of pain in his shoulder, but it passed off and he was able to dry himself one-handedly, with some stiff acrobatics.

"Here you go," MacTaint said, returning with a pile of rags. "They're me own. Of course, they ain't my best, and they may not fit so well, but beggars and choosers, you know. And take those frigging cannons with you. I don't want them laying about the place."

Getting into the clothes was an olfactory martyrdom, and Jonathan promised himself another shower directly he got to his apartment.

He got to his apartment later than he would have guessed, having to walk all the way, despite the five pounds MacTaint had given him. A few late-prowling taxis had come within sight, but they had not stopped at his signal; indeed they had accelerated. The clothes.

As he got his key from the ledge over the door, he heard his phone ring within. He fumbled at the lock in his haste because all the way home he had been thinking of calling Maggie to tell her it was all over and he was safe.

"Yes?"

Yank's phony American accent was a great disappointment. "I've been calling everywhere for you. Where have you been?"

"I've been busy."

"Yes, I know." There was a flabby sound to Yank's voice; he had not fully recovered from his booze-up on Vanessa's whiskey during his self-indulgent crisis of disgust. "I'm calling from The Cloisters."

"What are you doing there?"

"We just raided the place, figuring you might be in hot water. You left quite a mess behind you. The place is deserted—that is, there are no living people here."

"I assume Loo is going to cover all that up for me?"

"Oh, sure. Look, I'm on my way out to the Vicarage. Want me to drop by and pick you and the films up?"

"I don't have the films yet."

There was a pause. "You don't have them?"

"Don't panic. I'll have them in an hour, then I'll pick up Miss Coyne and meet you at the Vicarage."

"Miss Coyne's already on her way. I called her to find out if she knew where you were. She didn't, of course, so I told her we'd meet her there."

"I see. Well, don't bother to pick me up. If we drove out together, you'd talk to me. And I don't need that."

"You sure know how to hurt a guy. Okeydoke,

I'll meet you at the Vicarage. Don't take any wooden—"

Jonathan hung up.

He had bathed and changed and was resting in the dark of his room when MacTaint banged on the door.

"You wouldn't have a drop of whiskey about the place?" were his first words. "Oh, by the way . . . here." He handed Jonathan a cylindrical package bound up in black plastic fabric. "You know what you can do with your friggin' films?"

"Trouble?" He passed the bottle.

"I'd say that. Yes. Never mind the glass." He took a long pull. "Tell me, lad. Do you have any idea how much noise is made by busting open a bronze statue in an empty gallery hall?"

"I assume it didn't go unnoticed."

"You'd have thought the buzz bombs were back. Sure you don't want any of this?" He took another long pull, then he tugged the bottle down suddenly, laughing and spilling a little over his lapels. "You should have seen me scarpering my aged arse down the scaffolding, the canvas under my arm, and balancing your damned bundle. All elbows and knees. No grace at all. Bells ringing and people shouting. Oh, it was an event, Jon."

"Let's see it."

MacTaint took the Chardin from where it rested facing the wall and set it up on a chair in good light, then he dropped down onto the sofa beside Jonathan, his motion puffing out eddies of stink from within his clothes. "Ain't it lovely, though."

Jonathan looked at it for several minutes. "You have a buyer yet?"

"No, but . . ."

"I have five thousand."

MacTaint turned and examined Jonathan, his eyes squinted under the antennal brows. "Welcome back, lad."

"You're an evil old bastard, MacTaint." Jonathan rose and gave him the five thousand pounds he had set aside for the films, then he found the other five Strange had given him for expenses and handed that over as well.

"Ta," Mac said, stuffing the wad of bills into the pocket of his tattered overcoat. "Not a bad night, taken all in all. But I'd best be off. Lilla gets nervy if I'm out too late."

The Vicarage

Patches of mist on the low-lying sections of the road into Wessex were silvered by the full moon that skimmed through a black tracery of treetops, keeping pace with the Lotus as it twisted through back lanes, deserted at this early hour. Jonathan's shoulder was still stiff, and driving one-handed was tiring, so he maintained a moderate speed. It had been a difficult week. His reflex time had been eroded, and to keep himself awake he reviewed the events that had brought him to here and this—driving out to meet Maggie, the black plastic cylinder of amateur sex movies jiggling on the seat beside him.

Because he was deeply tired, people and events, words and coincidences of the past five days rolled through his mind, the connections obeying subtler laws than simple chronology. One event passed through his mind, then as he came around the bend of another occasion ... there it was. Obviously! The odd bits of tessera that hadn't fit in anywhere suddenly fell into place.

Maggie . . .

He pressed down on the accelerator and switched

off his driving lights so the plunges into wispy ground mist did not blind him.

He pumped his brakes and broadsided into the rough lane that led from the road to the Vicarage. As the car rocked to a stop, the door of the Vicarage burst open, and Yank rushed toward the car. The broad form of the Vicar filled the yellow frame behind Yank, something bulky in his hand.

Just as Jonathan ducked down, his windscreen shattered into a milky crystal web. A second bullet blew out the wing window and slapped into the back of the bucket seat. He grappled the .45 out of the map compartment, clutched open the door, and rolled out onto the damp grass. On the other side of the steaming undercarriage, Yank's foot skidded to a stop. Jonathan shot it, and it became a knee. He shot that, and it became an unmoving head and shoulder, the face pressed into the gravel.

The roar of the gun reverberating beneath the car covered the stumbling run of the Vicar, who now stood over Yank's inert body, a log of firewood poised ready to strike.

"Are you all right, Dr. Hemlock?" he called, wheezing for breath.

Jonathan got to his knees and leaned his head against the car. "Yes. I'm all right." The cool of the metal dispersed his dizziness. "Is he dead?"

"No. But he's bleeding badly. Seems to be missing a leg."

Jonathan could hear a crisp, pulsing sound, as though someone were finishing up pissing into gravel. "We'd better get a tourniquet on him. I've got to ask him some questions."

"You do have the films with you, I hope."

"Jesus H. Christ, padre!"

They carried Yank into the cozy den with its smell of furniture polish and wood smoke, and the Vicar set about attending to Yank with an efficient display of first-aid knowledge. He applied a tourniquet just above the missing knee, and before long the spurting blood flow was reduced to a soppy ooze.

"Oh dear, oh dear," the Vicar mumbled each time he noticed the damage the blood was doing to the Axminster rug.

Jonathan helped himself to the Vicar's brandy as he stood beside the fireplace, watching the older man work with quick, trained hands. "He's not coming around, is he?"

"I'm afraid not. Not much chance of regaining consciousness after a shock like that." The Vicar looked up and winked, and for the first time Jonathan noticed a purple contusion across his forehead.

"Yank hit you?"

The Vicar rose with effort and touched the spot gingerly. "Yes, I suppose so. I'd forgotten about it. We had a bit of a tussle. When he got here, he was the worse for drink. He said something offensive—I don't recall just what—and when I turned around, he was pointing a gun at me. He began babbling things about Max Strange, and needing the money to buy a ranch in Nebraska, and ... oh, all sorts of things. He wasn't quite right in the head, you know. The violence and danger of his double game had been too much for him. He was never the right kind of personality for this business." He winked. "Then your car drove in suddenly and took his attention. I grappled with him. He struck me down with his gun, and out he went. I took up a stick of firewood, but by the time I could come to your aid, it was not necessary. I could do with a drop of that brandy myself."

"Did he say anything about Maggie Coyne? Give you any idea of where she is?"

"I'm afraid not. You feel she's in danger?"

"She's in danger ... if she's alive at all. Yank must have told Strange about her. And Strange had a simple formula for dealing with spies and informers."

"You sound as though you *knew* Yank was in the pay of Strange."

"Only for the last fifteen minutes. The pileup of coincidences finally broke through my stupidity. Strange knew about your Parnell-Greene. He knew about me. He knew I had talked to Vanessa Dyke. Always a couple of steps ahead. He had too much information; there was too much coincidence. It had to come from inside. And Yank was at Van's house after she was murdered—no police, just Yank. He was pretending to be drunker than he was. Later, he wanted to pick me and the films up at my flat. It all fits in. But the coagulating agent was just a phrase—something one of Strange's men said after they had shot me full of dope. He told me I had struck out."

"Meaning what?"

"That's the point. The expression comes from American baseball. Only Yank would have used it."

"I see." The Vicar winked meditatively. "What shall we do about Miss Coyne?"

Jonathan pressed a finger into his temple and massaged it. "She could be anywhere. Her apartment, maybe."

"Oh, I doubt that. I've called several times in the

past two days. Never an answer. I was seeking information about you, because Yank had stopped re-
porting in—and now we know why. Finally, he did
call this afternoon to tell me that events had altered
your plans. He told me you had gotten the films, but
the situation was such that you could not carry them
on your person. He said you had mailed them. All
of that, I see now, was Strange's plot to neutralize
any action of mine. I was supposed to sit here awaiting the cheerful call of the postman, while they
made the sale and got away. And, of course, I would
have done just that."

Jonathan's concentration was still on Maggie.
"I've got to do something. I guess I could start at
her apartment, then—wait a minute! Why would
Yank want the films?"

"That's obvious, isn't it? Strange will pay heavily
for them."

"But Strange's dead. Yank knew that."

"I'm afraid you're mistaken there. Yank described
to me the rather gaudy mayhem you wreaked on the
staff of The Cloisters. He was proud of that, you see.
The virile fury of a fellow American, and all that.
And he mentioned that you had inflicted a ghastly
facial wound on Strange. A certain Miss Amazing
. . . or was it Miss Grace . . . well, whoever . . . she
carried Strange away to a sanctuary."

"Did he mention a name? A place?"

From the floor Yank gasped shallowly, then
moaned . . . like a child struggling to awake from a
nightmare.

Jonathan knelt beside him. "Yank?" he said
softly. Yank was under again. *"Hey!"* Jonathan
slapped the chill cheek.

"That won't get you anywhere," the Vicar said.

But Yank's eyelids fluttered. His eyebrows arched in an attempt to tug open the eyes. But they remained closed.

"Where's Maggie Coyne?" Jonathan demanded.

A moan.

"Where's Strange?"

Yank's voice was distant and mucous. "I . . . wanted . . . I only wanted . . . ranch . . . Nebraska."

"Where is Strange?"

"Please! Not . . . Feeding Station." Yank's body stiffened and relaxed. He was unconscious again.

The Vicar stood up with a grunt. "Ironic. He's frightened of the Feeding Station. Ironic."

"What's ironic?"

"He doesn't realize that you have saved him from that grisly fate."

"I have?"

"Oh, yes. There is almost no call at all for one-legged bodies." The Vicar winked.

The Cellar d'Or

After turning over the films, Jonathan retrieved the other .45 from the blinded Lotus. As Yank's car warmed up, he checked the load; there were only two bullets left. Enough.

A soft rain and low clouds blurred the limen between night and dawn as he drove through London streets that were desolate and gravid with despair. He pulled up before the Cellar d'Or. As he descended the narrow stone steps leading to the basement entrance, he could hear the whir of a vacuum cleaner within. The door was unlocked.

A black crone with a red bandanna pushed her vacuum cleaner desultorily back and forth over the black carpet and did not look up as he entered the bar. With the working lights on, the gold and black decor looked tawdry and cheap, and the air was stale with cigarette smoke and the smell of booze. Jonathan waited a moment for his eyes to adapt to the dimmer light.

"Close the door behind you, sir. It is cold this morning."

Jonathan recognized the basso rumble of P'tit

Noel's voice. Then he saw him, sitting at the back of the lounge.

"I am sorry, sir, but we have closed. Like ghosts, our customers fade away with the *cocorico* of the morning rooster."

Jonathan raised the revolver in his hand and walked back slowly toward P'tit Noel.

"It is odd, is it not, sir, that roosters around the world do not speak the same language. In Haiti, they say *cocorico,* while in Britain they—"

"Where's Strange?"

"Sir?"

"Don't screw around, P'tit Noel. I'm tired."

The Haitian rose languidly and blocked the entrance to the internal stairway, his Roman breast-plate muscles tense under the white knit pullover. Without taking his calm eyes from Jonathan's face he spoke in patois to the charwoman. "Vas-toi en, tanta."

The cleaner was clicked off, its whir dying with a Doppler fade, and the crone departed noiselessly.

"The gun is for me?" P'tit Noel asked.

"Not really. But I don't intend to grapple with you."

"Actually, I am a strong man, sir. I could probably absorb the first bullet and still get a hand on your throat."

"Not a bullet from this gun."

P'tit Noel looked into the big bore.

"Are they upstairs?" Jonathan asked.

"They were expecting someone. Not you. Someone with a package."

"He won't be coming. Listen, I don't care about

Grace. If she stands between me and Strange, I'll cut her in half. If she stands back, I'll let her go."

P'tit Noel considered this. He nodded slowly. "Mam'selle Grace has a gun. Give me a chance to get her out of the room. If you do not harm her, I shall leave you alone. The man is nothing to me."

He turned and led the way up the stairs and down a corridor. Raising a hand to gesture Jonathan back, he tapped at the door softly.

Amazing Grace's voice was strained. "Yes?"

"It is I, Mam'selle Grace. He is here, the one you await."

Jonathan pressed back against the wall as the lock clicked and the door opened. "Where the hell have you—Hey!"

P'tit Noel's hand snapped in with the speed of a mongoose and snatched Grace out into the hall by her arm. She screamed as her little automatic arced across the corridor and clattered to the floor. "Max!" Then she saw Jonathan, and fury glittered in her eyes. "It's Hemlock, Max!" She threw her diminutive naked body toward him, fingernails spread like talons, her lips drawn back revealing thin sharp teeth. "I'll kill you, you son of a bitch!" P'tit Noel swept her up as though she were weightless. It took all of his strength to hold her as she squirmed and snarled in his arms, her naked body oily with the sudden sweat of rage. "Let me go, you nigger bastard!" He began to walk clumsily toward the stairs, his awkward, savage burden screaming and kicking and clawing at him. But he could not bring himself to strike her, or even to protect himself from the punishment of her impotent, desperate anger. She dug her fingernails into his cheek and tore four deep furrows of red through the brown, but he only looked at her with resigned, unhappy eyes.

"Please, please!" She sobbed and panted promises. "I'll let you screw me if you let me go! Max! Max!"

He made consoling sounds as he continued down the stairs. She clung, pale-knuckled, to the railings, but the steady power of his momentum tore them slowly away.

Even after they disappeared down the stairs, Jonathan could hear her screams and invective. There was one last tormented wail, then the sound of sobbing.

A muffled voice spoke from within the apartment. Jonathan kicked open the door and dashed across the opening to draw fire. But no shot came. The muffled sound again. Incomprehensible words, as though someone were speaking through a gag. He pressed against the wall outside, the revolver before his face.

The words became distinguishable. The voice was a guttural whisper through clenched teeth. "Come . . . in, Dr. Hemlock."

Jonathan eased the door farther open with his toe and looked through the crack. Strange lay limp on the red velvet sofa, his shirt off and a wet towel covering half his face. He had both hands lifted to show that he had no gun.

Jonathan entered and locked the door behind him. He crossed to the bedroom, checked it out, then returned.

Strange's uncovered eye followed his every movement, hate and pain mixed in its expression. He spoke with great effort, his diction trammeled through clenched teeth. "Finish the job, Hemlock."

"I have."

"No. Not finished. I'm still alive."

"If you want to die, why don't you do it yourself?"

"Can't. No gun. Grace wouldn't help me. Too weak to get to window."

The eye glittered with sudden anger. "Do you know what you did to me?" With a convulsion of effort and a snort of pain, he tore the towel from the side of his face. The cheek was gone, and grinning molars were visible to just below where the ear would have been. The teeth were held in by tapered pink tubes of exposed root. And the eye, lacking support, dangled like a limp mollusk. The bleeding had been staunched, but the flesh oozed with a clear liquid and it had begun to fester.

Jonathan glanced away as Strange replaced the towel. When he looked back, the eye was crying. "Please kill me, Hemlock. Please? My whole life . . . devoted . . . beauty." The voice grew faint and the fingertips fluttered. The visible cheek had the subaqueous tint of somatic shock, and Jonathan was afraid he would pass out.

"What have you done with Maggie Coyne?"

The eye was dim and confused. "Who?"

He didn't even know her name. "The girl! The one Yank informed on. Where is she?"

"She . . . she's—" The eye pressed shut as he tried to clear his mind. "No. I have something to bargain with, haven't I?"

Jonathan considered for a moment. "All right. Tell me where she is, and I'll kill you."

"You give . . . word . . ." The head nodded as the tide of shock rose.

"Come on!"

The eye opened again, the lid fluttering with the effort. "Word as a gentleman?"

"Where is she?"

"Dead. She is dead."

Jonathan's insides chilled. He closed his eyes and sucked air in through his lower teeth. He had known it. He had felt it back at the Vicarage. And again as he drove through the sad, deserted city. It had seemed as though some energy out there—some warm force of metaphysical contact had been cut off. But he had conned himself with fragile fables. Maybe they held her hostage. Maybe she had escaped.

Strange's eye grew large with terror as Jonathan turned and walked aimless toward the door. "You promised!"

"Who killed her?" Jonathan asked, not really caring.

"*I* did!"

"You? Yourself?"

"Yes!" There was a flabby hiss to the word as air escaped through his cheekless teeth.

Jonathan looked down on him dully. "You're lying. You're trying to make me kill you in anger. But I'm not going to. I'm going to call for an ambulance. And I'll warn them you're suicidal. So they'll protect you from yourself. They'll fix you up—more or less. And it will be months before you find a way to kill yourself. All that time they'll be looking at you. Nurses. Doctors. Prison guards. Lawyers. They'll look at you. And remember your face."

Strange's swathed head vibrated with impotent rage. "You son of a bitch!"

Jonathan started toward the door, the revolver dangling in his hand. "See you in the newspapers, Strange."

Strange grasped the back of the sofa for support and pulled himself up. The effort caused the wet towel to fall from his mutilated face. "Leonard killed her!"

Jonathan turned back.

"I told you once, Hemlock, that I had a vice—expensive—subtler than sex. My vice is expensive because it costs lives. I like to watch the kinds of things Leonard does to women. Leonard was in particularly creative form with this girl of yours. And I watched! She didn't disappoint me, either. She had a strong will. It took a long, long time. We had to revive her often, but—"

Strange won.

He got his way after all.

Stockholm
28 Days Later

"... in fact, the word 'style' has been gutted of meaning. Overused. Misused. It's a critic's word. No painting has 'style.' Come to think of it, few critics do."

The audience tittered politely, and Jonathan bowed his head, losing his balance slightly and catching at the side of the podium. When he continued speaking, he was too close to the microphone, and he set up a feedback squeal. "Sorry about that. Where was I? Oh. Right! It is as meaningless to speak of the *style* of the Flemish School as it is to babble about the *style* of this or that painter."

"You miss my point, sir!" objected the young, terribly intelligent instructor who had introduced the subject.

"I don't miss your point at all, young man," Jonathan said, taking a sip from the glass of gin he fondly hoped passed for water. "I anticipate your obscure point, and I choose to ignore it."

At the back of the auditorium, the with-it young

American who was responsible for USIS cultural lectures in Sweden cast an anxious glance toward fforbes-Ffitch, who had flown over from London to see how the lectures he had cosponsored were going.

"Is he always like this?" fforbes-Ffitch asked in a thin whisper.

"I don't think he's been sober since he came," the American said.

fforbes-Ffitch arched his eyebrows and shook his head disapprovingly.

". . . but you can't deny that the Flemish School and that of Art Nouveau are *stylistically* antithetical," the bright Swedish instructor insisted.

"Bullshit!" Jonathan made an angry gesture with his arm and struck the microphone, causing an amplified thunk to punctuate his statement. He shushed the mike with his forefinger across his lips. "Of course, one can cite broad differences between the two movements. The Flemish painters chose in bulk to deal with natural subjects in a vigorous, healthy, if somewhat bovine manner. While the Art Nouveau types dealt with organic, hypersophisticated, almost tropically malignant *things*. But no painter belongs to a school. Critics concoct schools after the fact. For instance, if you want to look at 'typically Art Nouveau' treatments of floral subjects, I refer you to the Flemish painter Jan van Huysum or, to a lesser degree, to Jacob van Walscappelle."

"I'm afraid I don't know the painters to whom you refer, sir," the young Swede said stiffly, giving up all hopes of having his thesis supported by this acrid American critic whose books and articles were just then holding the art world in uncomfortable thrall.

The great majority of the audience was composed of young, shaggy Americans, this USIS center operating, as most of them do, more as a sponsored social club for Americans on the drift than as an effective outlet for American information and propaganda. Jonathan's lectures had broken the usual pattern of boycotting and sparse attendance that resulted from strong feelings against America's failure to grant amnesty to the men who had fled to Sweden to avoid the Vietnam debacle.

"It's a wonder there's a soul here," fforbes-Ffitch whispered, "if he's been drunk and nasty like this every night."

The American diplomat-in-training shrugged. "But it's been the best houses we've ever had. I don't understand it. They eat it up."

"Odd lot, the Swedes. Masochists. National guilt over Nobel and his damned explosives, I shouldn't wonder."

Jonathan's voice boomed over the loudspeakers. "I shall end this last of my lectures, children, by allowing our joint hosts to say a few words to you. They are obviously bursting with a need to communicate, for they have been babbling together at the back of the hall. I have it on good authority that your USIS host will speak to you on the subject: Why has the nation failed to grant amnesty to young men who had the courage to fight war, rather than to fight people." Jonathan stepped from the stage, stumbling a little, and the audience turned expectant faces toward the back of the auditorium.

The young USIS man blushed and tried to fake his way through, raising his voice to the verge of

falsetto. "What we really wanted to know was . . . ah
. . . are there any more questions?"

"Yeah, I got a question!" shouted a black from
the middle of the group. "How come all this Watergate shit didn't come out until after Nixon got his
ass reelected?"

Another American stood up. "Tell him that if he
grants us amnesty and lets us come home, we won't
tell anyone about the garbage he's made of the
American image abroad."

fforbes-Ffitch took this opportunity to say that
none of this had anything to do with him. "I'm English," he told two nearby people who didn't care.

By then Jonathan had walked up the side aisle
and had joined the flustered USIS man. He put his
arm around the lad's shoulder and confided in a low
voice, "Get in there, kid. You can handle them. After all, you're a government-trained communicator."
He winked and walked on.

"Well," said the USIS man to the audience, "if
there are no further questions for Dr. Hemlock, then
I ask—"

The hoots and boos drowned him out, and the audience began to break up, chattering among themselves and laughing.

Jonathan made his way to a display room off the
foyer. On exhibition were a lot of clumsy ceramics
done by star students and faculty of a well-known
California school of design, and brought there to
show the Swedes what our young artists could do.
One of the pieces had a title calculated to suggest
creative angst and personal despair. It was called
"The Pot I Broke," and that's what it was. Next to it
was a particularly pungent social statement in the

form of a beer mug featuring Uncle Sam with black features and bearing the cursive legend "Don't drink from me." But the star piece of the collection was a long cylinder of red tile that had drooped over during the baking, and had subsequently been titled "Reluctant Erection."

Jonathan took a deep breath and leaned his head against the burlap-covered wall. Too much. Too much hooch. He had been drinking for weeks. Weeks and weeks and weeks.

"Is it so bad as that?" asked one of the Swedish girls who had been looking around for him and was standing at the door.

Jonathan pushed himself off the wall and sucked in a big breath to steady the world. "No, it's great stuff. That's our subtle way to win you over. Dazzle you with our young art. A nation that can produce this stuff can't be all bad."

The girl laughed. "At least it shows your young people have a sense of humor."

"Don't I wish. Every time I see a piece of young crap, I try to forgive the artist by assuming it's a put-on—camp—but it won't wash. I'm afraid they're serious. Trivial, of course, and tedious ... but serious. I assume there's a party somewhere?"

She laughed. "They're waiting for you."

"Wonderful." He went into the foyer and joined a group of young Swedes exuding energy and good spirits. They invited him to come along with them to dinner, then off on a crawl of bars and parties, as they had done every night. They were attractive youngsters: physically strong, clear-minded, healthy. He had often reflected on how life-embracing the Swedes were on average, forgetting the traveler's adage that the most attractive people in the world are those one first sees after leaving England.

Outside the cold was jagged and the wind penetrating. While the young people waited, blowing into their hands, Jonathan said a very formal good night to the green-coated Beräknings Aktiebolag guard who patrolled the American Culture Center in response to repeated bomb threats. He felt sorry for the poor devil, stiff-faced and tearing in the numbing cold. He even offered to stand his watch for him.

A bar. Then another bar. Then someone's house. There was a heated discussion and a fight. Another bar—which closed on them. Someone had a wonderful idea and telephoned someone who was not home. Jonathan crowded with the four remaining students into a little car, and they drove back to the Gamla Stan to return him to his hotel on Lilla Nygatan, for he had been drinking heavily and had become embarrassingly antisocial.

They dropped him off on the edge of the medieval island, which is closed to private vehicles. Someone asked if he was sure he could find his way, and he told them to drive on—in fact, go to hell. When the red taillights of the car had disappeared into the swirling snow, he turned to find that a Swedish girl had gotten out with him. So. The party was still on! He put his arm around her—girls feel good in thick fur coats, like teddy bears—and they trudged around looking for an open bar or a *cave*. They found one, an "inne stället for visor, jazz och folkmusik," and they sat drinking whiskey and shouting their conversation against blaring music until the place closed.

They walked unsteadily through deserted narrow streets, holding on to one another, the snow deep on the cobblestones and still falling in large indolent flakes that glittered and spiraled around the gas lamps. Jonathan said he didn't much care for Christmas cards. She didn't understand. So he repeated it, and she still didn't get it, so he said forget it.

A little later he fell.

They were passing through the narrow arched alley of Yxsmedsgränd when he slipped on the ice and fell into a bank of snow. He struggled to get up, and slipped again.

She laughed gaily and offered to help him.

"No! I'm all right. In fact, I'm very comfortable here. I think I'll stay the night. Say, what happened to my overcoat?"

"You must have left it at the party."

"No, that was my youth I left at the party. How do you like that for a bitterer-than-thou tragic romantic riposte? Don't be swayed, honey. It's all hokum designed to get you into bed. You're sure you don't have my overcoat?"

"Come on. We'll go to your hotel." She laughed good-naturedly and helped him up. "Does it embarrass you to do something like that? To slip and fall when you are with a girl?"

"Yes, it does. But that is because I am a male chauvinist swine."

"Pig."

"Pig, then. What are you?"

"I'm an art student. I've read all your books."

"Have you? And now you're going to hop into bed with me. Proof of the adage that success has balls. OK. Let's get to it. Dawn is coming with a red rag among its shoulder blades."

"Pardon?"

"Shakespeare. A modest paraphrase."

There was a great rectangular weight in his forehead, and he tried to bang it away with the back of his fist. "How old are you, honey?"

"Nineteen. How old are you?"

He looked up at her slowly as the drink drained from his head. He was not well; but he was cold sober. "What was that?"

She laughed. "I said, how old are *you?*" The last vowel had a curl to it—a Scandinavian curl, but not unlike an Irish curl.

He looked at her very closely, glancing from eye to eye. She was a pretty enough little girl, but they were the wrong eyes. Not bottle green.

"What's wrong?" she asked. "Are you sick?"

"I'm worse off than that. I'm sober. Say . . . look. Here's the key to my hotel. The address is on it. You stay there tonight. It's all right. It's comfortable."

"Don't you like me?"

He laughed dryly. "I think you're just great, honey. The hope of the future. Bye-bye."

"Where are you going?"

"For a walk."

The sun rose brilliant and cold over the placid water of Riddarfjärden, a crisp yellow sun that gave light without warmth. A single tugboat dragged a wake of glittering, eye-aching silver through the thick black green water, its chug-a-da the only sound in the windless chill. Jonathan's eyes, teared by the cold and squinting against the light, followed the tug's deliberate progress as he leaned against the fence near the Gamla Stan tube stop. His hands were fisted into his jacket pockets, his collar turned up, his shoulders tense to combat the shivering. The brilliant, crusted white of the snow that blanketed the quay was unmarked, save for a long single line of blue-shadowed footsteps that connected his still form to a narrow alley between the ancient buildings that clustered up the hill behind him.

Fatigue made him sigh, and two jets of vapor flowed over his shoulders.

A girl stepped out into the sunlight from the dank cavern of the Gamla Stan tube station where she had passed the night sheltered from the snow and wind. She looked around disconsolately and pulled her surplus army parka more closely around her. She was burdened with a knapsack and a cheap guitar, and the American flag sewn to the butt of her jeans had come loose and frayed at one corner. Her monumentally plain face was gaunt, and her red-rimmed eyes showed hunger and misery. She looked at Jonathan with mistrust. He examined her with distant indifference. A grinning yellow sun-face sticker on her guitar advised him to "have a nice day."

London and Essex, 1973